"A masterf~~u~~ pounding m~~y~~ ~~. Mentink delivers~~ an explosive thriller where danger lurks on every page, with a volcanic back-drop that mirrors the simmering tension of this unforget-table story. Clear your schedule—you won't be able to put this one down."

Lynette Eason, bestselling, award-winning author of
the Lake City Heroes series

"*Fire Mountain* comes in hot! An eruption of taut sus-pense and a crackling romance that Mentink's fans will devour. A real stay-up-all-night read!"

Jessica R. Patch, bestselling author of the
FBI: Strange Crimes Unit series

"Dana Mentink is at the top of her game in this heart-pounding thrill ride. Danger explodes onto the page as Kit and Cullen fight to survive a volcanic eruption while relentless killers pursue them. An action-packed, gripping suspense, *Fire Mountain* will keep readers riveted until the end!"

Elizabeth Goddard, award-winning author
of *Storm Warning*

"An adrenaline rush! Dana Mentink's *Fire Mountain* hits the ground running, and the danger and action heat up from there. A flawless suspense with characters that will have readers turning pages and cheering for them to suc-ceed. I couldn't put it down."

Mary Alford, *USA Today* bestselling author

"A thrilling, adrenaline-charged sprint to the finish that romantic suspense readers won't want to miss!"

Susan Sleeman, bestselling author

"Dana Mentink's *Fire Mountain* is an explosive mix of danger and romance. With the backdrop of a deadly erupting volcano with a killer lurking in the shadows, two unlikely allies fight for their lives while protecting a baby. Every page crackles with tension and heart. Unputdownable!"

Darlene L. Turner, *Publishers Weekly* bestselling author

"From the opening pages to the very last, *Fire Mountain* by Dana Mentink delivers a riveting tale of suspense and compelling romance that keeps you on the edge of your seat."

Terri Reed, *Publishers Weekly* bestselling author

"Fasten your seatbelts. Kit Garrido and Cullen Landry are two of the most interesting characters I've seen in a long time. I cheered for them with each obstacle, and they had many. This story had me on the edge of my seat with each page! I loved this wonderful, fast-paced suspense."

Lenora Worth, author of *Undercover in Amish Country*

ELEMENTS OF DANGER #1

FIRE MOUNTAIN

DANA MENTINK

Revell

a division of Baker Publishing Group
Grand Rapids, Michigan

© 2025 by Dana Mentink

Published by Revell
a division of Baker Publishing Group
Grand Rapids, Michigan
RevellBooks.com

Printed in the United States of America

Library of Congress Cataloging-in-Publication Data
Names: Mentink, Dana, author.
Title: Fire mountain / Dana Mentink.
Description: Grand Rapids, Michigan : Revell, a division of Baker Publishing
    Group, 2025. | Series: Elements of Danger; 1
Identifiers: LCCN 2024047736 | ISBN 9780800746520 (paper) | ISBN 9780800747152
    (casebound) | ISBN 9781493450664 (ebook)
Subjects: LCGFT: Thrillers (Fiction) | Novels.
Classification: LCC PS3613.E496 F57 2025 | DDC 813/.6—dc23/eng/20241021
LC record available at https://lccn.loc.gov/2024047736

Cover design by Ervin Serrano.

Baker Publishing Group publications use paper produced from sustainable forestry practices and postconsumer waste whenever possible.

25 26 27 28 29 30 31   7 6 5 4 3 2 1

On May 18, 1980, Mount St. Helens in Skamania County, Washington, erupted. It is considered the most disastrous volcanic eruption in US history. While fifty-seven people lost their lives, many more were saved, thanks to the efforts of emergency management personnel and the citizen scientists who helped create a clear picture of the disaster in real time. This book is dedicated to the heroes, both officials and laypeople, who risked their own lives to protect their neighbors.

◼ ONE ◼

COLD AND ICE-PICK PAIN bored into Kit Garrido's temples. Her limbs were leaden, her body a deadweight in the driver's seat of her big rig. Grit coated her tongue and teeth. She tasted blood. Try as she might, she couldn't reach out to unbuckle her seat belt. Panic bubbled up inside her.

She felt movement. Someone yanked hard on the passenger door, unleashing pulses of pain.

"Ma'am?" A low baritone, rough.

A big hand skimmed her temple, calloused fingers hard like talons. Through her slitted eyelids, a male torso materialized, a large man in a heavy jacket. Warm ash drifted from his baseball cap and settled on her cheek, featherlight.

"What . . . happened?" Her voice was a croak.

"You crashed." His voice held the trace of a Southern accent. "Volcano's unsettled everything. Not safe to stay here."

Not safe? Crashed? Why wouldn't her mouth work fast enough to spit out the questions? Fear lapped at her insides as he fumbled for her seat belt.

"You've got to wake up. Now."

She forced her eyes farther open, grabbed the wheel. Cold wind raked her cheek. Wind? She lurched into full consciousness so fast her brain rocked in her skull. Green. Everywhere green mixed with brown, the trees of northern Washington all around, the rattling pine needles oddly muted by their coating of volcanic ash. A pine cone dropped on her lap through the gaping hole in the windshield. It left a sooty stain on her knee before it bounced off. She stared at it.

How . . .

He was talking, but she couldn't follow.

She touched her brown ski cap, then the flannel of her favorite long-haul driving jacket, the feel of the fabrics proving to herself she was alive. Somehow. A hiss of escaping steam commanded her to acknowledge what she desperately didn't want to see.

Her beautiful Freightliner truck was wedged cab first, jammed in a crevice between two crooked trees. In the sideview mirror she observed an enormous trench of gouged earth that marked her journey from the road above to the place of impact. The shiny yellow cab with its cozy sleeping unit, her home for three-hundred-plus days a year, was squashed like the face of a Pekinese. The pristine white trailer she'd washed that morning was no doubt damaged as well. She closed her eyes and pictured the bold font she'd painstakingly chosen for the Garrido Trucking logo. How absurdly proud she'd felt the day the lettering was applied. Her truck. Her business. Her life. Finally.

Muscles in her throat tightened, and tears started down her face.

Crashed. She'd crashed. Everything she'd worked for, gone. The pain in her head intensified. She stared around wildly. "But what happened? How did I wreck?"

The man shrugged. "Dunno. I'm not sure why you'd even be on Pine Hollow Road in the first place. Pretty ridiculous, considering."

Ridiculous? She bridled as the location sank in. Pine Hollow? Why there? Deep breaths. One, two, three, then she unbuckled and levered herself from the driver's seat. Pain lanced her left wrist. Broken or sprained? Her shirt was splattered with blood, though she couldn't feel any cuts.

"Easy," the man said, arms outstretched as if to catch her.

Why couldn't she remember what happened? She must have rolled out of her small office solo that morning, like she always did before picking up her load, the last load she dared haul out of a region under an evacuation advisory. She wouldn't have chosen Pine Hollow, a twisty route that would take her nearer the volatile Mount Ember. Everything she'd learned, the geologic facts she'd devoured, left her itching to escape. Had she lost control? Maybe she'd been knocked out by a falling boulder. Had the noxious gasses venting from the volcano's bulging side overwhelmed her? But why here?

The cold infiltrated her torn jacket, numbing her arms. Faraway, she heard the distant rumble of thunder or maybe another earthquake from the mountain preparing to blow. No sounds of vehicles, sirens, people. Eerie. Terrifying.

Her thoughts were muddy, slow. *Get help.* She patted her pockets in a futile search for her cell. Gone somewhere.

The satellite radio was her next choice until she realized it had been pierced by the branch that neatly skewered the windshield. Her throat went dry. A few inches to the left and it would have impaled her too. Ruined also was the precious old-school CB she'd rebuilt, which would have instantly connected her with a fellow trucker.

The man was still staring at her. He straightened and leaned closer. "Are you hurt badly? I can carry you."

She couldn't make herself answer, so he went on.

"Your radio's crushed, I see. My cell phone has no bars down here. Where's your phone?"

She jammed her knit cap on tighter. Hurt or not, she wouldn't let any stranger control the conversation, especially not in her rig. "I'll find it."

He shook his head. "You rest a minute. I'm gonna hop out and make sure your truck's not on fire or anything." He muscled his way back out the passenger door, the metal protesting with a bloodcurdling shriek.

She didn't see any sign of his vehicle through the filthy glass. Where had he come from? There were no helpful locals out and about under the present circumstances. Nerves tightened in her stomach. A trucker alone with cargo was vulnerable, a female trucker even more so.

Protect yourself. She fumbled for the crowbar, but the seat was collapsed on top of it. Instead she yanked the fire extinguisher loose, which made her head feel like it was going to detonate. Best she could do. She eased closer to the fractured passenger window.

The ground was a moonscape of ash and debris. The man eased along, a palm on the cab for support, and she got another chance to examine him. Long legs, cowboy boots, flannel shirt, Yankees baseball cap, and a scar—she hadn't noticed that before. It bisected his left eyebrow. He disappeared around the other side of the rig before returning a few moments later. The closer he got, the taller he was, probably six four and muscled. More than a match for her five-foot-five, hundred-ten-pound frame. The fear resurged. *Protect yourself.*

The extinguisher cut into her clenched palm. He drew close enough to the open passenger door for her to catch the light brown of his eyes, almost translucent like smoke. When he tried to climb aboard, she raised the extinguisher.

"Where did you come from?"

His lips quirked. "Originally? South Carolina."

That explained the drawl. "I meant . . ."

"I know what you meant." He shot a look at the ravaged landscape before he turned back. "Top of the ridge. My cabin's up there. I was on my roof and I saw you go over the shoulder. I was surprised six ways to Sunday. Didn't even hear you coming because the wind was howling, and I sure didn't expect any rigs to be in this area. Anyway, I hightailed it here in my truck. It's parked up a ways."

"I don't know you." A silly remark.

"Don't know you either. You from around here?"

She wouldn't tell him where she lived. "Close."

He pointed to the fire extinguisher and heaved out a breath. "Are you going to clobber me with that or not? I promise it's not necessary." He held up his palms. *How does anyone have fingers that long?* "You need first aid before we get out of here, and I'm the only one here to give it to you whether you like it or not." He plucked the kit from the pocket in the door and wiggled it at her. "You're bleeding."

"I don't need first aid."

He said something in reply, but his words seemed to come from far away, a rushing sound drowning them out as dizziness overcame her.

The extinguisher dropped to the floor, and she sank onto the driver's seat while he climbed in and slammed the passenger door. A wave of nausea enveloped her. Hastily he dumped out the first aid kit and shoved the container under her chin as she wretched. He handed her a clean handkerchief from his pocket with a neat C embroidered on it.

She stared at the precisely folded, pristine cloth.

His cheeks pinked. "I know. No one carries these things anymore. Mama insists, and she sends me a box of 'em every Christmas." He looked intently at her. "I'm fairly certain you have yourself a concussion."

He seemed like the kind of man who was certain about everything, the kind she avoided. Again he glanced out the window, and she saw the trickle of ground sloughing down the steep slope. The sky was already a sickly gray, rapidly darkening, thick with flecks of rock, minerals, and volcanic glass.

Powerless to the pain lancing her temples, she did not resist as he checked her pupils and pulse and smoothed a bandage across her brow.

"Cut up here near the hairline. Just a little one. Not deep. Probably won't scar."

"Who are you?"

He offered her a bottle of water from his back pocket. "Drink some."

"Stop helping me," she snapped. "Answer my question. Please."

"You're bossy." His voice was teasing, but there was tension in his mouth, his muscled shoulders. Other thoughts were distracting him. Her too.

"Who? Are? You?" She clapped her hand on her skull as if a knife were cleaving her temples.

"Be still. No sense adding to your pain. Name's Cullen." He looked toward the direction of the road. Another rumble blasted through the haze.

"Cullen who?"

He scrubbed a palm through his crew-cut hair the hue of a tarnished penny. "Cullen Landry. Should I call you Kit?"

She blinked, stomach tight. "How do you know my name?"

He pointed to the stuffed bear nestled next to the ruined radio, the name Kit embroidered on a heart held in its paw. "Not rocket science. Figured that's you, right? Short for anything?"

Her face went hot at his mention of her teddy bear. "I . . ."

A gust of wind blew a wisp of ash through her ruptured windshield.

"Last name Garrido like on the side of the truck?" he said.

She allowed a small nod.

"All right then, Ms. Kit, we can get to know each other better later, but the sun's setting, and right now we got other problems."

"The volcano," she said absently.

"That's way up there on the list. This road's been red-zoned."

"Red? When I left, emergency services said yellow everywhere except the northern side of the mountain." *When I left . . . which was when, exactly?*

"There's been a lateral eruption on the flank. Earthquake swarms, the mountain's continuing to bulge out, it all adds up to a mega eruption."

She studied him, swallowing another wave of nausea. His chin was stubbled, face tanned.

He shifted. "To save time, can you tell me if anyone knows you're here?"

"I probably talked to my office guy before I left." *For where?*

"Probably?"

Her brain felt dazed, like a bird that hit the window glass midflight. "I don't remember exactly." It pained her to say so.

The crow's feet deepened, bracketing his eyes, puckering the eyebrow scar. "Okay. Let's backtrack. What do you remember? Your age? Address? Anything?"

Her chin went up. "Of course I know that. Kit Garrido, age thirty. I live in a trailer in Tulley Valley, where my trucking office is." Instantly she regretted rattling off the information to a complete stranger. So much for playing it close to the vest. She really must have a concussion.

"What were you driving?"

"This." She flapped a hand at her ruined vehicle, her life savings crumpled and wrecked. Tears blurred her vision. "A Freightliner Cascadia." Her rig. Her everything.

The muscle in his jaw jumped. "I meant what cargo? For

14

whom? Do you remember that part? Maybe they'll alert someone when you don't show up with the delivery." Sweat trickled down his temple. Odd since she was so cold her toes had gone numb.

What was her cargo? And her destination? "I can't recall at this moment." And she wasn't sure she should tell him anyway.

He peered around as if he could find someone else to answer his questions. "You're sure you don't have your phone on you? In a pocket or something?"

She gritted her teeth. "It was in the charger next to my seat." At least, she figured it was since that was where she always kept it.

He was still scanning the horizon, lost in thought. His gaze wandered back over the contents of her cab, the wrecked steering wheel, the imploded glass. Eyes narrowing, he suddenly went still for a long moment before he let out a low whistle. "We've got more problems than a math textbook."

She felt like laughing. "Besides the fact that I was in a crash and now we're stranded somewhere in an evacuation area near a volcano that's about to erupt?"

He scrubbed a hand over the back of his neck. "Yeah, besides that."

She tried for a calming breath, but it hurt coming in and going out. "Like what?"

He pointed. "Take a look for yourself."

At first she could not understand the significance of the little round hole punched in the driver's side window or the second one two inches below it. "Are those . . ."

"Bullet holes. Yes, ma'am."

She gaped. "Someone . . . shot at me?"

"Appears that way. Could explain why you crashed."

"Who would do that?"

"Great question. Carrying precious cargo?"

"I don't—"

He cut her off with a sigh. "Remember. Right."

A shooter had tried to kill her? Steal her cargo? And was possibly still out there? Cullen stood motionless, watching her. He was a stranger . . . with no vehicle visible that she could see.

He indicated something else with a jut of his chin. She looked. A splotch of red caught her attention, and she gasped. The small print on the passenger window was a bloody, partial outline of a hand. Cold inched along her nerves.

His brows drew together, lines bracketing his forehead. "Not your blood. You were still strapped in when I arrived."

"And not yours?"

He held up his calloused palms as if she were attempting to rob him. "No blood, and that's a tiny print. I got big hands."

Someone had pushed their way *out* of her truck. Someone bleeding. "I was alone. I never travel with anyone else."

"Until today maybe."

"No. I was alone."

"Ms. Kit, we can talk about that after we're clear of this location. Gotta get out. Take us 'bout a half hour to reach my truck. Let's stick to the trees in case whoever it is hasn't left."

Before she could reply, he'd climbed down again and started to scour the ground. Without a moment of warning, the slope let loose with a noise like thunder. Cullen barely managed to scramble back inside and slam the door. They flung themselves in the seats and held on. Soil rolled and pummeled her rig, shaking and rattling. A brown avalanche rushed by the wreck.

Debris shot around them, rocking the trailer. Unbelievable. They would die here in her truck, the machine she loved that had given her an independent life. A boulder slammed into the roof, the percussion swallowing her scream. Would the roof give? Cullen leapt up, pushed her behind the driver's seat, and crouched beside her. Her heart thundered so hard she was sure he could feel it, his wide chest pressed against her shoulder. The percussion of the earth piling all around them was like the onslaught of a hurricane.

Time stood still. Five seconds? Ten? Fifteen? And then it stopped.

Her breath came in harsh gasps.

He crept to the window. "Well, you're not driving this rig anytime soon, but it appears we won't be buried alive just now."

She forced her lungs to do their job. "We can dig out. I've got a small shovel."

He opened his mouth to answer when a strange noise emanated from the sleeping area. They both jerked as if they'd been touched by hot lava.

That sound . . .

It couldn't be what she thought it was. Her brain was misfiring. It had to be the concussion. But the noise continued, and Cullen looked as if he'd heard it too. The hairs on the back of her neck prickled. "What . . . what is that?"

His intense stare added to her unease. "You said you never carry any passengers."

Passengers? "I don't." She gaped.

He shoved aside the curtain to the sleeping area and crawled inside. She was immobile as he returned a moment later, eyes wide with shock, holding a car seat. The seat held a baby in pink pajamas who wriggled, let out a cry, and strained against the straps of her carrier. The toothless mouth opened wide like that of a newly hatched bird.

Kit could not summon a single word.

"Her seat was belted to the chair in your sleeping area." He looked from the baby to Kit, his expression hardening with suspicion. "Well?"

She blinked, nerves screaming. "I . . ."

He cocked his head. "How exactly did this baby get into your truck, Kit Garrido?"

▫ TWO ▫

LORD, ALMIGHTY...

The rest of Cullen's prayer tapered off.

A baby.

Mechanically, he rocked the infant, seat and all, back and forth in his arms. He shot another look up toward the road, trying to process, ignoring the sputtering woman in front of him.

The fussing baby had instantly rocketed to the top of the priority list. Had Kit abducted the parent and child? He'd consider that if it wasn't for the bloody handprint and bullet holes. The shots had originated from outside the vehicle.

Was she transporting them? Helping them flee? Or abducting them and the plan went wrong? The scenarios would have to wait.

Options, Cullen.

He wished he'd told his brother his intentions. If Gideon knew the current situation, he would cuss up a storm about Cullen's carelessness and roar in, skirting any police involvement with utter contempt for the raging volcano.

19

Gideon was listed in the dictionary under "fearless." But he was prepping to teach a wilderness class in Olympia and he'd already let Cullen know he was a complete fool for staying in spite of the evac notices.

Fool or not, he wasn't going to leave his six acres of property no matter what the scientists or newscasters or his brothers said until he was sure his handful of friends had gotten to safety. He'd already moved his own horses to his parents' farm and assisted with a neighbor's sheep relocation. His conscience kicked at him. Maybe there was more to his decision than stubborn allegiance to friends and property. Leaving felt a lot like dying, and he'd already done that once.

Think, why don't you?

Kit kept on with the questions, which he ignored as he tried to put a plan in place. *Head on a swivel, Cullen.* No matter who'd been involved in abducting the baby or the baby's parent, he'd see to it they wouldn't get another chance at the kiddo. Adrenaline buzzed his nerves. A flashbulb pop of memory sizzled before he could stop it.

"Gotta breach it!" he'd shouted. *"They're smothering in there."*

The abandoned truck, the women inside calling out feebly.

"Get back." His partner at his side on the radio. *"Wait."*

He'd barely heard her. He'd factored in the hinges and the precise point to hit the door, but not the crude, improvised explosive.

An explosion, the heat. Flying pieces of metal.

Officers down.

20

The baby grabbed at his chin, and the memory evaporated, leaving a sheen of sweat on his brow.

Kit was propped in the corner, tracking his every move, her expression still dazed. Either she was an exceptional actress, or she really didn't have a clue how the baby had come to roost in her rig. Possibility three: She honestly couldn't remember that she'd been involved in a crime. Somebody should make a TV show about this. He'd watch it, simply to see how they'd explain it all.

The baby was gearing up for a good holler. No time to sort it all out. *What's it gonna be, Cullen?* If the three of them could reach his truck, they were likely still an hour from the nearest evacuated town along an unforgiving road. As if to underscore the danger, the ground pulsed and rumbled. Mount Ember was not joking around. The seismic monitoring of her swelling sides was the topic of every news station. He'd listened to a reporter that morning zealously expounding on the possible dangers of pyroclastic flows, air currents filled with searing gas and pulverized rock that could travel at hundreds of miles per hour. Most of it was white noise to him. The gist was that Ember was going to follow in the historic footsteps of her nearby cousin, Mount St. Helens, and blow her top.

A puff of air through the bullet holes swept another trickle of ash into the cab along with a spatter of rain. He drew back farther into the sleeping area with the baby, shielding the infant. If someone was desperate enough to shoot a truck driver on a red-zoned road, they'd likely be committed to sticking around. To track the person who'd left the handprint? Recover the baby? The parent? He texted his brother a quick message. The little dots swirled and swirled with no result. The message would not send.

Another tremor shook the ground. Thunder from a burgeoning spring storm or Mount Ember getting ready for the main event? It'd be pure folly, he decided, to lead Kit and the baby to his truck with the unsettled rubble all around them and the light failing. But if they stayed put, who would reach them first? National Park Service? Local cops? Or the shooter?

He could hike back up to his vehicle alone, go for help. Even solo, trekking over unstable ground in polluted air was going to be a problem. As big a problem as leaving the two behind in the truck? A concussed woman and a baby? That notion made his stomach churn.

With the weather worsening, he decided they had to shelter and pray that time was on their side, at least survive until dawn when they could try to hike for help. He had his revolver in the truck. Not enough firepower if Big Guns came calling but better than nothing. The baby would be warm and breathing relatively clean air at least.

Kit was now shuffling around the cramped sleeping area, staring at the baby as if she were a rattlesnake. He unbuckled and extracted the screaming infant from her carrier, turned down the pink comforter on the compact bed, and laid her on the mattress.

"Hey there, Tater Tot. You came through that crash like a champ, didn't you?" He brushed his palm over her fuzzy scalp, along her spindly arms and legs, detecting no signs that she'd been injured.

He thanked the good Lord above for car seats and sturdy straps. Car seats, he knew for a fact, were built solid as space shuttles these days. Another lash of pain stung his heart.

The baby looked to be less than a year old, maybe nine months and change, as he considered his partner's child when she'd been a similar size. He recalled the "Honorary Uncle" shirt he'd worn proudly when he'd arrived to watch Baby Mia.

The stowaway baby hoisted her legs, pulled one sock off, and managed to grab her tiny toes. He almost laughed at the oddness of it, this itty-bitty human, perfect and whole in the aftermath of a horrible wreck.

Kit's mouth had actually fallen open as she stared at the infant, her pert lips a circle of disbelief. "This is . . . impossible."

He let her eyes catch up with her mouth before he spoke. "Her seat was strapped onto your chair back here. Do you remember doing that?" He watched her expression, body language, for any tell that she was lying. He didn't think she was. Then again, maybe she'd honestly forgotten her crime.

"No," she whispered. "I don't."

When she swayed, he guided her to sit on the mattress next to the baby. He was confused. She was confused. The only one at all satisfied was the baby now sucking on her impossibly small toes.

"Could be that was her mother's handprint on the door," he suggested. "I'm guessing a woman, by the size of it."

"But . . . why would a mother leave her child in my truck?"

He decided to rock the boat. "Maybe you kidnapped the mom and baby, put them in your rig to get them out of the county. Someone was trying to rescue her and shot up the rig. Mom escaped and went for help."

She would have slid off the bed if he hadn't grabbed her forearm.

"What? That's completely asinine." She stopped, looking from him to the baby, arms folded around her middle as if her stomach ached. "I didn't kidnap any baby. I've never seen it before."

"That you can recall anyway, and it's a she. I've named her Tater Tot until I hear different. We'll get her to the cops quick as we can."

Fire sparked her ink-dark eyes. It suited her better than the dazed look.

"And why should I believe a word *you* say? Maybe you shot at my rig, tried to kill me and the mother and take the baby."

He laughed.

"It's not funny."

"If I wanted you dead, I would have killed you when I climbed in and you were still half conscious, wouldn't I? Maybe cut your throat? Strangled you?"

She blanched but didn't flinch. *Knock it off, Cullen. She's a civilian, remember?* A moment later it flashed on him that he was too. "My truck's a half mile uphill from here. In the morning, if no help arrives, we can try to reach it, but for now, when the dirt settles, I'm gonna climb out and see if I can get a signal. I'll try to keep a line of sight to your rig in case the shooter returns."

Her brows crimped. "Are you some sort of cop?"

The burn of it . . . after almost a year. "No," he said finally. Best he could do.

24

The baby flung the other sock off. He gathered it up and slipped both back on, then stroked her head to check if she was still warm enough. "Hey, Tater Tot. Keep your socks on, huh? It's cold in here." *And only getting colder. Ticktock.* "I'm going to look for your phone, Kit. Could be yours works better than mine. Can you babysit?"

Kit gasped. "Are you serious? I don't even own a houseplant."

"Don't let her roll off the bed. You can do that." He didn't wait for her reply. "Does your rig have a GPS built in?"

"Yes. It can be tracked from my office in case there's trouble."

Trouble. Right. "Any employees? Would they be checking on you?"

She sighed. "I only have one. Normally, Cliff would keep tabs on me, but this was supposed to be my last run before evacuation. He cleared out yesterday."

Of course he did. Cullen grabbed a flashlight from a clip attached to the back of the passenger seat and beamed it around the darkened interior. The light caught some scattered pencils, a hair scrunchie, paperwork. He scanned. "Manifest says you were hauling office supplies."

She groaned. "Great. My tombstone will read 'Rest in peace with the paperclips.'"

He chuckled. *Witty.*

With a twinge in his knee, he eased to his hands and knees and beamed the searchlight into all the dark corners of the cab. Where was that phone? She kept a neat truck. No gum wrappers or loose change. Only a set of binoculars and a bound book of paper maps. He grabbed them both.

"Cullen." She'd almost shouted it, and he realized she must have been talking to him while he searched.

"What?"

"Do you think I was transporting this baby's mother somewhere? Like she asked me for a ride?"

He spared a look at her from his cramped position between the seats. "Can you propose another explanation?"

"Well, I'm *not* a kidnapper."

"But you see how it looks, right?" he resumed. "You were transporting a baby you claim to know nothing about. At least the bullet holes and blood trend in your favor. I photographed both, by the way."

"Do you suppose . . . I mean . . . Do you think the mother was hurt bad? Or the shooter got her while I was blacked out?"

That notion made the acid surge higher in his gut. He could swallow a lot of things, humiliation, loss of purpose, being stripped of his cop family, but the fact that whoever did this might have gotten away with it was intolerable. At the end of the day, justice was the only thing worth striving for. "I don't know." *Yet.* "Aha." With a crow of victory, he plucked her cell phone free from a dark crevice.

For the second time that day, he saw her smile, a gorgeous, radiant expression that dimmed the longer he held the phone. It was smashed, a piece of the screen missing. When he tried to power it on, it remained stubbornly dark.

She was on her feet. "This is not happening!" she shouted.

He wanted to holler right back that it most certainly was and he wanted no part of it. He'd screamed the exact same thing as he was bundled into an ambulance the last night of his career. Rage didn't change anything.

The baby had begun to full-out wail again.

He picked her up and cuddled her to his chest, patting her diaper, which reminded him she probably needed to be changed. "Could you please take it down a notch? You're upsetting Tot."

With fists balled in anger, she pressed her lips closed.

The baby reached out petal-soft fingertips to touch his lower lip. "Let's focus on what we know. This area is off-limits. Cops are busy setting up blockades and evacuations. No help is coming, thanks to the volcano."

Worry crawled across her features, making her look much younger than thirty. He swallowed. At thirty years old, he'd had the world by the tail, or so he'd thought. People who loved him, a job that gave him identity and purpose and a means to change the world for the better. Acid crawled up his throat. What a difference a decade made. He shook the thought away. "Let's get you two settled so I can take a hike, so to speak."

She nodded absently, the fire gone out of her, which made him feel curiously sad. "Go now," she said. "Sooner is better."

"Easy for you to say. It's gonna be like hiking in quicksand." He held the baby out to her. "Tot will need a change and a bottle soon, if she's at all on par with my . . ." He swallowed. "My friend's baby. I'm hoping there's a diaper bag aboard or it's gonna be a long night."

Kit looked at Tot as if she were a hand grenade with the pin pulled. "This is completely crazy. I'm a truck driver. I shouldn't be involved with any of this."

"Me neither," he growled, patience fraying, "but right now we gotta focus on her." He offered the baby again. She made no move to take her.

Her gaze was fogged with pain and fear. "The bullets might have been an accident. Someone trying to scare away a looter. There's been ransacking in some areas."

He exhaled, summoning a gentler tone. "If it was an accident, then we won't have any further trouble from Big Guns. It's just us versus a volcano." Her eyes shifted, and he knew she was ticking off the facts she could not account for, the baby, the bloody handprint, two bullet holes, not merely a stray shot that found her truck.

Slowly, she lifted her arms and accepted the bundle of wiggling baby who'd begun to fuss. "She's crying."

"Yep, I can hear that. I'm gonna take a quick look around to see if there's a bag of supplies." The wails increased.

"Cullen, what do I do?"

"Haven't you ever babysat before?"

"No."

There was something clipped about that word, more substance to it than he had time to investigate at the moment. *Ticktock.* He activated the flashlight again and played it around the tumbled sleeping area. Kit's clothes were neatly contained in drawers and a collapsible laundry hamper that had overturned. Cleaning products were still perfectly stowed, a stack of trucking magazines flung everywhere. There was also a massive crack in her thirty-inch television that she eyed mournfully.

"There." Kit spoke over the baby's wails, pointing under the pink comforter he'd flung aside. "That's not mine."

A duffel bag. He hauled it out, preoccupied with other

details. How long before the cops might possibly arrive, pending his success at getting a signal? There was an outside chance Gideon might check in on him in light of the more recent explosions. And a slim possibility that his brother had tried to call him and might dispatch help when he got no reply. Slim was better than none.

He unzipped the bag. "Score. Baby stuff." The contents were jumbled and looked to have been flung quickly inside.

Kit didn't answer for a moment. "Cullen, do you think Tot's mother is alive?"

The silence thickened between them. "I don't know." But the cop in him insisted otherwise. The missing mother had cared enough to strap in her baby and pack supplies, but had not returned to the wreck? He extracted a diaper and looked at Kit. "Care to do the honors or should I?"

She shuddered. "You."

He laid Tot on the bed, stripped off the soiled diaper, and applied a new one, proud that it only required one readjustment to get it perfect. Kit reached in the bag and handed him a baby-sized hoodie.

"How about this? It's getting colder in here."

It took both of them to wrestle the kid into the garment. In a nifty side pocket of the duffel was a baby bottle and a bunch of powdered formula packets along with a single jug of distilled water. *Thank you, God.* He squinted. The printing was too tiny on the packet.

"Can you, uh, read this?"

Incredibly, she smirked. "My dad had to hold things far away when he hit a certain age too."

He scowled. "I'm only forty."

"Don't worry. Forty is the new thirty." She read the

instructions and even mixed the bottle for him after sanitizing her hands with a wipe, then continued her perusal of the duffel bag's contents.

He settled into the chair with Tot on his lap. When he lifted the nipple to her lips, Tot latched on like a hungry bear. While she drank, he continued his examination of the sleeping area and noticed a small crate of books, a half-dozen volumes neatly secured with bungee cords. *Volcanoes of the Pacific Rim*. *The Living Planet*, the earthquakes and volcanoes edition.

"Bookworm?" He motioned to the crate with his chin.

"Just learning."

"About volcanoes?"

"Sure. Don't you want to know what's unfolding around you?"

"Only in small doses." He admired Tot's robust guzzling. "Good thing she's not picky about her beverage temperature. Do you want to take her now while she's occupied?" But Kit's attention was elsewhere.

"The bag," she said.

"Uh-huh." He was trying to recall the topography around them. If he couldn't get a signal, he'd continue on to the truck, drive up a ways. A mile north in the direction of his cabin there was a granite peak, one of many in the foothills of Mount Ember, sprinkled all along the Cascade Range. If the seismic activity hadn't destabilized it and he could make it to the top, or even halfway, he might get a signal. Call Gideon first? Sometimes it was easier to get an outside connection if the systems were overtaxed. That would leave Kit and the baby alone for a longer period. They should have a contingency plan, get some supplies together in case they had to flee. A disaster in the making, but if Big Guns came back . . .

She spoke louder this time. "The duffel bag."

His focus snapped back to her. "What about it?"

She was on one knee, peering at it. "It's too heavy for a few baby supplies. I pack duffels all the time for multiple nights, and they never weigh this much."

She pawed through the contents, burrowing past the tiny clothes, small Tupperware containers, and mini formula packets. When she pulled out a plastic-wrapped bundle, he let out a low whistle.

She stared.

He stared.

The baby sucked.

The fading sun illuminated the fat stacks of money gripped in Kit's hands.

◼ THREE ◼

KIT'S PALM WAS SWEAT-SLICKED as she removed the money from the duffel and set it on the floor. Three bundles altogether, neatly secured. She quickly counted one. Not new bills but plenty of them. She alternated between ogling the money and the baby madly sucking at her bottle, impossibly small on Cullen's lap. Tot had flung out a fist to capture her foot as if she were responsible for keeping the toes attached to her body.

Ten thousand dollars, more or less. Kit was gnawing on her thumbnail, a habit she thought she'd conquered long ago. She checked the stacks again. It was still ten thousand dollars bound with rubber bands in the precise way she would have done if she'd ever possessed that much cash.

None of it made sense. If only the shrieking pain in her skull would let up so she could think. With as minimal movement as possible, she snagged a container of Tylenol from her first aid kit and swallowed several with the aid of a small container of orange juice she'd intended as a midafternoon pick-me-up.

Cullen still hadn't said a word. When Tot's milk was

halfway gone, he expertly tipped the child upright and patted her back in one fluid movement. Kit wouldn't have expected such proficient nurturing nor the warm feeling it gave her which she immediately checked. So he was good with infant care. So what? He was a stranger. Maybe he'd been the one to stow both the baby and money in her rig. She didn't remember a thing. This might have all been one ill-executed plan by the guy humming softly across from her.

"Well?" she demanded, pointing to the bundled bills.

"Well what?"

"What do you have to say about this money?"

"Shouldn't I be asking you that? It's in your truck."

She glared. "Do you have any theories you'd care to share?"

He pursed his lips. "Might explain why Big Guns was after the woman. She ripped him off. Ten thousand isn't a ton, but it can be depending on the circumstances." He paused. "Some people don't take kindly to losing what they feel is theirs." Something sizzled like a lit match behind his irises and then vanished.

They stared at each other.

The baby let loose a massive burp. "Attagirl." He wiped her chin with a rag and returned her to the patting position. "I better go."

His stomach growled, and he grimaced.

"Hey. Got anything I can eat while I hike? I'm starving."

Food was the furthest thing from her thoughts since her own stomach was tumbling in queasy circles. If she'd learned one thing from all her long hauls, it was to always travel with a variety of food choices, prepackaged and organized by time, a.m., afternoon, p.m., late night. Should she feed this man? Her silence lingered too long.

"If you don't want to, I understand." He didn't appear like someone who understood. In fact, he was giving off hurt-little-boy vibes. She'd never been able to abide seeing someone go hungry. Plenty of homeless people had been the recipients of her food. She found herself taking the bologna sandwich she'd stowed on the afternoon shelf in the mini fridge.

"Here."

His mouth curved in a wondrous smile as if she'd handed him a steak and lobster feast.

"Yeah? You sure you don't want it? That's awful nice of you."

"Don't get too excited. It's only got mustard, because I can't stand mayo, and there's pickles if you want, but I don't put them on until I'm ready to eat because they make the bread soggy." Was she really going on about mustard and pickles?

"Perfect. I eat pretty much anything that isn't nailed down, and that sounds plenty gourmet to me. Rip off a hunk. We should ration, in case." Since he was still patting the baby, she unwrapped the sandwich, took a plastic knife from the drawer, and sliced off a quarter.

He devoured it in one massive bite and sighed. "Delicious. I haven't eaten since last night, and that was stew out of a can."

A man that big wasn't going to get far on a single mouthful. She gave him another quarter with a shrug. "You'll need the energy."

Droplets of rain hammered the metal cab.

He ate and quirked a brow. "Not to be a delicate flower or anything, but do you have storm gear? It's gonna be a trek, and the ash is mixing with the rain. Gotta slog through all that debris out there, and it'll stick to me like skin on a pudding."

First her sandwich, now her clothes. She shifted uneasily. Still, it was going to be a dangerous enough undertaking for him without adding wet clothes to the mix. She pulled out the raincoat she'd bought on impulse at the thrift shop from its spot under the bed and tossed it over his knees.

His brows zinged up. "I, uh, was picturing a yellow slicker, like the Gorton's fisherman guy."

"Desperate times." She didn't allow a smile, but when he handed her the baby and shrugged on the raincoat, his wrists hung out of the too-short sleeves as if he were wearing a child's size. The dark blue material with yellow rubber duckies reached only a few inches below his belly button. Baseball cap jammed on, coat unable to zip over his broad chest, and a smear of mustard on his chin, he was a sight. She angled her shoulders so he would not see her smile in the glow of the flashlight.

The baby was beginning to squirm against her shoulder. A rush of panic followed when she realized she'd be in charge of this creature until he returned.

"How long do you think it will take?"

"No idea. Couple hours, maybe? I'm gonna have to move slow. Ground's a mess. Two things while I'm gone."

Now he was giving orders? "What?"

"Numero uno, see if you can get her to sleep."

"How do I do that exactly?"

"You'll figure out something. When you lay her down, put her on her back, not her tummy, and make sure she doesn't smother or get tangled in the blankets. Second, work on packing some supplies in the duffel, okay? Dry clothes, food, flashlights, first aid kit, whatever you can fit. In case."

"In case of what?"

He didn't look at her. "A hasty departure."

She blinked. "There's nowhere to go. We have to stay here until we're rescued." Besides, this truck was her heart and soul, and she wouldn't leave it until they pried her rigid dead fingers from the steering wheel.

"Hoofing it is a last-ditch scenario. Hopefully the cops or a rescue unit will show. Maybe some emergency workers will see the truck's skid marks or my abandoned vehicle and call it in." His tone hardened as he glanced at her. "Big Guns might have taken off and this baby's mom is okay, but . . ."

But if she was able, why hadn't she returned to the rig for her baby?

It was almost completely dark except for the glow from the flashlight she'd wedged between the mattress and the crumpled wall. Strange shadows marbled his expression, carving hard lines around his features.

She gritted her teeth and cradled the baby. "I'll pack if I can."

Before she realized, he'd bent toward her.

Her heart thudded. Was he thinking about . . .

But he kissed the baby on the downy crown of her head. "Be good for Auntie Kit, huh, Tot?" And then he opened the door, disappearing into a gust of windblown ash.

The baby cried as if she knew he'd left. Kit felt like crying too. Her temples were pincered in an agonizing vise, and aches and pains had begun to overwhelm the flimsy comfort of the Tylenol. In particular, her left wrist was throbbing. The infant's sobs lasered into her skull. The little thing was all rubbery limbs and head thrashes.

She mimicked what she'd seen Cullen do, patting with a combined walk and jiggle up and down motion as she minced along the minuscule area between her tiny table and sleeping alcove. Louder and louder the baby screamed, drowning out the patter of raindrops on the roof and her own thoughts. Her head ached. Did all babies shriek with such intensity? Fear tightened her throat. Maybe there was something wrong. The crash might have caused internal injuries. Babies were fragile flickers that could so easily be snuffed out. She swallowed.

"I'm sorry your mama isn't here." Where was this baby's mother? Father? Out there lost? Buried alive? Shot? She patted and joggled and soothed with the only kid song she knew, "Jingle Bells." The screaming didn't stop. Something had to be wrong. She'd be forced to go get Cullen. But should she leave the baby alone in the truck while she went to fetch him? Strap her into the car seat maybe? Or carry her along, out into the night, worrying about noxious gasses and landslides?

The baby's massive burp cut across her panic. It was so startling, Kit stopped walking. Through the blanket, the small arms and legs relaxed, as if a stopper had been pulled to drain out the discomfort. Slowly, Kit walked and joggled some more, quietly singing "Jingle Bells."

Before the verse was over, Tot was asleep.

Victory flooded Kit's soul. After a mental fist pump, she gingerly laid the baby on the mattress, tummy up, far away from any smothering fabric. Job one, complete.

Job two, packing for an escape. An escape from whom? To where? She had to think, in spite of her muddled brain. Cullen's plan wasn't going to work for her. She had no intention of leaving, but she'd make sure he was supplied if he insisted. The contents of the mini fridge yielded a few more snacks, which she added on top of the money in the duffel along with the food and water she'd brought and a tightly rolled blanket and the flashlight.

She tried to replay her actions that morning. It was all a depressing blank, and it remained so as the minutes ticked into an hour and beyond. How many more before Cullen was able to pick his way over the treacherous ground and return?

At least she could while away the time trying to unscramble her brain. *What's your normal routine then?* Maybe dredging up what she could recall would jog loose what she couldn't. Thankfully, those details were still reachable.

On a regular day, she'd arrive at 6:00 a.m., inspect the truck, load the mini fridge, and queue up a new audiobook on her phone. She'd go over the cargo details with Cliff, confirm departure and arrival times, while he took messages off the computer or answering machine that would hopefully lead to more jobs so she could give him the raise he'd been hounding her for. Mostly she'd be scouring the broker sites to secure a load for the trip back home. Every moment her truck was empty was a dollar she wasn't earning. The volcano would have put the kibosh on regular business, though. She'd probably been working on spreading her net, looking for work that would keep her out of the area until the eruption danger was over, examining load sites for attractive delivery locations.

She imagined the throb of the engine when she fired it up that morning. Thrilling, no doubt, like it always was. She'd have picked up her cargo early since she intended to drive out and not return until the all clear was given. She had no doubt plotted where she'd stay overnight. The cleanest truck stops with showers and security were a priority so she could sleep in her rig undisturbed, hopefully. Didn't always work. A single woman of small stature attracted plenty of unwanted attention from opportunistic thieves and even lonely truckers.

The trip two months ago . . .

She shivered. Why wouldn't that memory vanish from her mind along with whatever else she'd forgotten?

Try again. Remember, Kit.

She must have stopped for a hitchhiker. Not her regular practice, but if it had been a woman and a baby? Begging for a ride in a volcano dead zone? Her brain waves were a hopeless tangle. She sat morosely and closed her eyes to try to rest her aching skull. While it would have been a relief to sink into sleep, she merely rested as best she could, listening for sounds of Cullen's return.

When her worry made it impossible to lie still any longer, she removed the antique travel clock from its velcroed spot on the shelf next to her mattress and checked the time. Impeccably precise, as was the father who'd given it to her. Seven fifteen. Cullen had been gone for hours.

The baby slept, arms flung wide as if nothing in the world could hurt her.

Risking a peek out the window with her flashlight, she saw nothing but a swirl of gray as the wind lifted the ash blanket and hurled it airborne. She squeezed a couple more water bottles into the duffel bag. Removing the money would allow for more supplies, but she couldn't see leaving it behind in her crumpled truck. Cullen could get it to the cops.

The baby remained quiet, so Kit picked up the spilled magazines and returned them to the shelves and swept the broken bits of glass into a plastic dustpan. Ridiculous, no doubt, but she felt better for it.

The travel clock read seven forty-five. She eased around the mattress and pressed her face to the grimy window. How much longer would they be stuck here? What if they ran out of bottles and diapers? Food? What if Cullen fell or became overwhelmed by fumes? What if no one came?

What if someone did?

A sizzle of lightning lit up the sodden meadow and the rocks beyond. A plume of something drifted through the air. Another belch of ash from Mount Ember. Cullen came into view, a pale shadow. Her heart sped up, relieved, until she realized he was moving fast, jogging toward the rig, slipping and skidding in spurts, sinking shin-deep into the debris before yanking himself free.

She flung the door open for him and he scrambled in, wet rivulets of muck dripping from the raincoat.

"What's wrong?"

He peeled off the jacket and thrust it at her. "We gotta bolt for my truck. Put this on. You can shelter Tot inside, keep her dry as best you can."

She was summoning a question as he jerked a look around.

"You packed. Good. I'll carry the duffel." He stopped his rapid-fire commands when she seized his wrist.

"I'm not leaving my rig."

"No choice."

"I—"

He cut off her answer by taking her elbow and propelling her to the driver's side window. Crammed shoulder to shoulder, they stared through the fractured glass.

"I don't see anything," she whispered, unsure why she spoke in a hushed tone.

"Watch." His murmur tickled her ear, the chill of his cold cheek against hers prickling her skin. Her searching gaze found only an impenetrable sprawl of velvet night.

He pressed one wide finger to the window glass. "There."

Above them, where a sliver of road was visible before it became lost by the steep slopes of Mount Ember, two gold pinpricks trailed down the mountain, flickering in and out of view as the terrain rose and fell.

Her breath caught. *Rescue.*

"Headlights," he confirmed. "Saw them during my trek. Never did get a signal either."

They were lost, out of contact with the outside world. But maybe not. "It's probably the police or the National Guard." She pressed an eager palm to the window. They'd be rescued. She could call in a desperate favor and get her truck towed. The baby would be all right. The National Guard or park service could find the missing mother.

"I don't think so, Kit."

They stared as the vehicle moved steadily down the mountain, no strobing lights yet, but maybe that would happen shortly. She could feel the tension in the muscled wall of his chest pressed against her shoulder.

Again they sank into silence, gazes drawn to the appearing and disappearing headlights. They caught sight of them again on a short stretch of road before the vehicle sank out of view.

"He's probably two miles from here before the road takes the plunge. No emergency lights, not an official vehicle."

The baby stirred on the mattress, whimpered.

One more time the car appeared, moving toward them at an unhurried pace. As they watched, the headlights flicked off, the moonlight catching the darkened vehicle for the briefest of moments until the clouds sealed out the light again.

Her stomach contracted, her fantasies of rescue popping like soap bubbles. There was no good reason why someone would want to approach without being seen. Only bad ones.

"Not cops." Cullen looped the duffel strap over his shoulder. In a fog, she shrugged into the wet jacket, grabbed the teddy bear and travel alarm clock, and stowed them in her pockets before she scooped Tot up. The baby protested being zipped against Kit's chest inside the rubberized raincoat.

Cullen turned off the flashlight and shoved it in his back pocket. Wordlessly, he led her through the dark belly of her truck to the passenger side.

Too fast.

It was all happening too fast.

She followed, the baby an alien weight pressed against

her. Each step was torture. How could she leave her rig? Her everything?

At the door, he climbed out, standing below, arm extended to help her.

She looked at him, burdened like a pack mule. Was she really going to do this? Run into the night with a stranger and a baby with a volcano threatening to bury them alive?

But the vehicle with no lights, the bullet holes, the blood . . .

With her ruined truck behind her, she clung to Cullen's hand and stepped down into the darkness.

▪ FOUR ▪

CULLEN TRIED TO KEEP HOLD of Kit's elbow to prevent her from foundering in the debris. They staggered up the slope with all the grace of two people in a bizarre three-legged race. When she stumbled, he held her steady, the baby's cries swallowed by the rain. When he lost his footing, she grabbed the back of his jacket, which staved off a face plant.

He didn't bother to keep track of the approaching car. Big Guns, presumably, was winding his way closer every moment. If they didn't make it to his truck before company arrived, he'd have to hold them off somehow. At the moment it required all his concentration to achieve the first part of the plan. The sifting ash coated his face and stung his eyes, went up his nose. He prayed the raincoat was enough to protect Tot's lungs. His own were burning.

Kit fell forward over a concealed rock, and he barely caught her, almost falling himself.

She looked at him, her face luminous with a coating of silver dust. "How much farther?"

"Five minutes. Almost there." It was likely closer to

ten, but five sounded friendlier. His mother had always told her three boys everything good would happen in that mythical five minutes. He was a full-on preteen before he finally realized her trick. They kept battling, hands clutched together. He was wet and filthy, and Kit was having trouble yanking her legs from the mess when at long last he spotted the outline of his trusty old Dodge. *Sweeter than a valentine.*

"There she is."

The sight lit a fire under both of them, and together they surged up the final steep section and crested the road.

"I'll drive," he said as he hustled to the passenger door. "You keep trying to get a signal on my phone."

"But the baby," she panted. "We left the car seat. How do I . . ."

He yanked the door open and practically lifted Kit inside, tossing the duffel bag at her feet. "Gonna have to make do. Buckle yourself in and hold on to her best you can."

He hauled the seat belt as far as it would go and held it for her while she settled and snapped it into place. The windows were an absolute mess, and he swiped off a smattering of branches as he raced around to the driver's seat.

"Thank you, God," he breathed as the engine coughed to life. He released the brake and eased onto the road. The tires flung plumes of ash upward, which were again batted down by the rain. Nothing in the rearview, not yet. He increased the pace. Each foot of elevation they climbed made him hopeful they'd get a signal.

"Now?" He pointed to his phone. "Got anything? Are you checking?"

"Of course I'm checking," she snapped.

Obviously not the time to micromanage. He applied his mind to plans while she continued to monitor the cell phone.

"There's a turnoff to the highway in about a quarter mile. We'll . . ."

The rest of the itinerary died on his lips as an SUV appeared around the bend behind them. No headlights. He wouldn't have even seen it coming if a sudden, faint thread of moonlight hadn't burst through at that moment. Stomach clenched, he accelerated. So did their pursuers. Smothering an oath, he pressed the gas to the floor. Sludge churned underneath them, spewing to either side.

The road was a minefield of potential obstacles, and he prayed they wouldn't have a tire blowout. Kit grabbed the armrest, braced her legs, and clung to the squirming lump in her jacket. Tot wriggled and cried against Kit's belly, undulating like the iconic scene from the *Alien* movie.

No matter how fast he pressed, the followers kept pace, inching closer.

He gritted his teeth, straining forward as if that would increase their speed. "Truck's not fast enough."

Kit's eyes went wide. "Are they going to . . ."

Cullen had only seconds to shoot out an arm and pin Kit in place as the car rammed them from behind. The impact was violent, and even with his restraining forearm, Kit was thrown forward. "Protect Tot's head best you can!" he shouted, gas pedal to the floor. He gained a few feet from the SUV, but the gap was already closing between his truck and the more agile vehicle.

His cop brain took notes. One assailant or two?

Minimum two, he decided, could be more in the rear seat, but he pushed that worrying fact to the back of his brain. Reality check. They weren't going to make it to the turnoff that led to his property. Cold sweat speckled his brow. He risked a two-second stop and quickly grabbed the gun from under Kit's seat, ignoring her stare. Then he floored the gas again. If it came down to him against two or possibly more armed men, he didn't give them stellar chances.

His teeth ground together, gritty from the ash in his mouth.

If you win, it's gonna be the hardest thing you've ever done in the entirety of your miserable lives, he promised their pursuers. Was it the money they were after? Then they could have it. But not the baby. And not Kit.

Ahead was a fire trail that split the meadow neatly. No way he could get his truck up there. Rock and a hard place, a cliff on the other side and killers behind. The ash coated his tongue with bitterness. Their only advantage was he knew the trail, hence he was able to navigate easier over the dips and hollows. It allowed him to increase the distance between them. A sudden offshoot to the road helped as well, a short hairpin turn tucked behind the shrubs that brought them back onto the main route in short order but forced the SUV behind them to slow to a crawl.

Kit was trembling now, from cold or fear or both.

His tricks would not work for long. He would have to make a stand. As he fought the wheel, he spelled it out. "I'm gonna stop and jump out, leave the engine running. Give me a few seconds, then you drive as fast as you can, take the first turn you come to, and follow the road straight up. Where it loops around the mountain, that's where my cabin is. Door's unlocked. Bolt yourself inside. Hide there. Call for help if you can."

"What? Why?"

Because we're circling the drain with no escape in sight. Not a great option, her and the baby alone, but he could not come up with anything better. He clutched his gun. "Only chance we got is if I can get to them before they come for us."

"Cullen, there is zero chance that's going to work."

It was the first time she'd said his name. Why did it sound nice, rolling off her tongue, even if she was disagreeing with him? Better than when his brothers or bowling buddies said it.

"Hey, if it goes fine, I'll meet you up there." He winked. "You done real good with Tot so far, Kit Garrido. Honest. You're going to handle this now. Turnoff's hard to spot so look lively. Ready?"

"No." She snatched at his jacket sleeve. "You can't go off and get murdered and leave me. Do you hear? That's not fair, and I won't stand for it."

He almost laughed at the schoolmarm tone she'd drummed up, which must have been an effort since she was simultaneously trembling with cold and patting the squirming bundle in her jacket.

"I'm open to suggestions, but they're going to be on us again in a hot minute."

"I need to think." She chewed her thumbnail. "We could . . ." Her mouth opened in a round *O* of surprise as she looked past his shoulder. "Who's that?"

A dirt bike careened down the fire trail. Cullen risked

turning on his headlights for a better look. The rider was wearing street clothes, caked in debris from his helmet to his sneakers. He was skinny with a fringe of hair trailing down his back.

Cullen flicked the lights off again and kept moving, squinting, gun in hand. "Who in the Sam Hill . . ." They needed another pursuer like a hole in the head. Likely he was a wing man to the people in the SUV. The bike flew onto the main road in a slurry of debris, like some snippet from an action movie. Guy or gal was a skilled biker.

His nerves twanged. They were good and truly sandwiched. The only avenue available was to mow the biker down with the truck. He'd thought it was a solid plan until the guy pulled a gun from his pocket.

"Down," he shouted to Kit.

He gunned the engine, moving the truck forward while trying to keep his head out of bullet range. The shot came, and several more. Answering fire from the SUV. The dirt bike swerved off the road and vanished back up the fire trail in a swirl of ash. What had just happened? Why weren't they dead? He squinted in the rearview mirror while Kit craned to see behind them.

"The SUV is stopped. Why?" she whispered.

Since the air was thick and swirling, he rolled down the window and cautiously stuck his head out to get a closer look. A puff of wind stirred the debris cloud on the road, clearing so he could snag one precious glimpse that sent him into deeper confusion. "Tires. Evel Knievel shot out one of their tires."

"How do you know his name?"

He did a double take. "I don't. Haven't you heard of Evel Knievel?"

"No."

He sighed. Figured.

She craned to peer into the darkness. "So was he a good guy or bad guy?"

"Question of the hour." He rolled forward once more, trying to work it out in his head. Who was the newcomer and why had he enabled their escape? "You sure seem to have a lot of people interested in you."

"Not me. The baby or her mom."

"And that's your whole deal? You're a trucker, nothing else?"

"What else would there be?"

He shrugged. "Nothing." Maybe. "Never met a woman trucker before."

"There's a first for everything."

He chuckled, scanned the rearview mirror for any sign of Evel returning. Evel might have saved them now so he could plan his own ambush later. No way he was an innocent in the whole thing. "Until we know for sure what's going on, we're going to assume anyone in our proximity with a gun is a bad guy." He didn't wait to analyze further but rumbled along the road until he found the point he was looking for. The rock pillar marking the way had been leveled and partially buried. All the better. It made the turnoff even more difficult to detect. "Can't risk any more driving to snag a signal. Gotta get some shelter pronto."

"Still going to your cabin?"

"We can hunker there, try to call someone." He didn't add the second part. From his place on the top of the knoll, he could make a better stand against the guys who'd tried to ram them, and possibly against the mysterious rider. With his rifle and his knowledge of the terrain, the playing field was more even. It would be a sweet plan, if they weren't on a mountain getting ready to blast itself to smithereens. God was in charge of that little detail.

Could you put a hold on the main event until we get out of this mess, God?

"Why is the guy in the SUV trying to drive us off the road?"

"They."

She jerked a look at him. "What?"

"There are two in the vehicle at least."

"The guys who shot up my rig?"

He thought of the handprint inside Kit's cab. Might have been a minor cut. There hadn't been too much blood. Was Kit's mystery passenger connected to the men in the SUV?

The baby cried, muffled by Kit's jacket. She unzipped it enough that Tot popped her head out, flushed cheeks damp with tears, mouth wide to voice her outrage. Crying was a good indicator that she was whole and healthy. At least that part had gone okay. Cullen kept his mind on his driving, and the wails increased until his ears rang.

"Are we almost there?" Kit called above the wailing.

"Around that peak that looks like a thumb." He wasn't going to risk using his headlights, so he rolled slowly, the familiar curves and turns ghostly now under their ashen blanket.

Kit peered into the darkness. "Nothing but trees. You like your privacy."

"Yeah. I like visitors too, but only the kind I invite. My bowling team, for instance. Or my brothers, but they get on my nerves pretty quick when they stay over because they make themselves way too comfortable and eat all my snacks. You?"

"Me?"

"You like visitors?"

She cocked her head as if she'd never thought of the question before. "Not really."

"Why?" he said when Tot paused to refill her lungs.

"I . . . I just don't." She rubbed a fist over her forehead.

He left off the conversation as the road steepened. Exactly three and one eighth miles and he was pulling up at his neat two-story cabin, rolling the truck down into the below-level parking area, which was also where he stocked the firewood for the stove. The siding was almost luminous in ash, the windows and roof filmed over with debris, but the structure was intact and defiant. *It's like you, Cullen. A hot mess but still standing.* Beyond it the acres of pastureland were empty without his graceful, meandering horses. He'd never noticed before how quiet his place was, minus his herd.

Quiet and lonely. His heart thudded painfully, but his animals were safe at least, housed on his parents' farm in Shelton, near his middle brother's Olympia home. But he'd come back to the brewing cataclysm in spite of the family protest. Because he couldn't bear the way his mother constantly tried to get him to talk about what happened? Or some delusion that he could actually save his property from ultimate destruction? The excuse of helping his friends?

"Nice place," she said, and he couldn't restrain a flush of pride.

"Worked hard on it." Sweat equity including sixteen stitches, and it would soon all be snuffed out by Mount Ember.

As long as they didn't get erased with it, he told himself. He unbuckled, hastened around to take the duffel and help extract Kit and Tot, but she'd already hopped out with the sniffling baby. He led them inside through the basement door and locked it behind them, not a customary practice, but he was glad he'd installed a sturdy deadbolt anyway, considering. He guided her up the short flight of stairs to the kitchen, where he pulled the blinds and turned on the under-cabinet lights, resisting the urge to fist pump. "We still have power. I wasn't sure." Enough illumination, but not so much that his place would be a beacon in the darkness for those trying to find them.

Tot's outrage had died down to exhausted hiccups as he put the duffel on a chair and helped Kit out of the raincoat. She immediately thrust the baby at him.

"Come here, Tot." He kissed her fuzzy head, and she crammed three fingers in her mouth. "You worked yourself up a head of steam there, didn't you?" He pointed Kit down the hallway. "Bathroom's through there if you need it. Light switch on the left. No exterior window so it should be all right."

Kit nodded and hurried off.

While she was gone, he strolled the baby in circles around the hardwood and worked through the myriad thoughts clamoring for his attention. His phone still had no signal. He texted his brother again anyway. Who else?

Lon? His bowling friend holdout who'd refused to leave the area until he got all his sheep moved? Cullen had spent two solid days making that happen until he stank of sheep and had burned through three tanks of gas hauling the trailer to a location safe from volcano. Lon undoubtedly had left that very morning.

Another bowling buddy, the crusty Archie Esposito, might still be in the area, but he had no way to reach him, since the man refused to carry a cell phone. The best bowler on the team, Archie took every opportunity to remind Cullen. He better have gone or Cullen would have something to say about it. Archie was a self-described stubborn old coot.

You're the stubbornest, Cullen.

But if Cullen hadn't delayed leaving, he never would have seen Kit's rig careening off the road. Prickles danced up his spine. Didn't bear thinking about what might have happened to her and Tater Tot if they'd remained in the crushed rig. He joggled over to the front windows that looked out upon the pasture and pulled the curtains closed.

After they fixed the tire, the two guys in the SUV would figure out where he'd turned off sooner or later, if they had any smarts between them. He intended to be ready for the reckoning that was going to happen. The tightening of the muscles in his stomach felt oddly pleasing, reminding him of who he used to be, the good part that did things for people and brought others to account. That part.

With Tot against his shoulder, he climbed the narrow staircase and stood in the darkened bedroom, using the night vision binoculars from his bedside table to scan out the window. Nothing moving out there in the falling rain that he could detect. He checked the camera he'd fixed on the gnarly pine by the stone marker. By some miracle, it was still operating and his phone receiving the feed.

No one coming.

Yet.

He carried Tot back downstairs, calculating. He had the gun he kept in his truck and a rifle on the premises.

With his free hand he began pulling things out of the duffel bag and staging them on the kitchen table. The empty bottle that needed washing, a clean diaper, and something that looked like pajamas with footie things built right in. He was surprised when he found Kit's teddy bear that she must have shoved in at some point. His lips curved in a smile. All tough edges and angles, but Kit was attached to this raggedy toy. Gently, he stowed it back in the duffel.

When Kit emerged from the bathroom, he got a good look at her. Her clean face was heart-shaped with delicate features and graceful brows. Her intelligent eyes roved the room, soaking in every last detail of his home. He figured she didn't miss much. The fringe of her bangs poked out from below her brown cap, which she must have tried to wipe off in the bathroom. Slight build, strong for her size. Her jeans were ripped at the knee and filth coated her boots to her upper thighs. The woman desperately needed a change of clothes.

"How are you feeling?"

She blinked. "Me?"

He arched a brow at that one. "You seem to be the only other person in the room besides me and Tot."

"My head hurts. And I'm hungry and I don't like being dirty."

"That about sums it up for me too, minus the headache." But his knee was hollering, and lots of other parts.

"Are they going to follow us here?"

"Eventually, but it's all clear for now. I figure we have a couple hours before they fix the flat and locate the turn to my place. I'll see them coming. I've got a camera."

She nodded, and it seemed to cause her pain.

"Let me get a blanket to lay her down. I'll wrangle us something to eat and find you some pain relief while you shower."

She recoiled. "Shower? I don't . . ."

"Rude to point out to a lady, but you're a mess and so am I. Even if I'm wrong about the timing, I've got a sensor on the drive that will alert us if anyone drives up so we'll have some notice."

"What are we going to do if that happens?"

He felt the coiling again in his stomach. "You will protect Tot, and I will take care of the intruders."

She pursed her lips. "That sounds . . . intense."

"Confronting killers usually is." And the outcome was never guaranteed. He knew that all too well.

"You think they . . . the people in the SUV are after the baby or Tot's mom? Or maybe the dirt bike guy is?"

He shrugged off the question. No sense speculating. His gut told him they were going to find out sooner rather than later. He threw a quilt on the floor and set Tot in the middle with a ring of plastic keys from the duffel clamped in her tiny fist. Her limbs flexed as if she was relieved to be free of her raincoat cocoon.

"Five minutes," he said, but this time he meant it. From the closet, he procured a set of lady's sweats and handed them to her along with a clean bath towel.

She accepted with a raised brow.

"They belong to my sister-in-law who is a bit of a scatterbrain and leaves things here when she and my brother visit. Probably too big but better than my clothes." He added a pair of men's sweat socks. "Socks will be huge on you, but maybe you can hike them up. Dry at least."

"Thank you," she said quietly, eyes downcast. "I . . . didn't say that before. I should have." She too was thinking about what might have happened if they hadn't unexpectedly met up in the middle of an evacuation zone.

He nodded.

When he heard the shower running, he dumped a can of soup into a pot and opened a box of saltines. Not gourmet, but quick and filling. Then he changed Tot into a clean diaper and her fleece jammies. Only three diapers left in the duffel. That would be a problem soon enough.

And where was a baby going to sleep exactly? Could they stay put long enough for that to happen? Deep down he had a streak of optimism that simply would not die. This would work. Even if Cullen couldn't see a way out, God could. And that really was the only reason Cullen could face each day, that inextinguishable spark that shone through his pain. Sometimes it was so minute, he could hardly see it.

With Tot happily gumming her plastic toy on the quilt, he returned to the closet once again for his rifle.

Another scan from the upstairs window indicated no cause for concern, and the driveway camera was quiet.

He carried the rifle with him downstairs and stowed it in an out-of-the-way corner along with a backpack that he kept at the ready for emergencies. Of course, when he'd first prepared it, he'd been thinking wildfires or floods, not volcanoes and killers, but the supplies would help anyway. He added a carton of ammo and zipped it closed.

The baby had gone quiet, sound asleep with her arms flung wide as if she hadn't a care. Lovely. He washed the bottle, plunged it in boiling water to sterilize it along with the nipple, and let it air dry. A single bottle was going to be as big a problem as the three diapers if they had to flee or the hot water gave out.

Kit emerged wearing the sweats, which sagged low on her hips until she hoisted them up to her waist. He tried not to notice that her middle was toned and smooth. He handed her a rubber band.

"This might help." He waved a vague hand at her confusion. "You know . . . cinch up the slack."

"Oh." She gathered a bunch of material and secured it with the rubber band. "Weird but resourceful."

"We can put that on my tombstone. Next to your 'Rest in peace with the paperclips' motto."

Her sudden smile was a surprise.

When the soup was ready, they sat at the table, and he thanked God for their survival. Kit sat uncomfortably through the grace, which he pretended not to notice. Her discomfort was secondary to his need to express gratitude. By all rights they should have been wiped out any number of times in the past eight hours, yet here they were with food and shelter and a baby that was very much alive. There was that spark again.

The weak light from the under-cabinet lamps dulled the bruise rising on Kit's forehead around the bandage.

"How's the head?"

"Pounding like a drum. How's the knee?"

He twitched. She'd noticed the limp? "I . . . it's okay."

"Old injury?"

His mouth refused to answer for a moment. "Yeah. Job related."

"What's your job?"

"Now, I raise horses."

She blew on a spoonful of hot soup and waited. The expectant silence was worse than the throbbing in his patella.

"I was a cop. Call went bad. I got hurt and retired." So few words that contained a whole world inside them.

She tipped her chin up, and he knew she sensed the scarred place he was trying to cover up. For the briefest tick he had the urge to spill it all. Instead, he ate a spoonful of soup and burned his mouth swallowing too fast. He cleared his throat and checked his phone. "Cameras are still operational, so that's a relief."

"We have to find a way out. Mount Ember is going to erupt. Soon."

"Until first light, we can't go anywhere. Roads are way too treacherous."

She fiddled with her water glass. "But what's the long game? We can't stay here and wait for the mountain to explode or for them to find us."

"Nor can we drive around in the dark without wrecking or broadcasting our location. Before first light we go."

"Where?"

"Not sure."

She stiffened. "We need a plan, a detailed plan. I always have one."

He folded his arms. "I'm thinking your plan for today didn't include Tot and shooters."

She shrank into the baggy sweatshirt. "No, it didn't." The edges of fear crept over her face.

No, Kit wasn't a fly-by-the-seat-of-her-pants type. He slid over a bottle of aspirin he'd grabbed from the kitchen. "This will help with the headache. I'm thinking we drive up the road to Pinnacle Point. Chances are good we can get a signal there, or at least see how the roads look."

She swallowed the pills with a swig of water. "Isn't it better to make for the nearest town?" She squinched her eyes shut. "Grandlake, right? We can get help there maybe. Someone must have stayed behind."

"It's fifteen miles from here, along a closed road, and the town's evacuated. We're better off heading to Pinnacle."

"I don't agree."

"Why?"

"Because if Tot's mom is alive, she would head for town, not farther into the wilderness."

And that dried up his argument. It was possible Tot's mom didn't know the area and she was lost and wandering. More likely she was dead. But if there was any shred of a chance they could find her by heading to the nearest town . . .

"All right. Compromise. We get a signal first. Then we head to Grandlake."

"Okay."

"How about some shut-eye? Guest bedroom's down here. I'll bunk upstairs with Tot and scan every hour to check our security and see if by some oddball chance the signal's been restored."

"You need sleep too."

"I'll get it. Cat naps."

"I'll switch with you in a few hours. Unless Tot's screaming, and then you can have as much time as you want with her." The corner of her mouth curved enough to let him know she'd made a joke. Not as stoic as she pretended to be.

"Fair." The soup was gone, but he stared at the stray noodle at the bottom of the bowl. The decision was made then. After a quick stop, they'd ride to town.

The thing he didn't want to say aloud thrashed in his brain.

Town was exactly where the killers would think they'd go.

And it might not be too long before they arrived to finish what they'd started.

▪ FIVE ▪

THE BED FELT STRANGE, the blankets too light, the room too large. The loss of her rig, the cozy sleeping area in particular, carved like a dagger into her soul. Her sturdy Freightliner represented her future, security, everything, and now it was a mangled mess being gobbled in inches by a hungry volcano. The wind shrieked around Cullen's cabin as one day progressed toward the next. Maybe the three of them would be buried soon too. Or their pursuers would arrive first.

If the men were only interested in the money, they could have it. She kicked at the blankets. What had she done to deserve any of this danger? Being shot at? Her rig wrecked? Chased into the night with a stranger when she was minding her own business, hauling office supplies for goodness' sake.

The bloody handprint surfaced in her mind.

A woman so desperate she'd leave her baby . . .

Kit's self-pity waned. Tot's mom didn't deserved whatever had happened to her either.

Kit was certain the men, whoever they were, wouldn't

be satisfied with the cash. Her gut told her there was something else, deeper, uglier at play that she didn't understand, something more personal than money.

She tried praying, but her thoughts kept skittering off as she repeatedly dozed and startled awake again. What could she do? How could she protect herself?

She scooted to the periphery of the mattress, clutching at the edge to hold herself in place. The moon broke through the storm and stabbed its way under the roll-down blinds. Cullen hadn't cluttered up the place with too many personal touches. There was a clock by the bed, an old, tarnished brass thing with a fat round dial that ticked its way through the hours. The face was cracked and a piece of the metal facing broken off. Faded lettering on the top read, "You survived ten years. True blue, through and through."

True blue. Even if he hadn't told her, she'd have pegged him as former law enforcement. He had that authoritative aura about him of a man who wanted to fix things and knew how. It usually rubbed her the wrong way, being with people who automatically assumed the leader role, but realistically she'd likely be dead if he hadn't intervened.

Unusual circumstances. As soon as you get clear of this red zone, you won't need any more help from Cullen. Tension tightened her gut, but she pushed it down. Her life was working smoothly before, wasn't it? She'd had it all under control.

Until you wrecked your truck.

She blinked hard at the tears that pooled in her eyes, gathering the unraveling strands of her control. She'd regroup. Maybe salvage the rig somehow if the volcano allowed. The notion made her heart leap. The wreck might not be as bad as she thought. She knew people who specialized in difficult tow jobs. She'd go back, examine it more closely.

But how, when there were people actively hunting her? Her mom would say to pray about it.

Vienna Jackson Garrido, with the dark slice of hair and trim figure, always smelled of coconut hand lotion. A church deacon, she was so sure of herself and her place, so willing to speak of a grace and forgiveness she couldn't or wouldn't offer to Kit's father. The hypocrisy left Kit with such discomfort that she'd never again set foot in a church after she left home.

A vise of pain squeezed her left eye and radiated through her forehead. *Focus on remembering Tot's mom.*

A lifetime ago, she'd picked up cargo, somewhere. She'd buckled in and driven toward her destination away from the evacuation zone, but some incident caused her to change her plan entirely, a thing she rarely ever did.

That had to be where Tot's mom entered the picture, and she'd picked her up. Kit concentrated on that. What had she looked like? What had they said to each other that resulted in Kit driving her rig along the twisty Pine Hollow Road instead of hightailing it to the freeway as she'd planned? Had there been any indication the woman was being followed? Pursued? That she or the baby were in danger?

All Kit got for her efforts was a deeper throbbing in her skull.

Snap.

She jerked to a sitting position, pulse pounding. What

had made the sound? The mountain announcing it was about to sweep the cabin away? Feet still swaddled in Cullen's borrowed socks, she shuffled as she crept to the window, lifted a corner of the blinds, and peered out.

The surface below could have been lunar terrain, acres of bumps and craters all concealed under a silver silt blanket. A pile of debris several yards from her window shifted. She pressed her nose to the glass, cupping her hand for a better look. A racoon waddled across Cullen's back deck, his gray fur blending with the night so only his white markings and paws stood out clearly. At an unhurried pace, he meandered along, eventually disappearing under the pasture fence. She blew out a breath, pressed her forehead to the cold glass.

The masked bandit made her think of her father's unceasing efforts to protect the fish in her mother's small pond from the nighttime marauders. Trash pandas, her father called them.

Each one of his plans to foil the hungry rodents had grown more elaborate: motion-activated lights, protective nets, a fake plastic owl that fooled none of the racoons, nor the hawks as far as anyone could tell. *"I'm real sorry,"* she remembered him saying, his arm looped around her mother's shoulders as they surveyed a shining detached fin, all that remained of her little koi family. Kit could hardly believe all the fat, luminous fish had been snatched away.

Her mother had sighed, brushing at the tears with the back of her hand. *"You tried."*

That tender moment was the last she remembered between them, as shortly thereafter the police had knocked on their door, investigating funds gone missing from the investment firm where her father was employed.

The inquiry led to her father's confession and his eventual arrest. The marriage had buckled under the weight of shock and shame. Their family had collapsed too, because, though her mother would not divorce Sid Garrido, she would never forgive him either, no matter what her religion insisted. He'd begged for forgiveness, never offered one word of excuse for his crimes, only remorse and soul-deep regret. Her mother was unmoved by any of it. Kit wondered if maybe she'd lost both of her parents in that moment.

Crack.

The memory evaporated. She stared into the night. That noise hadn't come from the waddling racoon. Outside, the wind plowed the ash into sooty drifts, and she stared until her eyes burned. Was that . . . Adrenaline whipped her nerves. A shadow of something, no, some*one*, disappeared around the corner of the porch. Everything in her wanted to scream. *Alert Cullen.* She reached for her phone, the dead screen mocking her.

In a panic she flung open the bedroom door and ran across the living room, sprinting for the stairs to the upper floor. She was three strides from the bottom step when the kitchen door smashed open. A glance over her shoulder proved a dangerous mistake. She clipped the corner of the rocking chair with her hip and fell to her knees.

A man exploded from the kitchen and crashed into her, bringing her flat to the floor. He grabbed her hair, his own trailing against her cheek as he leaned over her.

"Where is she?" he whispered savagely.

"Get off me." Kit wriggled and squirmed, but he held her fast, his knee crushing the small of her back. Her heart slammed in her chest. "Cullen!" she yelled, but he slapped a palm over her mouth.

"You're going to tell me where you took her."

Kit was suddenly engulfed in the memory of her assault at that late night truck stop in Tacoma. The pressure of his weight against her, his hands fumbling with her clothes, his calloused fingers reaching to seal off her scream.

She did what she'd done then, turned her fear into rage, a rage so hot and incendiary it was uncontainable. Back at the truck stop, she'd bitten, screamed, and kicked so violently she'd thrown the guy off balance long enough to make it to her rig. She could still hear his meaty palms slapping against the driver's door in rhythm with the vile names he'd spat at her seconds after she locked herself in.

On Cullen's living room floor, the man pulled her hair tight and breathed hot against her neck. His ponytail drifted across her cheek. Long hair? The man riding the motorbike? The torch of anger lit her from the inside out. When he shifted, she bit his palm until she tasted blood. With a yowl he loosened his grip on her hair, and she rammed her head into his face. Bone crunched, and he reeled back with a cry of pain.

"Cullen!" she screamed, rocketing to her feet, but he was already racing down the stairs with his rifle.

He leapt down the last two steps, hit the bottom, feet planted, rifle aimed. "Hands up or you're dead!" he hollered.

The man was on his knees, but he raised his palms while Kit scuttled over to Cullen, who was standing on shaky legs.

Cullen shot her a quick glance. "Bleeding? Hurt?"

"No." She swiped at her mouth. "It's his blood. I bit him before I headbutted him."

Cullen quirked an admiring grin. "Nice job. Bashed him up good. Turn on the lamp."

With shaking hands, she flicked on the small table lamp and backed against the wall so Cullen wouldn't see that she was on the brink of collapse. Palms pressed to the wood paneling, she tried to slow her panicked breathing.

You're okay. You're in control.

Cullen shot a glance out the window. "Motorbike outside. Snuck in around my cameras. You the one who shot out the SUV tires?"

The man didn't speak, so Cullen moved a step closer, gun aimed at his head. "Slide out the gun from your waistband with two fingers and ease it down on the carpet. If you move fast, you die fast. Got me, Evel?"

Not reacting to the nickname, he did as directed. Cullen seemed outwardly calm, but he was breathing fast.

Cullen gestured with the gun. "All right. Now that we've got that taken care of. Sit in that chair, hands in your lap."

Kit felt her stomach uncoil a fraction as the man complied.

Cullen did not lower his weapon. "Who are you and why are you breaking into my cabin?"

The lamplight revealed him to be in his late twenties, her age maybe, as tall as Cullen but thin and wiry. His clothes were filthy but not threadbare. He remained silent, drops of blood flowing from his bitten hand and his nose.

"He asked me where she was," Kit said.

Cullen frowned. "She who?"

"I don't know." Kit understood what Cullen wanted to know. Was the stranger after the baby or the missing woman? Or both?

Cullen took a step closer. "You're going to start talking."

Evel tipped his blood-smeared face to Cullen. "Who are you two?" he countered, eyes blazing. "How'd you get the baby? Where are they?"

Cullen's head cocked ever so slightly. "You're confused about the situation here, fella. You broke into my house, and I've got the rifle. Means you answer the questions, not ask 'em."

The stranger's leg muscles bunched as if he was going to spring from the chair. Instinctively, Kit braced to defend herself, but Cullen took a step closer, and Evel sank down again.

"She's mine. They're mine. I want them back," the man said.

"That explains nothing," Cullen said. "Right now, we got a whole bunch of people interested in this baby and her mom. Dunno who's being truthful, and that means you're gonna have to do some serious talking. Cops are notified. On their way now."

"No, they aren't. All the communication's knocked out."

A tiny beeping yanked their attention.

"What's that?" Kit said.

"Front camera alert." Cullen pulled out his phone and handed it to her. "Check the screen."

As she did, her stomach contracted to a fist. "A car . . . the SUV, coming this way."

"How many inside?"

She squinted. "I can only see . . ." She gasped. "The image disappeared."

Cullen muttered. "Lost the remaining signal." He turned to her. "Know how to shoot?"

"No."

He yanked the lamp cord from the wall. "Here. If he moves, whack him with this." He ran out the front door, grabbing binoculars on the way. She went all-over cold when the man moved in the chair.

"They're coming and they'll kill you," he said.

The hair rose on her arms. "Who? And why?"

"She can hurt them."

"Who?" she repeated.

He swiped at the blood still seeping from his nose. "Annette."

Annette who? she wanted to scream. *Is that the baby or the mother?* But before she could get anything out, Cullen was back. "Can't tell how many. We've—"

Evel surged from the chair, running for the stairs. *Tot . . .*

Kit grabbed his jacket as he barreled by, spinning him around, right into Cullen's fist.

Evel collapsed, groaning.

Cullen pulled out the fallen man's wallet. He flipped it open and yanked the driver's license free, jamming it into his own pocket.

A scrap of paper fluttered to the floor. Kit just managed to grab it before Cullen snagged her wrist.

Evel sat up with a groan. Flashlight beams splayed into the darkened interior. He staggered upright and lurched into the kitchen.

"We have to stop him," Kit called.

"No time," he said, pulling on her arm. "They're around the side of the house." The small light over the mantel was suddenly extinguished.

"They cut the power," she whispered. "They're coming." Her skin felt too tight for her body. Wordlessly, she raced upstairs after him and snagged the sleeping Tot and her duffel bag. Cullen grabbed his pack and bolted the bedroom door.

Locking us in? "What are we doing?"

From downstairs came the sound of a door being slammed open, boots trampling the wood floor of Cullen's living room.

He hurried to the small bedroom window and wrestled it open.

She struggled to understand. "The . . . roof?"

"We're not escaping without a firefight unless we get creative." He climbed out onto the level section of roof, banging his forehead on the sill, his wide shoulders barely squeezing through. Hand extended, he crooked his neck to see her.

"Fast, Kit. We gotta move fast."

With great difficulty, Kit climbed over the sill, holding Tot in a death grip. At the edge of the flat portion, the eaves dropped away at a frightening angle. They both sat down on their bottoms.

The shingles were slick, and the loose socks caused her to slip. Cullen grabbed her arm. "You hold Tot. I'll hold you."

Together they skidded and slid their way to the very edge of the roof, where her toes encountered the gutter. Fifteen feet, maybe. Too far to jump.

"How are we going to get off this roof?"

Cullen pointed. "We'll climb down the drainpipe. It'll deposit us near the garage. We'll get to my truck."

Shimmying down drainpipes with a baby in the dark. A completely ridiculous and risky plan, but what was the alternative? Return to the house for a shootout? Deliver the money and hope they wouldn't be murdered?

"They're coming and they'll kill you."

From the window she heard the sound of boots kicking at the bedroom door. They'd be through in a matter of seconds.

She peered into the darkness. She'd survive the drop if she fell, but Tot? What if they bungled the transfer? She clenched her teeth. "Will the downspout hold?"

Cullen gave her a "hurry up" gesture and tossed the pack and duffel onto the ground, then slung his rifle over his shoulder. "You go first in case I'm too heavy. I'll lower Tot down to you."

She eased over the roof and gripped the cold metal. It was gritty against her palms. Her socks reduced her traction, and she quickly shimmied them off. Her toes screamed at the freezing metal, but with the improved friction she was able to slither down. When her feet landed on a slimy spot of grass, she could hardly believe she'd done it.

"Here's Tot," Cullen whispered. He held the baby by the back of her outfit, leaned his torso into the gap, and extended his arm to its full length.

Kit stretched until her spine cracked, her hands woefully short of the dangling baby.

Tot's limbs twitched madly as he eased her down a couple inches more. The baby was ready to scream.

"I can't reach."

"Gonna let go. Catch her."

Catch her? Panic rippled her limbs. "No, don't."

But he counted down from three and let go. The baby dropped from his fist and thudded softly into Kit's arms with a squeal. "Shhhh shhhhh," she soothed, trying to calm them both. Wood splintered inside as the bedroom door was kicked off its hinges.

"They're through, Cullen," she called. "Hurry."

Cullen scooted onto the downspout. He looked like he was acting in some sort of clip from a bad B movie, his giant frame clinging to the spindly metal conduit. No doubt the guy was athletic, but he wasn't exactly graceful.

As he fought for a hold, boots sliding, the metal shrieked. The drainpipe sheared away from the cabin. Cullen toppled like a felled pine, landing on his back in a swirl of debris. Immediately he rolled onto all fours and staggered to his feet. "Go. I'm okay. Get to the truck."

He delayed a moment, but she didn't stop to find out why. With Tot clamped to her front, she ran to the garage. Every rock and stone found the soles of her bare feet, but she kept on, finally ripping open the driver's side door of Cullen's truck and tossing in the duffel before getting in with Tot.

Tot cried as Kit looked anxiously for Cullen. Where was he? One minute and she heard shouts from the house. Had he passed out? Broken his leg and been unable to make it to the garage? She'd have to go back for him.

Hand on the door, she flung it open just as Cullen sprinted up and leapt into the truck. He cranked the engine and slammed it into reverse.

"Down," he roared a second before bullets sprayed at them from the roof. The SUV guys had discovered their escape route. She could see their dark shapes dropping from the roof, one, two. The truck lurched. Cullen cleared the garage, and then he pivoted in a U-turn. He floored the gas. They streaked down the drive until he slammed on the brakes.

The SUV was parked in the middle of the cement, blocking their escape.

Tot chose that moment to wail. The sound pierced her eardrums like an arrow. Behind them, flashlights moved along the drive, bobbing as the two men ran to catch up with the truck.

Cullen was still for a moment, then he wrenched the wheel and plunged off the road and into the pasture. She barely maintained her grasp of the baby.

"Can your truck handle this terrain?"

"We're gonna find out."

"Is there an exit in this direction?"

He didn't answer. They surged on, bumping and pitching. In the sideview mirror, the SUV's headlights activated. Their attackers had reached their vehicle. The pursuit was on again.

She couldn't talk. They were jostling so much she could barely think. Bare feet braced, she wedged herself in the seat and caged her arms around Tot. As much as Cullen sped up, the SUV managed to make steady progress in closing the gap between them.

Ahead, a sturdy split rail fence barred their way. He turned parallel to the fence until they reached a metal gate. He braked, leapt out, and hurried to open the combination padlock. Like a linebacker, he shoved the gate aside.

"How's this helping?" she started when he got back in,

but he drove through, jumped back out to close the gate, and locked it behind them. In a flash they were moving again, the ground more uneven than before.

"I know my land," Cullen said. "They don't. The gate will slow them down long enough for us to get to the bridge."

"And the bridge leads to . . ."

"We'll get to my friend's place outside of Grandlake. He was uncertain about evacuating, but even if he did, he has a landline. Might work."

"*Might* work?" They were banking their lives on a flimsy notion like that? Over the growling engine she heard metal smashing metal, a shriek that hung in the air. The SUV guys were attempting to bash through the gate.

Evel's rasping voice replayed in her thoughts. *"How'd you get the baby? Where are they?"*

They? The baby and Tot's mom? She had to be the key to whatever the murderous men were after, and it wasn't just the money in the duffel. *"She can hurt them."*

Tot screamed and Kit held her steady. How long before the attackers would be upon them again?

◾ SIX ◾

CULLEN WOULD NOT ALLOW HIMSELF to think about what had almost happened in his cabin. "Narrow escape" didn't even capture it. The SUV guys hadn't wasted a moment fixing their flat and tracking them. And Evel had actually busted through the kitchen door. Cold swamped him from the inside out. Evel could have killed Kit if she hadn't unloaded on him. A smile curled his lips. Kit was impressive.

He snaked an admiring glance at her, his cheeks warming when she caught him looking.

"What?" She clutched the baby defensively. "I'm holding her as tight as I can without squishing her."

"Not that. You're doing fine. Kudos on the way you handled Evel back there. That was excellent."

She blinked, smiled faintly, and lifted a shoulder. "He had it coming."

"That's for darn sure."

She shifted on the seat. "He said 'She's mine. They're mine. I want them back.'"

"Did he drop any names?"

"Annette. And he said she could hurt them."

"If Annette is Tot's mom, she's clearly been trying hard to escape and she must have found something to serve as insurance."

"Evel could be lying." She voiced his own question. "Is she running from him? Or the SUV guys?"

"Maybe both. Whatever she did, stealing that money or running away, she made some people angry." *Angry enough to kill.*

"She's not anybody's," Kit said fiercely.

"What?"

"He said, 'They're mine,' but they aren't anyone's property, Annette and Tot. I don't have to be acquainted with Annette to know that." She jiggled the baby more vigorously.

"Agreed." The emotion in her voice tightened the muscles in his belly. Kit was a force, an enigma. He wished they could sit down across from each other so he could look into her delicate face and understand who she was and what she'd been through. It'd be a fascinating story, he had no doubt.

Concentration was required elsewhere. He attempted to avoid the big dips that might take out the axle, but he was flying blind with the darkness and the debris.

"You . . ." He lost the rest of it as they slammed into a hidden crevice and out again, his cranium impacting the roof. She yelped, and Tot let loose a screech as he struggled to correct but not before another tooth-rattling jostle.

"Sorry."

"Where are we going?" Kit said over the baby's screams.

"There's a bridge over the creek. Only shortcut to Grandlake from here." *If we don't blow a tire first.* He wondered again how the SUV guys had managed to change their flat so quickly. Must have some mechanical skills. Definitely advanced tracking ability since they'd been found again in speedy fashion in spite of the conditions. The only glimpse he'd gotten had been two guys, one trim and dark-haired, the other with a bush of unruly curls protruding from under his knit cap. Only two? He prayed there were no more wolves circling, waiting to join in the hunt. Bad enough the motorcycle dude had made an escape.

They bumped their way past the trees and up a gradual slope that reassured him they were headed in the right direction. Thick clumps of pines grew sparser as they rose in elevation, and he tried not to listen to his brain screaming, *This isn't safe, you dolt!*

His breath caught as they took in the massive bulk of Mount Ember silhouetted against the shrouded moon. Normally her steep granite sides, rising some nine thousand feet into the sky, would be visible only occasionally, her top sporting a crown of snow that remained year-round. Now the magnificent slopes were misshapen, the eastern side bulging out like a grotesque pimple. Farther south there was a giant pockmark where none had been before. He felt like they were traversing an alien terrain. They were only ninety miles south of Seattle, but they might as well be on Mars.

Kit peered out the driver's side window to get a look. "I heard on the news Tuesday night that the steam explosion made a two-hundred-fifty-foot crater. The bulge in her side is growing six feet a day as the magma rises up the cone of the volcano. Geologists are predicting the main eruption within days. There'll be an avalanche and mud-flows from the melting snow. Smoke, ash, catastrophic ground movement. The red zone is expected to be fully impacted."

"The red zone was extended fifteen miles last I checked." She nodded. "Maybe twenty now. Emergency Services keeps updating it."

Kit had to be thinking what he was. They were well within that deadly distance and moving deeper into the explosion zone with every mile. The town of Grandlake where they were headed was settled squarely in the foot-hills of the angry monster, as was his cabin. Was there another way? Find the nearest cleared road and try to get off the mountain?

"In the articles I've read, scientists are predicting total devastation within the evac area." She spoke calmly, as if she were delivering a weather report.

"I'm not sure I want to know all that." In his peripheral vision he caught her puzzled head cock.

"Why wouldn't you? It's all relevant information." The baby's cries had settled to low whimpers.

"Facts aside, I prefer to leave room for the 'what if.'"

"The 'what if'?"

He edged them around an endless series of fallen trees. "Sure. We're being chased by killers and we have this un-identified baby and a volcano threatening to go bananas, but what if we get out of this unscathed?"

He heard her dismissive sniff.

"There's practically zero chance of that happening, Cullen."

"Yeah, but what if we succeed in spite of everything?"

"Rose-colored glasses aren't going to keep us from dying."

"I prefer to attribute it to experience. I've seen God do plenty of miracles, so why not another one here and now?"

She didn't quite roll her eyes but almost. "We're on our own. God's not interested in three insignificant people."

"You're not insignificant," he said quietly. "And neither is Tot."

She rested her cheek on Tot's head, her shoulders softening for a moment before she spoke again. "We're probably not going to get out alive, but if the 'what if' gives you comfort . . ."

It did. This moment, these days, his life, would be over when God said so. Not a moment before. He'd learned that when the truck door had come flying off its hinges, missing him by inches.

But not missing his partner, Daniela. There'd been moments, plenty of them, when he'd wished he'd taken that impact instead of her. He realized with a jolt that if God had answered that prayer, Kit and Tot would likely be dead. There was a reason Cullen had been climbing down from the roof of his cabin at the very moment Kit's truck hurtled off the road. That was too massive a coincidence, and he didn't believe in those. He swallowed, gripped the wheel tighter.

Let's see what you're up to here, God.

Eventually they reached the far end of the pasture where he let them out through another gate and locked it behind him. He'd never secured his fields before, until he heard reports of animals being stolen a few months back. Painful to put locks on, he'd thought at the time. Now he was grateful.

"Another mile, but it's steep."

She nodded, braced her bare feet against the floor. The meager moonlight had succumbed under a thick haze. The tires kicked up a coating of muck that the wipers smeared instead of cleared as they headed away from his land.

"It's like driving through a bowl of chowder," he muttered.

The river would be swollen, both with the aftermath of a recent storm series and the deposited debris from the continuous earthquakes. Once they were over, it would be a fairly straight shot to Archie's place. Another thirty minutes, tops.

He prayed they would find something to help. A working phone, a search and rescue safety patrol, heck, even an old CB radio they could use to contact the outside world. He felt acutely the loss of his rifle, dropped when the drainpipe had given way. He hadn't had a moment to reveal that setback to Kit. The woman had enough on her plate, didn't she? They were down to one handgun.

The air was choked with a cloud of fine dust. Reluctantly, he rolled the window down just far enough for him to stick his head out. "Sorry. I gotta see where I'm going. Hold your breath if you can. Keep Tot covered."

It was the odor that warned him first, a fragrance of freshly moved earth that swelled above the acrid tang, as if a backhoe had recently plowed up the compacted ground.

Stop! His brain shouted the command. After a hard brake, he put the truck in park and got out. He blinked, shone his flashlight across the soil as he tried to absorb what he was seeing. Great chunks of the riverbank were gone, along with the bridge supports. *Not six feet from my front tire* . . .

His boots sank a few inches into the loose debris as he tiptoed closer.

The bridge itself was knocked sideways, sticking out like a severed limb from under a tomb of fallen rock. Even as he watched, the detritus rattled and slid as if the volcano were reminding them it was far from finished.

Hands on his hips, he stared.

There was no way to cross the river, not in the truck.

Kit climbed out. "Tot's on the floor and she's not happy that we stopped. What's the delay?" With her elbow crooked over her mouth to protect her lungs, she took in the ruins.

"No way across." *Captain Obvious. Regroup. Now.* "New plan. We'll have to hike."

"No way. Can't we find another route?"

"Too steep and wooded here. Only other choice would be to retrace back to my cabin. And we know who we'd encounter if we chose that option."

Kit's breath puffed white in the air. "How far?"

"Good news is they won't be able to cross either, and they don't know the way around, I hope. They'll double back in their vehicle. Buys us time."

"How far?" Her tone was weary but hard-edged with determination.

"Four miles, maybe five."

She groaned. "That's not tenable. Tot's cold."

He touched her shoulder and felt the shivers she'd been trying to suppress. "I'll carry Tot and the bags. We'll stop when we need to. Take it slow."

Her eyes were wide glimmering points of light in the gloom. She wouldn't express her fear and frustration, but he felt it anyway, a current of dark emotion. *This isn't going to be the end*, he wanted to tell her. *We're not going to hunker here and wait to see if the killers or the volcano get us first. Not. Going. To. Happen.* He hadn't felt that stubborn flash in a long time.

Look where it got you before.

He pushed that thought away, muttered a silent prayer, and started to unzip his jacket to put over her and Tot when engine noise cut through the darkness.

Found. How? There was no way . . .

In unison they raced back to the truck. With no rifle, what was he going to do? The handgun was their only protection. He drew it from the holster.

Thoughts tumbled as they scrambled. Was it safer for Kit and Tot to stay in the truck, a bull's-eye target? Or hide in the cold wasteland, breathing in who knew what? And how would Kit and Tot find shelter if he didn't survive? Maybe they should attempt to reach the trees that hadn't been consumed by the landslide. Make it harder for the SUV guys, anyway.

Kit got to his vehicle first, tugging open the passenger door.

He was still frantic for a better plan. *Lord, how are we going to play this?*

She slid in and scooped up Tot from the floor. Before he could take aim, he was blinded by headlights.

A crackly voice rang out as someone exited the four-seater ATV. Cullen could barely make out a tall man and the outline of a shotgun aimed squarely at him.

"You just halt yourself right there, mister," the voice said.

Cullen blinked in disbelief. "Archie? Is that you?"

"Who's that? Stay still and speak up."

"It's Cullen Landry, sir."

A stream of colorful language followed as the man trudged forward. Up close, Cullen saw the familiar straggly beard and battered hat.

Archie heaved out a breath and hugged Cullen in a spindly armed embrace. "No way did I figure on finding you here."

Cullen whacked him on the back. "You have no idea how happy I am to see you. What are you doing with a gun, sir?"

Archie was blind in one eye and had a cataract forming in the other. He wasn't supposed to be driving, let alone shooting. "Been looters around. Stealing everything they can get their hands on." Archie shoved back his hat with a thumb. "What in the ever-lovin' world are you doing here, Cullen? And after you beat *me* upside the head about evacuating. This is gonna be the best story I ever heard, somethin' tells me."

"Give it a minute, it's going to get better." Cullen's relief was heady as he returned to the truck. "It's okay," he said to Kit. "Archie's a friend."

Kit shot him a wary look but got out with Tot.

"This is Gunnery Sergeant Archibald Woodruff Esposito, retired," Cullen said. "Archie, this is Kit Garrido."

To her credit, Kit managed a polite smile as Archie stood military straight with only a slight stoop to his shoulders. "Hello, ma'am. Very pleased to meet you."

"And the baby's named Tot," Cullen added.

Archie's mouth dropped open as he took in the baby she held close. His startled gaze hopped back to Cullen. "Son," he said slowly. "Thought we knew each other fairly well. Never heard you talk of a family."

"Long story. No time to hash it out now. Short version is we got some unfriendlies after us. We need help."

"Unfriendlies?" Archie's grizzled brows shot up. "Looters?"

"Worse."

"What's worse than filthy looters?"

"Tell you on the way to your house, sir. We need to get the baby someplace warm."

Archie's expression turned mournful. "No can do, Cullen. My place is under twenty feet of rubble. Got out with only the proverbial clothes on my back before the cliff let loose. And don't you dare give me any flak because obviously you didn't clear out either."

Cullen bit back a howl of disappointment. "No flak from me, sir. Where are you sheltering then?" He prayed Archie wasn't going to say he'd been roughing it in a tent somewhere. He wouldn't put it past the former marine, who seemingly had no concept of the fact that he was eighty-plus years old. But if they didn't get a roof over their heads soon . . .

"I've been holing up in the library, of course," Archie said. "No one there. Just me and the books. That's where I saw your truck lights from the upper floor, and I drove out to take a look-see."

Not going to find the safety he'd hoped for at Archie's. His plan morphed to fit the new facts. Shelter. Number one priority. "All right. The library it is." Anywhere he could get Kit and the baby warmed up and fed, out of the acrid air. There would be some supplies in town they could scavenge, hopefully. "Library phone in service?"

"Landline worked last I tried."

Cullen felt a surge of elation. Archie was the only person on the planet who didn't own a cell phone, but with the old-fashioned connection they could contact the police, his brother, anyone. Finally, something was breaking their way.

Cullen holstered his handgun, grabbed their meager supplies, and urged Kit forward. He helped her and Tot into the back seat of the ATV, which he figured was the safest spot if they hit a tree or whatever.

"Archie is the Grandlake volunteer librarian and a stubborn one at that. He doesn't believe in evacuations, do you, sir?"

"This from the hypocrite that didn't take his own advice." Archie cheerfully craned his neck through the driver's side door to spy the baby in the back seat. "Going to be bumpy, ma'am, but I'll try to drive as safe as I can."

"Uh, how about I drive, sir?" Cullen announced. When Archie wound up to retort, Cullen pointed behind them. "You're lookout. If you see any signs of pursuit, holler. And you've got the shotgun. Better under these conditions than my handgun."

Reluctantly, Archie acquiesced. He grumbled, but due to Kit's presence he reined in his usual stream of profanity.

Cullen executed a careful turn and took the path where Archie pointed. It was rough, all right. Definitely only suited for an ATV, so their pursuers would have a difficult time following. "Can't believe the bridge is wiped out."

"Surprised me too, but Mount Ember doesn't have to answer to anybody, does she?" Archie said. "Could be an advantage, though, right? More problems for the unfriendlies. Are they locals? Do they know the terrain?"

"Uncertain, but my hunch is no." Cullen drove slowly through the swirling darkness. Yes, the destroyed bridge could be an advantage, until their pursuers found a workaround. Or Evel did.

He felt Archie's shotgun against his shin. He wasn't sure Archie had brought a lot of ammo with him when he went to the library. If not, they could retrieve some from the hardware store if they could get inside. Did that make him a looter too? No, a survivor and a protector. Plus, he'd leave money, whatever cash he had in his pockets along with his cell number.

A wash of loose dirt trickled down in front of the tires. If the volcano erupted, none of it was going to matter anyway.

Cullen tried to keep the ATV on the smoothest parts of the route as they crept their way to Grandlake. The painted welcome sign boasted a population of three hundred fifty, and it appeared three hundred forty-nine of them had the good sense to evacuate. Cullen had made regular trips to Grandlake, more an outpost than a hub, but the place was almost unrecognizable. Every pane of glass, sidewalk, and driveway was dulled by grime, like a scene from some apocalyptic horror movie.

Sturdy plywood covered the gas station windows. The coffee shop and minuscule post office stood solitary and empty. There were houses, small buildings, a few farms on big, wild plots adjacent to the town, but no doubt the residents had all been convinced to go. Eerie.

"Not a soul here 'cept me," Archie said, his voice hushed.

Cullen couldn't resist a tease. "That should tell you something about your life choices."

"Uh-huh. Says the guy racing around with a baby and a woman in a red zone." He sniffed in disgust. "There wasn't any place safer you could have taken them? One thing for a man to be stubborn, but when he has a family . . ."

In the rearview, he saw Kit start.

This was going to take some explaining. "Tell you later, sir."

"This I gotta hear." Archie's tone held a trickle of glee. The old man had always loved being privy to the drama of others. This story should serve up a double helping.

Cullen pulled the ATV to the side door of a two-story stucco building crammed between a shuttered tire store and a bait and tackle shop. A dirty sign in the window read "Grandlake Library and History Museum." It was a pretentious name for a dilapidated structure. Most residents knew that if you strolled into the room designated for the museum, volunteer librarian Archie wasn't going to let you out until he was satisfied you'd seen every rusted tractor part, crinkled black-and-white photo, handmade fishing lure, and faded newspaper in the museum's crowded glass cases. Cullen had only made that mistake once, though Archie tried to suck him in whenever he spotted him in town.

The skin on the back of Cullen's neck prickled as they waited for Archie to unlock the door. The sense of urgency rose with every passing second. Cullen had to bend to avoid braining himself as they entered, and he threw the bolt once they were inside.

"No electricity, but we got the lanterns. There's a small generator, which I haven't fired up yet. Saving it." Archie looked at Kit and the baby. "But now seems like the proper time."

A generator was more than he could have hoped for. He couldn't stifle his grin.

Archie handed Cullen a lantern, which he activated, then he bustled outside, and in few moments the generator purred to life. Cullen flicked on the heater and one small lamp and pulled down all the blinds. Kit did not need his urging to scoot close to the heat register with Tot.

Cullen moved a chair from behind the checkout desk and plopped it practically on top of the metal grate in the floor. "Here. You two warm up. I'll get hot water soon as I can and fix Tot a bottle."

She sank down with a sigh, flanked by floor-to-ceiling shelves of children's books.

Archie returned with a cardboard box full of clothes and set it down next to Kit. "Library lost and found," he crowed. "You wouldn't believe what people leave behind. Once I found a set of dentures and a six-pack of raisins in the same day."

"Oh, thank you," Kit said with fervor as she handed Cullen the baby and took the box.

Cullen offloaded Tot in the arms of a startled Archie, but the old man pulled the tiny girl close and immediately started to talk to her.

"A seasoned grandpa," Cullen said to Kit. "He's got seven."

"And number eight coming in the spring. We almost got ourselves a baseball team." Archie smiled at Tot. "This one's a pretty pumpkin. Not bad for your first effort." He winked at Cullen.

Cullen's cheeks burned. "Oh, she's not mine."

He raised a grizzled eyebrow. "Ah. Well then." He turned to Kit. "You get the full credit in the looks department."

"She's not mine either."

Cullen chuckled at Archie's gaping astonishment.

"We'll explain the whole thing, sir, but Tot needs a dry diaper something fierce." He fished one from the duffel. "Would you care to do the honors while I fix her bottle? You said you've got a microwave in the break room, and Tot hasn't had a warm bottle since I don't know when."

That seemed to snap the trance. Archie spread the towel Cullen handed him on a table and laid the baby gently on her back. "No proper bottles, you poor lamby pie? We'll get you fixed up with that warm milk. Don't you worry your angel head about it. Grandpa Archie's got it handled."

"Too bad people don't lose their shoes and socks at the library, but I found a flannel shirt I can wear." Kit tossed a man's barn jacket to Cullen. "This one will almost fit you. Better than my raincoat anyway."

He chuckled and stepped into a minuscule break room where Archie had told him about a microwave and sink. Perfect, since he could keep an eye on them all while he shook up the formula.

While Archie crooned to the baby and undid the snaps on her outfit, he jerked his chin at Kit. "There's an employee bathroom right behind the checkout desk if you need it, miss."

"Please, call me Kit."

"Only if you'll call me Archie."

Kit smiled. "Archie it is. I found some clothes that will work for me, but the only baby-sized thing is a sunhat and a toddler-sized snow jacket."

"I have an idea about that, Kit," Archie said. "And you need some shoring up too. We can't have you trekking around in bare feet."

While the bottle warmed, Cullen prowled the cupboards but couldn't find anything big enough for Kit to put her feet into for a warm water soak. His level of respect for her continued to rise. Their escape had been surreal. Barefoot and without a proper jacket, she'd somehow kept Tot from injury. He recalled that he'd actually dropped the baby off his roof into her arms. Cold sweat pricked his forehead. Thanks be to God that Kit had risen to the occasion. Point of fact, she'd been an absolute dynamo since he'd found her in her wrecked rig. He'd met a lot of strong women in his day, starting from his mother and extending to a long line of exceptional cops, but Kit topped the list.

Into the last clean bottle went one of the two remaining packets of formula. He found a clean mug, warmed the water, and shook up the milk.

Warmth. Food. That handled, he'd beeline for the phone.

Kit emerged from the bathroom, clutching the flannel shirt around herself. "Thanks for changing her, Mr. Esposito."

"You will call me Archie, young lady. No arguments."

With a smile, she reached for the bottle Cullen brought, but Archie took it first.

"Now, let an old soldier handle the grub. I'm a pro. You drink some water, and if you're hungry, there's cookies I keep stashed in the break room and a half bag of corn chips."

"Food of champions," Cullen said with a laugh.

"Beggars and choosers." Archie settled Tot on his lap and watched in delight as she clamped onto the nipple. "Look at that. Eating like a professional. Never seen anyone with such a healthy appetite. Phone's behind the desk."

Cullen practically sprinted to the ancient rotary device. It took him a second to remember how to work one, but he kept his back to Archie to conceal his hesitation. When he untangled his brain, he dialed the emergency number. A busy signal. He disconnected and tried again. Same result. Not surprising.

Kit drew close, handing him a cookie on a piece of paper towel. She had another for herself.

"Thanks." He was pleased for some reason that she'd thought of him. "Emergency line's overwhelmed. I'm going to try my brother." He dialed. "Ringing."

Her eyes lit up, a hue somewhere between black coffee and the coat of the most beautiful quarter horse he'd been privileged to own. His stomach was doing flips as the phone rang once, twice. Before it got to three, his brother answered. Blood surging, Cullen gripped the phone. "Gideon . . ."

"If it isn't my baby brother. Where are you?"

"Grandlake, ten miles from my cabin."

"Why?" His brother's tone sounded lazy, soft, but Cullen wasn't fooled at the unspoken *Why are you there? Why didn't you evacuate like any sensible person would have?* The edge was there under the velvet.

"In a minute. In case we lose connection, I need to tell you some things right away."

Gideon was quiet as he relayed the information about

the crash and their pursuers. "Kit Garrido is here with me and the baby. We nicknamed her Tot."

"Identity of the dirt bike guy?" Gideon asked.

Cullen fished around in his back pocket and examined the driver's license he'd seized. "Name's Kyle Wallace, out of Los Angeles. I like Evel better."

"What?" Gideon said.

"Never mind. We don't know what any of the men want with Tot's mom."

Kit's eyes flew wide. "Wait a minute."

"Hold on, Gideon," Cullen said.

She pulled the paper from her pocket. "I found this when you took the license."

Archie listened in as he read to his brother from the paper.

"Gideon, it's a copy of an article ripped from a newspaper, the *Washington Trib*, dated June 7, five years ago. No more text except for a caption. 'Annette Bowman was . . .' and the rest is torn off. Woman looks young in the photo, maybe late teens."

The static on the line made him work harder to hear. A series of rattling thunks indicated the wind-driven debris was striking the upstairs windows. "Gideon, the mountain's about to blow."

"I'm aware."

Cullen could hear the tapping of keys. "There's an evacuation area twenty miles south of you," Gideon said. "National Guard has a command post there, and a helicopter. Can you make it?"

Twenty miles? "Not with a baby and the roads wrecked."

Kit was still staring at the clipping of Annette on the desk. Cullen realized it had been a few seconds and his brother hadn't replied. "Gideon?" He held the receiver, gut clenching. "Can you hear me?" He tried again and once more until he gently placed the receiver back in the cradle. "We lost the landline."

Kit stared at him, and he knew she was wondering the same thing he was. How were they going to get to an evacuation zone twenty miles away? He tried to plaster a hopeful expression across his features.

"On the positive side, someone in the outside world's got the dirt," Archie said.

"Yes," Kit echoed. "Your brother will send help, right?"

"Yes, he will." *But will it be in time?*

Archie put Tot to his shoulder and patted her back. His troubled gaze indicated he wasn't optimistic either. Tot fussed for a few minutes while he and Kit ate their cookies and drank a bottle of water each. He would have liked a second one, but he didn't know how Archie was fixed for supplies, and they'd need plenty of water to prepare Tot's bottles until . . .

Until what? What exactly was the endgame now? With extreme effort, they could possibly cover the twenty miles in the ATV, but with the landscape buckling around them? Men in active pursuit? And a baby to protect?

Kit wandered back to the heat register and pressed her toes to it, still obviously cold. It was almost 2:00 a.m. and she was clearly exhausted, but sleep would have to take a back seat to warmth. They'd be here through the night at least; might as well secure some creature comforts while they worked on the next phase of action.

"You mentioned a supply plan, sir?"

Archie nodded. "The convenience store across the street.

Leonard and Mary run it, and they gave me a tongue lashing for not evacuating, but they said to help myself to whatever before the volcano blew me up." He jiggled Tot, who was fighting sleep and sucking at the same time. "Appears to me that since this baby doesn't belong to you, it's likely you're not traveling with a full complement of gear."

"That's an affirmative." He hesitated. "I can explain . . ."

"Later. Leonard and Mary's store's got a baby section." Archie eyed Kit's battered feet. "Some boots too, for the weekend warriors who don't arrive in this area properly supplied. How about we go take ourselves a lookie-loo?"

"Is it okay to go out there again?" Kit's gaze flicked to the lowered blinds.

"They can't have gotten here so quick, if at all," Cullen said. "But the ground's a mess. Want to stay put and I'll be your personal shopper?"

She shook her head. "We should stick together."

He wasn't sure if that was the wisest plan, but considering the woman had almost been murdered several times since the previous afternoon, he wasn't going to quibble.

Archie pointed to Kit. "Meantime there's a box of Band-Aids and a first aid kit under the checkout desk. Don't want that cut on your foot getting infected, huh?"

Cullen felt bad that he hadn't noticed the scrape.

Kit obeyed orders and fetched the supplies, then sat on the floor and folded her legs in a way he could never even come close to. She disinfected and applied a bandage. Those little toes, so small. He'd been told his toes looked more orangutan than human. She caught him staring, and he hastily glanced away. *Admiring toes right now, Cullen? What is wrong with you?*

95

"All right. We can do a supply run, but Tot needs to finish her bottle first." Cullen was surprised when Archie handed over the baby.

"While she's topping off her tank, I got me an idea. Be right back." Archie hustled into a back room, and Cullen heard the hum of machinery.

"What's he doing?" Kit whispered.

"Dunno, but Archie's a wily one." He urged Tot to drain the formula, her luminous eyes fixed on his face under heavy lids.

The wee fingers reached up for his chin, and he lowered his head to accommodate. The tender touch tore open the wound as he remembered what he'd had and how much he'd lost. Daniela's infant daughter was gone from his life, just like her mother was, and he missed that tiny tot more than he'd ever thought possible.

Your own fault. He felt Kit looking at him as she re-packed the first aid supplies, so he got up under the pretense of burping the baby.

Just rock the baby. Stay in the now, not the what-used-to-be.

"Oh yeah," he heard Archie crow. With Tot asleep on his shoulder, Cullen found the dusty work area where Archie sat on an overturned crate in front of an archaic-looking machine.

"What is that thing?"

"That, you uneducated rube, is a microfiche reader, which was the bee's knees in research tools before the invention of the internet. These microphotographs contain entire issues of newspapers." He smirked. "Newspapers are periodicals containing current events and—"

96

"I know what a newspaper is, thanks. Tell me what the 'oh yeah' was for."

"Because it so happens that we have two decades of the *Washington Trib* on microfiche, and this old dinosaur found the article from which your picture of Annette was torn." He poked a thumb into his chest.

Cullen gaped. "You're joking."

"Nope. I figured it was worth looking. Pulled up all the June issues for the last ten years. Got a match on the second one. Easy as pie." Archie grinned. "'Cuz the only thing better than a marine is a librarian marine."

"You're right about that."

He grinned. "Take a look here."

Cullen peered over his shoulder at the grainy paper shown on the dim screen.

Archie held up the ripped article Kit had gotten from Kyle's wallet for comparison. "That there's the very same article as the piece the motorcycle guy was carrying. See? Photo matches perfectly and the caption."

Stunned, Cullen scanned the tiny words in the first paragraph, wishing he had his reading glasses, a fact he wouldn't disclose under pain of death and dismemberment. He looked for the zoom option, but as he bent, Tot complained. Archie took her while he moved in closer.

He read until he got the gist. His stomach dropped to his shoes.

Archie's grave expression told him he'd read it too.

Kit appeared in the doorway. "What did you find out?"

He exchanged a look with Archie.

What was the best way to tell her that the trouble was even worse than they thought?

◼ SEVEN ◼

KIT PRESSED IN NEXT TO HIM and started to scan the article.

"Read it aloud, would you?" Cullen eased back. "Too crowded if we're all trying to see the screen."

Uh-huh. Likely he was struggling to see the print and didn't want to underscore it by enlarging it any more, but she wouldn't bother teasing him about that now. Instead, she made the image bigger, sat on the crate and read, picking out the important facts and making note of them in her mind.

Seventeen-year-old Annette Bowman had run away from her single mother's Washington home after a dispute five years prior. She'd hopped a bus and headed for Seattle, and her mother never saw her again except in a photo she'd found of her daughter on . . .

Kit went cold.

. . . an online escort service, which had since gone out of business. It was tied to a person by the name of Nico Phillips, who had been questioned by the police and released. A photo of the man was included, dark hair, handsome features, easygoing smile.

She could hardly get out the words as she continued reading. "'Police believe Annette Bowman may be the victim of sex trafficking.'"

Kit sat back, trying to assimilate the information. Annette had to be Tot's mother. Didn't seem likely she'd risk her life for anyone other than her own child. Had she been coerced into the sex trafficking business by Nico Phillips? At the tender age of *seventeen*?

The cookie she'd eaten turned into a chunk of lead in her stomach. She closed her eyes, trying to remember the woman, Annette, and what she'd asked of Kit, what Kit had agreed to. A ride out of town? She got one fleeting memory of desperate blue eyes framed by blond hair, the shade too brassy to be natural, pushed back by dark sunglasses atop her head. Annette?

"She could have been trying to escape this Nico guy." Kit hadn't realized she'd spoken aloud.

Cullen laid a palm on her shoulder. "You still don't remember?"

Kit shook her head miserably. "An impression is all. I have this sense of a young blond woman, really panicked, waving at me." The urgency billowed in her gut. The photo in the article was taken five years prior, so Annette was now twenty-two. Kit, at twenty-two, had been desperately trying to ignore the failings of her husband and dealing with an unexpected pregnancy she hadn't realized she wanted until that had failed too. It had taken her years to claw her way to a standing position again. There'd been a litany of loans, hungry nights, and weeks of barely making rent before she finally had to grovel and ask for help from her mother.

She knew what it felt like to be lost, scared, and alone.

With a baby to protect, all those terrors would be amplified.

"So Annette ran away from home and got mixed up with this Nico guy. It's possible he's the one who's after her." Cullen stood behind her, his reflection somber in the blurry screen. "That'd be my guess. Let's say you stopped and picked her and Tot up before whoever is after her shot at your rig because they knew she'd hitched a ride from you." He stared at the photo of Nico. "Might be him. I didn't see him well enough to make an ID when he ambushed us on the road. Dirt biker Kyle might be working for a competitor. Or he's a friend of Annette's? A sympathetic john she got in touch with who was helping her escape?" He paused. "The father of her baby even?"

Friend or enemy? No way to tell.

Kit stopped herself from chewing on her thumbnail. They looked at the screen again, at the photo of the smiling young Annette taken during her high school years, before her innocence was stripped away. Her lips were curved into a half smile, cheeks full and dimpled. Kit's reflection and Cullen's were superimposed on the monitor, as if they were all part of a bizarre family photo with the smiling girl . . . a girl who'd grown into a woman in spite of dire circumstances. Annette could have been forced into the servitude of this vile man, but she'd perhaps gotten something to use as leverage against him.

"Still, it's pretty extreme for this guy Nico to follow her into this mess. Travel into an area with a volcano ready to explode? He'd take his chances with all that just to get her back? Or the ten thousand dollars?"

When Cullen didn't answer, she spun on the box to face him. "You were a cop. You know this stuff. Tell me what you think."

He shook his head. "Hard to say."

She felt a flash of anger, frustration, fear. "What's your theory then?"

Cullen's brow was furrowed with concern or exhaustion. "She could have something damaging, or thinks she does, but with guys like that . . ." He blew out a breath. "They see their women as property, not people, and he wants his property back. To set an example for the others, maybe."

Disgust made her dizzy. She recoiled, and he grabbed her hand. She saw compassion in his smoky irises.

"I'm telling you how human traffickers think, Kit. You asked, and I'm telling you. I've seen women and girls locked in overheated trucks, dying at the hands of people like him. I . . ." He broke off, swallowing, his grip on her hand intensifying, and she realized he was fighting off a dark memory.

He squeezed her fingers, and she squeezed back. For a moment, they clung to each other, connected by a shared horror. *His property.* Her gaze drifted to Tot in Archie's arms. Was the baby Nico's property too? Or biologically his? Father or not, did he believe he owned the child? That he could treat her like a piece of luggage to handle the way he saw fit? Was he actually the one involved in the whole situation? The dizziness continued, and she closed her eyes, held on to Cullen, and breathed slowly until it passed.

When she opened her eyes again, Cullen appeared controlled, sympathetic, and she considered how long she'd been holding on to him. She let go.

"We should get those supplies," Archie said quietly. "Figure out a plan. Rest tonight. Too dangerous to do diddly in the dark."

Numbly, she followed him to the front. Archie swaddled the sleeping baby in the toddler-sized parka she'd taken from the lost and found box. While it was too enormous to work for Tot's clothing, it was a decent makeshift sleeping bag. Tot didn't stir, only the fuzzy crown of her head visible after Archie's careful tucking.

Kit's heart thunked with the fear that Tot's mom had been abducted by a horrible man. If Kit had only been more aware, spotted the person who'd shot up her rig, maybe Annette and Tot would have been able to escape. She dismissed the guilt. *You're a truck driver, not a secret agent.* And likely she'd been fully focused on volcanic hazards. Had Annette even told her the truth in the first place? Or had she concocted a story to convince Kit to give her a ride? She'd obviously said something compelling to induce Kit to leave her planned route. It was all one maddening blur. She felt Cullen watching her again.

She curled her toes, still cold in the borrowed socks, trying to force more circulation. "I'll carry her, Archie."

"Nah. Grandpa Archie's on deck. You've earned a rest."

In spite of her turmoil, Kit arched an amused brow at Cullen as they followed Archie out. Cullen leaned close to whisper in her ear. "Hard to believe his marine buddies called him Bone Buster. That's not precisely the term, but there are some things a man shouldn't say in front of a woman."

She smiled, the tickle of his stubble against her ear making her nerves buzz. "Archie's a natural. Much better than me."

"Hey, back at my place you managed to catch Tot like a pop fly to center field."

Her eyes rounded in remembered panic and she slugged him in the shoulder. "Don't ever, ever do that again, by the way."

He laughed and held the door for her. "I'll try to steer clear of any more baby tossing."

Archie was already halfway across the street. "Get the lead out, you two. Baby Tot needs to get tucked in for the night. Been hauled around enough for one day, I should say."

Cullen took in the muddy mess on the street and Kit's unshod feet. "Hop on," he said, crouching. "I'll piggyback you."

Piggyback me? "I . . . uh . . ." She scanned in search of some other alternative. She didn't want to be that close to Cullen or anyone else. Her toes ached though, and rocks and debris would surely shred her already tender soles. There was no way to know how much longer they'd need to hole up until help arrived, and ruining her feet wasn't going to make things easier. Practicality won over pride. *Deep breath. Let the nice farsighted rancher carry you across the street, Kit.* "I guess that would work."

He balanced carefully, and she climbed onto his back.

For a man his size with a full-grown human clinging like a limpet, he moved easily, and she tried not to pay attention to the way her arms fit around his wide shoulders. He was so . . . solid, in a moment when everything was shifting and sliding and changing. It had been a very long time since she'd felt like there was any dependable man in her life. She resisted the urge to lay her cheek against him.

The sheer incredulousness of the situation almost made her laugh aloud. The previous morning she'd likely set off thinking she was going to drive straight out of the danger zone, collect a fat paycheck, and head someplace warm with sunshine and trees. A run-down secondhand bookshop and a decent sushi restaurant to while away the hours would be a bonus. Now she was piggybacking across the street to scrounge vital supplies from a boarded-up store at the suggestion of a crotchety marine librarian who was crooning to Tot as if he were a combination of Frank Sinatra and Mary Poppins. There was no stranger scenario than that. And Cullen seemed to have some rosy notions that God was going to deliver them from it all. Leaving room for the "what if," as he called it.

Her father had said many a time, *"There's your plan, and God's plan, and yours doesn't count."* The stab of sadness made her curl tighter around Cullen, and she found her cheek coming to rest on the crown of his head. Not because she liked him but because they'd become unwilling partners in the whole elaborate disaster unfolding around them. Dad would no doubt have said God planned for the odd pairing, but she wasn't accustomed to leaving things to God.

Yeah, well, how are you doing planning out your own life at the moment? The memory of her crumpled truck brought a lump to her throat as they clomped around a fallen log occupying the middle of the street. She'd temporarily forgotten how abruptly things could be stripped away. She lifted her shoulders and held her face to the cold sky.

"Move it, Cullen," Archie called. "If that hillside goes, we'll be safer inside than out."

"Yes, sir." Cullen picked up his pace, causing her to tighten her hold.

She darted a look at the barely visible landscape at the end of the street. The trailer she called home was in a quiet suburb fifty miles away from this town. She'd never been to Grandlake, but she could see the appeal. It was nestled in a valley with picturesque views of the foothills trickling down from Mount Ember. They were more like mountains than hills, and if the volcano belched loose another mass, gravity would speed it right down in one lethal flow.

Cullen coughed. "How about a little looser?"

She forced her arms to slacken around his neck. "Sorry."

He made good progress, and Kit was already squirming off his back before he could lower her properly.

"Thanks for the lift."

"Anytime, Kit Garrido."

Her name sounded significant on his lips. She wondered what he really thought of her, the woman he'd met under such bizarre circumstances. He'd said he admired her courage, but there was a difference in her mind between courage and desperate self-preservation. What other choice was there besides fighting to survive? That didn't require bravery, just a deep-seated instinct.

Archie handed the key to Cullen, who unlocked the heavy wooden door. The interior was cold and dark, but they'd brought flashlights. The simple mom-and-pop shop was a combination grocery and convenience store, complete with an old-fashioned cash register with actual keys. A candy bowl on the counter offered wrapped green-and-white mints. Her flashlight beam revealed aisles crammed with everything from canned goods to basic first aid to clothing and books.

Cullen picked up the clunky rotary phone at the check-out.

"Nothing," he said in disgust. "Worth a try, though."

Archie jutted his chin. "First stop, shoe department." He plodded down the second darkened aisle, which Kit and Cullen illuminated with their flashlights.

Kit sighed. "When I was a kid, I dreamed about being locked in a shopping mall overnight and being able to pick out whatever I wanted. This is as close to that dream as I've ever gotten."

Cullen smiled. "Me too. Read this book once about two kids who hole up in a museum."

Kit straightened. "Really? I know that one."

"A gem," Archie called over his shoulder. "*From the Mixed-Up Files of Mrs. Basil E. Frankweiler*. Grandkid-dos loved it."

"That's the one." Cullen glanced at Kit. "You read it?"

"Many times." Thrilling, for some reason, that these two men she now depended on for survival had read the same childhood favorite.

Cullen sighed. "When we get out of here, I'm finding myself a copy of that book."

"Me too."

"Might as well see the positive side of the adventure." Archie clomped to the shelves filled with winter boots and a collection of socks.

Cullen snagged a wooly striped pair and tossed them
to her. She could hardly stop from caressing them. Warm,
dry socks. She would never again take them for granted.
After she reached safety, she intended to buy up the first
few packages she came across and donate them to the
nearest homeless outreach.

He chuckled as he took in her expression. "I've got a
new appreciation for socks now too."

But how would she pay? She'd crammed her wallet in
the duffel, but she didn't carry much cash.

"I got it," Cullen said quietly, as if he'd read her mind.
"Don't worry about the money."

Impossible. There was never an occasion in which she
did not worry about money. Her thoughts jumbled up. "I
have a debit card, but only a little cash. I could—"

"I said I got it, Kit." He looked squarely at her, his
intense gaze glittering in the flashlight glow. "Pick what
you need." It was a command more than a suggestion,
and she didn't like it.

"I'll reimburse you for everything if . . ." She exhaled.
"When we get out of this."

"Not necessary."

Her chin went up. It was very necessary. "I'm paying
you back, Cullen."

He started to argue, then shrugged. "All right. When
we blow this popsicle stand at some point, we'll settle up.
Right now, we get on with it. Deal?"

She nodded, dropping to the floor to pull on the socks
before she scanned the shelves for boots. Most were far
too big, but there was one pair that would work with
the thick socks. She laced them up before they moved to

a small area of clothing. The footwear felt clunky and stiff, her numbness making her gait clumsy, but the bliss of having something between her feet and the floor was indescribable.

A sweatshirt, extra socks, jeans, and jacket later and she was set. She declined another hat. "I've got mine." She fingered the worn brown cap.

"We could get rained on. 'Chill the head, close to dead' was Gideon's favorite saying on our wilderness hikes. He loves nothing better than trekking to nowhere with only a small pack and his confidence. I learned early on when Gid said 'We'll only go ten miles' it was going to be closer to twenty. He's a SERE instructor for the Air Force now."

Gideon obviously shared the Landry confidence. She acquiesced when he added a chunky black ski cap to her pile. Wouldn't hurt to have a spare, and she was too tired to argue. Arms full, she waited for Cullen to make his choices.

He acquired a few pairs of dry socks and a heavier jacket, hat, and pants.

"Grub next," Archie said. "Only got a loaf of bread and peanut butter at the library besides the cookies and chips. Best take some food while we decide on moves."

The edible offerings were mostly of the snack variety. They collected cheese crackers, packets of nuts, and as many water bottles as they could carry. She could not resist acquiring some sugary treats while Cullen snagged chips.

"Because who doesn't need some crunchy, salty cheesiness when you're outrunning a volcano?" he quipped, waving a bag of Doritos at her.

"What about Tot?" Archie said. "Gotta get some munchies for her."

Kit was startled. "Like, actual food?"

Cullen groaned. "Oh yeah. I forgot about that." He explained, "She's about nine months or so, to my mind. She'll be eating some solid foods, more than likely. There was a baggie of some cereal stuff in her duffel."

Archie nodded sagely. "Yeah. I think I saw a glimmer of teeth when she was hollering, a nice neat pair coming in on the bottom."

Teeth. The baby had teeth. What else did this kid need that she was unaware of? Prickles of panic ribboned up her spine. What if they didn't provide it? Bad enough the baby was at risk due to their situation, but what if Tot was harmed out of pure ignorance? Smothered by her blankets? Given an improperly sterilized bottle? Dehydrated or vitamin deprived?

Calm down. Cullen knew about babies, even if she didn't. The pink book cover flashed in her memory. *Your Baby, Month by Month.* She'd never gotten past chapter 3 when the fetus was still plumping and doubling like rising dough, now the length of a peapod, now the heft of a small lemon.

Her ears replayed the soft whoosh and rhythm she'd heard at the doctor's office, a tiny heartbeat.

Two hearts beating in one person. Breathtaking and terrifying.

Until there was only one again, the other just an echo of memory.

"You okay?"

Cullen was looking at her over the top of his pile. She jerked, stuffing away the dark thoughts. "Yes. Tot needs solid food along with her milk. I get it."

"These were the exact ticket for my grands when they were getting teeth," Archie said, taking a mini box of Rice Krispies from the shelf and shaking it. "Easy to eat, and the dog cleaned up all the bits that didn't find their target."

Kit took the cereal.

Archie sailed on. "Next stop, the baby aisle. Think they got more infant foods there."

In a daze, she followed Cullen and Archie around an endcap filled with Sterno, camp stoves, and emergency lanterns, tidily displayed. She admired the shop owners' sense of order. Not the slightest sign that they'd hastily evacuated.

Cullen selected several items from the shelf. "We'll get a variety of foods," Archie was saying. "'Cuz we don't know what Tot prefers since we just met her and all."

It was comical to hear the men compare the formula labels and discuss the merits of sweet potato versus butternut squash.

"She's not gonna like spinach," Archie said. "No human likes spinach."

Cullen eyed the little jar and its green contents. "Worked for Popeye."

"He was a swabbie, not a marine." Archie's insult dripped with good-natured distaste.

Cullen put the spinach back. "How about peas instead?"

"Yes, peas will do. Oh, and here's Cheerio-type things. We gotta have that. You pour a handful of those out, and it teaches her how to grab stuff and feed herself if the Rice Krispies things are too small," Archie insisted. While they debated with all the seriousness of a United Nations inquiry, Kit edged past them a few paces and gathered warm outfits that appeared to be Tot's size, socks, blankets, a jacket, a cap knitted to resemble a strawberry, and several packs of diapers.

Archie looked up from perusing a shelf. "Okay, so we got bottles and plenty of formula and food. Some clothes and a supply of diapers. She use a binky?"

Kit frowned. "A what?"

"A pacifier," Cullen translated.

"Oh." Did Tot use one? She hadn't seen any in the duffel bag, but there might have been one buried in her car seat when they'd snatched her and run.

"One way to find out." Cullen ripped open a packaged pacifier and offered it to Tot, who'd begun to fuss. She gulped it like a baby bird after a worm. All three of them watched Tot suck contentedly.

"Guess that answers the binky question," Cullen said. "Look at her go on that thing."

Kit rolled her eyes at Cullen. "You mean we didn't have to listen to her wailing for hours after you dropped her off the roof?"

"What?" Archie's eyes went as round as Oreos. "Dropped her where?"

"Uh, that sounded worse than it actually was," Cullen said.

"No, it didn't." Kit enjoyed Cullen's discomfiture.

"Never mind," Archie said stiffly. "I don't wanna know." He gathered Tot closer, mumbling something under his breath. Their last acquisition was two sleeping bags for Cullen and Kit.

"We got enough for now," Archie said. "Can always come back if things remain stable."

Stable. The word jarred. Did that mean if the volcano didn't go ballistic or the men didn't show up to kill them?

On the reverse trip, she returned under her own steam to the library, lugging a bag of items that Cullen had meticulously listed on the whiteboard behind the counter along with his name and cell number. He'd laid down the cash he had and inked the remaining amount in the form of an IOU. The mom and pop would be astonished to know they'd supplied three grownups and a baby when they came back . . . if there was anything left to return to.

Her cheeks went stiff in the frigid wind. The temperature was dropping steadily. Grateful her feet were protected, she hustled inside. As the door closed behind her, she thought of Annette. Was she alive? Out there somewhere in the elements? Had she been caught? By Nico? And if he was after Annette, why was he also terrorizing them? Did the person after them think they'd recovered her after she bolted and were helping her flee with his money?

A darker thought slithered through her brain. Maybe he'd already killed her and was coming for his other property. The cash and . . .

Tot.

An iron band formed in her chest as she watched Archie unwrap the sleeping Tot and gently transfer her into the warmer pajamas they'd picked out, yellow with rubber duckies that reminded Kit of Cullen stuffed into her raincoat. The cloth legs were too long, Tot's toes not quite reaching the ends. The baby winced, squinching up her mouth as if she would cry out, but she didn't.

You're no one's property, Tot.

And she realized in that moment that she'd fight any man to her last breath if he tried to take the child. It would be the hill she'd die on. Her truck and this baby, those were the two things that mattered, and one was out of her control . . . but not Tot. It felt strange to have a stranger's baby suddenly rearrange everything, but Nico had done the same when he snatched Annette away from all of her girlish plans and aspirations. What had it felt like to Annette's mother to worry and grieve every single day of her life for her missing daughter? She thought of her own mother, a woman she'd come to realize was not a perfect, larger-than-life figure but a fragile human with weaknesses and flaws of her own. The hurt of what she'd done to Kit's father still throbbed, but maybe a bit less painfully. They still had time to work through what had happened. Didn't they?

Cullen was fiddling with an ancient-looking transistor radio he'd found, trying to get a news station for an update on the volcano. He twisted the metal antenna to the right and then the left before he sat back with a frustrated sigh, glancing at her.

He frowned. "We forget something at the store? I can go back."

"No." She busied herself unbagging the groceries. "Mind wandered is all."

Archie laid the sleeping Tot on a mat in a section of floor in the children's library that was padded with foam tiles. Kit wanted to cover her with blankets, but that urge had to be resisted. Hopefully Archie's generator would keep the heat at a reasonable comfort level.

She organized the foodstuffs on the counter in the break

room, baby foods, baby supplies, adult snacks, water bottles neatly lined up. When she'd finished, the radio crackled, and Cullen gave himself a silent fist in the air as he adjusted the volume.

The broadcaster's voice was tinny and distant. "As Mount Ember steams under her snowy blanket, scientists sent up choppers again this morning to get new aerial photography of the summit. Most ominous of the findings was that the bulge on the east side of the mountain continues to grow. This bulge has already moved some three hundred feet up and out from where it was at this date last year. Couple that with swarms of earthquakes numbering into the thousands, and the alarm levels are increasing. Local county sheriffs have enacted blockades on the two major roads leading to the mountain, and the FAA has extended their no-fly zone from five miles to ten. All residents are urged to evacuate immediately due to . . ."

The radio dissolved into static. Cullen grumbled under his breath. No amount of fiddling with the dials brought it back. He stared at the device, fists on hips.

Archie slurped from a cup of instant coffee he'd prepared. "Much as I am loathe to admit it, seems you were right, Cullen. Ember's gonna burst. I should have departed last week."

"You and me both."

"Make that three of us," Kit said. "But if we hadn't stayed . . ." Her gaze went to the sleeping baby.

"The Lord knows what he's about, that's sure," Archie said quietly. "Planning time?"

"Planning time," Cullen confirmed.

Kit exhaled slowly as they gathered around the checkout desk. "Our best chance of survival is to make it to the evacuation zone?" It was more a statement than a question.

"Because we're on borrowed time here." Cullen sought her gaze.

She nodded. "Everything I've been reading predicts that when the bulge fails, it will unleash a massive mudflow that will inundate everything downslope, including this town."

"Now that's a downer of a forecast," Archie said.

"With the ATV we have a chance." Cullen arched a brow at Archie. "Fuel?"

"Twenty gallons at best."

"It'll do."

It would have to. Otherwise . . . what? They'd die miles away from the evac zone? Stranded in poisonous gas clouds? Crushed by falling trees? She glanced again at Tot, so small in her fuzzy pajamas.

"Guess I should come along," Archie said. "You all need a nanny, appears to me, or you might be dropping her from roofs again."

Cullen grinned. "Yes, sir. We surely do."

Archie went to a high, dusty shelf crammed with different-sized packets, selected one, and unfurled a brittle paper topographical map. Since they'd turned off most of the lanterns, Cullen held one out.

Archie slipped on a pair of thick glasses. "All subject to change thanks to Ember's shenanigans, but the fire trails are our best bet to clear out with the ATV. Evac zone is where now?"

"Gideon said south, twenty miles," Cullen said.

Archie pressed a calloused finger to the paper. "That'd

be here, Lodgepole Meadows. Three main routes to get there, 'cept one is already obliterated thanks to the earlier landslide." He snagged a pencil and followed each route with the tip. "Which way you think?"

Kit absorbed the tiny lines and squiggles. She prided herself on being able to read a map since GPS wasn't always 100 percent reliable. "This one looks fastest but closer to the fallout zone."

"Right. Flame Ridge is a straighter shot, but parts are already obliterated." Archie refocused on the second route. "Silver Canyon is our other option. Connects the town of Twinfork to the old lumber mill where Granddad used to work. I went with him a time or two. They built a tunnel from the town to the mill so the workers could have a shortcut underground. Used to pretend I was one of Snow White's dwarfs when I'd pop out from behind the waterwheel and scare the workers." He chuckled.

"Dad put the kibosh on that quick. Bad idea to be giving men a fright when they're working with saws. Anyway, they bored that tunnel because otherwise it'd be a steep journey, so that's what we're in for. Steep." He smoothed the map. "Key here indicates there's four thousand feet of elevation change, forested mostly in the beginning, and there's lava boulders."

"Sounds like a good time to me," Cullen said, rubbing at his elbow.

Archie peered at him over his glasses. "Does that sarcasm indicate you would like to disagree with Kit and myself?"

"No, sir. I'm not a hiker, and I've lived in these parts less than two years. If I'm gonna hare off into the mountains, it's gonna be on a horse on a clearly marked trail. If you two think Silver Canyon is the safest way to the evac zone, I defer to your expertise."

"All right, then. Silver Canyon or bust." Archie yawned and checked the aged wall clock. "Almost two thirty." He pointed to Kit. "You, lay yourself down in the break room and get a couple hours of shut-eye. I'll take the first watch until four. Real nice view of the foothills from upstairs, and I got a sweet telescope up there." He stopped suddenly, turning to her. "Blows my mind that I was watching out that window for looters and instead I found me a family of three."

"Oh . . ." she started. Not a family, not them. Just . . . united strangers.

"I know you aren't a blood family, but people can be put together in unexpected ways." Archie grinned. "Someday I'll tell you how I met my late wife. She married beneath her and that's certain. Cullen," he called quietly over his shoulder. "I'll wake you at four and you can take over watch. We can aim to leave at half past five."

Kit opened her mouth to offer to take part of the watch, but in truth, she was fighting to stay conscious. And a suspicion was dawning on her that Archie was relishing his part in the mission to save her and Tot.

"I'll get up around five and pack the supplies in the ATV," she insisted.

"No need, I can—" Archie started.

"Let her," Cullen said. "She's an unparalleled organizer."

She wasn't sure if he meant that completely as a compliment, but her senses were thrumming with fatigue. At that moment she would give anything to lie down.

Archie gestured her into the break room.

He showed her a curtain that could be slid over the threshold. "Not much, but some privacy anyway."

Privacy. The word thrilled through her. "But isn't this where you've been sleeping? I don't want to take your place."

"Don't give it a thought. Like I said, I got me a nest upstairs where my recon station is set up. Cullen can hunker in the checkout area in case Tot cries, and you'll be cozy as a bug in a rug in here, even if the couch is lumpier than last year's gravy." Chivalry. The oddest place to encounter it, in an old library, underneath an angry mountain. She could not remember when she'd felt quite so thankful for the kindness of strangers.

She spread out the sleeping bag on the dilapidated couch. "Thank you, Archie."

"You're welcome." He paused again. "You've done great taking all this on when you were just minding your own business, driving your truck. No marine could have done better. It'll all be behind you soon," he said quietly. "Good night."

When he was gone, she collapsed on the couch, his words ringing in her ears.

All behind you soon.

Everything.

Her stomach tensed. Then what would be ahead? What lay in the frightening future for Kit without her truck? Without her plans?

"Knock knock." A knuckle tapped on the wall.

She jerked as Cullen popped his head in.

"Before you settle in, I thought you might want your flashlight."

118

She took it.

He turned to go.

Her nerves burned with fiery panic. *All behind you.* "How far away is my truck from here?" she blurted. "I mean, in hours."

Cullen frowned. "Your rig? With the bridge out, likely a good six hours. Why do you ask?"

The wild plan unspooled along with the words.

"After you and Tot get to the evacuation zone, I want to go back to my rig, mark the exact location so I can get it towed out later in case the GPS tracker dies. Or . . . there are some emergency lanterns in the convenience store. I'll leave one, as a beacon. Then I can meet you at the evac zone." She was babbling. Her elaborate plan wasn't the least bit logical, but she couldn't stop.

His eyes were wide in disbelief. "That's a bad idea."

She narrowed her eyes at him. "I wasn't asking for your opinion, and I didn't say I expected you to come with me. As a matter of fact, I wouldn't want you to."

"You can't go back there." His anger made him grow even larger in the cramped space. "You won't survive."

Her tone was cold. "Like I said, this is about me. You don't have to like the plan because you're not a part of it."

"It isn't a plan, it's a death wish."

She glared. "Quiet. You'll wake Tot."

He paused, lowering his volume. "Listen to me, Kit. We're sitting on a mountain-sized bomb about to detonate. You know that. You've studied it. Our only choice is to pray we can make it to the helicopter and get out alive, you, me, Tot, and Archie. Your truck doesn't matter anymore."

Her chin went up, and she straightened on a flood of emotion. What did he know about her? About her rig? The way she'd lost everything, everyone? Any of it? "It matters," she hissed. Tears threatened, and she blinked furiously against them. She would not blubber, not with Cullen, this man foisted on her by circumstances she could not control. She folded her arms as if she could shield herself from the volcano, from him, from the truth that meant she'd be devastated. Again.

Unable to look at him, she stared at the "Libraries are good for circulation" magnet stuck crookedly on the door of the mini fridge. Jaw clenched, she willed him to leave.

Instead he sighed, stepped forward, and wrapped his arms around her.

She was so shocked she couldn't move.

It was both startling and comforting. All she could do was breathe, and tremble, and feel.

"I'm sorry for my tone," he said quietly into her ear. "What's going on here . . . it's beyond what anyone should have to absorb. Your truck means the world to you, I understand, but your life means more. Once we get out safely, I'll help in any way I can to make things right." To her amazement, he kissed her on the temple, then her forehead, his lips warm and soft against her skin. "Get some sleep. Archie and I can take care of Tot if she wakes. See you in a few hours."

He padded away, pulling the curtain across the break room area.

She stared, transfixed by the warmth of his embrace, the wake of his touch. Confusion sparked through her.

"I'll help in any way I can to make things right."

Why did his words make her want to cry?

It wasn't the tenderness, the earnestness. Perhaps the novelty of being cared for by a man? She hadn't dated since her marriage dissolved. More like exploded. Rusty social muscles. That was it. Or was she merely an overwrought woman in an impossible situation whose emotions were all over the board?

Get some sleep.

Those three words made the most sense in her depleted condition. She climbed into the sleeping bag, finding the most level spot on the misshapen sofa.

A rolled-up sweatshirt served as her pillow.

For the first time in a very long time, she laced her fingers together. "God . . . Annette and Tot . . . don't let them down." An awkward prayer, wasn't it? More of a demand? Completely lacking in whatever a proper prayer was supposed to have, probably. Another habit rusty from long disuse.

"They're nobody's property," she added.

Whatever else she'd intended to say to God vanished as the world faded around her.

◼ EIGHT ◼

CULLEN DREAMED HE HEARD someone talking to him. *Go away, whoever you are.*

When he was grabbed by the shirtfront and shaken, he swam into consciousness with an instinctive fist curled, ready to punch.

"Hit me, Cullen my boy, and I'll gut you like a pike," Archie whispered amiably. "Tot's changed and back to snoozing and it's your watch. Roll out, son." Before Cullen got his second eye open, Archie had departed to his sleeping bag.

Cullen groaned. The hard floor, which had been a source of agony throughout the night, was magnetically pulling him back, but he fought against the lethargy and hauled himself to his knees. Another ungainly maneuver rendered him upright, but his body didn't agree with the commands of his brain. Every inch of his miserable flesh, from his eyebrows to his heels, throbbed and ached and burned. He had to clamp his teeth together to keep from out and out lamenting. The downspout episode when he'd fallen like a sack of rocks had been more costly than he'd realized. "Lord God, gonna need help." He curled a palm around the edge of the checkout desk for leverage.

A fragrance caught his nose, offering a sliver of hope. Coffee.

He turned his head toward the smell of salvation. Where? How? He didn't care. The only thing that mattered was the quickest way to get some down his gullet. He staggered toward the scent, smashed his socked foot on the corner of the desk, and jackknifed forward, toppling a lantern with his elbow. It seemed to tumble in slow motion toward a clattering landing that would mean the end of baby Tot's peaceful slumber.

But the crash didn't come. Instead, a slender palm darted out and deftly caught the lantern, then set it safely back in place. Better yet, the other hand delivered a mug of steaming coffee to the same countertop. He blinked, but the beautiful sight did not vanish. Not a dream.

"I woke up, so I got started packing. I made coffee while I was at it," Kit whispered. "Want some?"

"You are now my new heir and executor. The brothers will be officially dropped from my will in favor of you," he said reverently.

Her laugh was barely audible. "Wonder what I'd get if I could make you a latte. I'm a very skilled barista. I have an espresso machine in my rig. Come on."

Toe throbbing, he hobbled after her, scooping up the coffee and lurching into the break room, where he tried not to collapse on the card chair like a demolished building.

She turned on a lantern. "Did you sleep?"

He held up a finger, drank, and exhaled. The hot liquid teased his senses back to life. He took a second, life-affirming gulp. "Okay. I will now be able to entertain questions. Barely. I must have managed to snooze for a while since Archie had to wake me by grabbing me around the neck. You?"

Shadows clung to her face and darkened her eyes to midnight. "A little. I was busy trying to work my way through all the 'what ifs,' as you'd say."

Was it his imagination or did she seem slightly less guarded with him? He was relieved his frustration and fear hadn't led him to explode at her the night before. Some intuition, some unaccustomed urge had made him drop his authoritative schtick and offer comfort. Weirdly he'd felt comforted too. Could be he'd learned a thing or two from his horses. The finest ones, the most majestic and proud, were the tenderest inside. They needed to be understood, rather than managed.

Sapphire popped into his head and heart simultaneously, the black bay with the white starburst who chewed the wooden door of her stall, upended any box or bag she encountered, and got between him and any of her sister mares if she didn't like what he was about. Sapphire was a hot mess.

And beautiful.

Ferocious.

Perfect, in her own way.

Would Kit approve of him comparing her to his finest horse? He had no clue.

I understand you better than you think, Kit Garrido.

The silence had lingered longer than it should so he drank more coffee and looked around at her neat bundles of materials. "Is that a camp stove?"

"Yes. Archie brought his equipment and some dehydrated pouches to add to the stores. I repacked Tot's duffel with the essentials on top so we don't have to hunt around for stuff."

He was sure she'd repacked her bear too.

The adult clothing was rolled into neat packages and tied with string. Food was arranged in a see-through plastic bag with smaller parcels tucked inside. Organized, like he'd said.

"Some nifty packing."

She shrugged, but he thought there was a smile there too.

"My dad could get an entire week's groceries stowed in a single shopping cart and roll it to the register. It was like some massive game of Tetris. The checker was always delighted."

"Your dad live close?" Not a safe question. He realized as soon as he'd said it and she pulled back in the chair, deeper into the shadows. *More coffee, Cullen. You need more coffee.*

"He died eight years ago. My mom lives in Washington, but we're . . . I don't see her often."

A world of understatement in her words. "I'm sorry for your loss." And for the estrangement with her mother. Too many families with missing pieces, holes, and fractures that let in the water.

His family on the other hand was about as close as any five people could stand to be without losing their minds. The Landrys consisted of two patient, easygoing parents who'd learned that worrying about their three rowdy boys was counterproductive, and the sons who had a quarterly conference call entitled "The State of the Parentals" to ensure their folks weren't in need of something they were failing to disclose. Maybe his family was idyllic, or it could be he simply preferred to think of them that way.

"What about yours?" she said.

"Mine? Oh. Typical farm stock." He told her about their property near his brother. "Took the horses there last week."

"Why didn't you stay?"

He paused midsip. Why hadn't he? "To be sure my friends all got out, like I said. Had to help move a buddy's sheep."

She cocked her head in that way that made him feel like she was looking underneath his skin into places he'd rather she wouldn't.

"The folks wanted me to bunk at their place as a matter of fact," he admitted. Came near to begging, where his mom was concerned, but staying for any length made him uneasy. His mother's constant smothering of the questions she desperately wanted to ask raked his nerves.

Why must you go on punishing yourself?

When will you restart your life, Cullen David?

He wasn't punishing and he had restarted. Built a cabin and joined a bowling team, for goodness' sake. Had his own ball and shoes and everything.

"You don't restart by turning away from everyone you knew before the accident." His mother always referred to it as "the accident," as if he'd rear-ended someone or slipped on the ice.

Guilt licked at his insides. Yeah, he'd quite literally put distance between himself and those he'd known before, including his parents. His brothers. There'd been excuses about not visiting, avoiding fishing trips, camping vacations, holidays.

It was easier to breathe around people who hadn't known him before.

Kit was still waiting for a response.

Tit for tat. She'd told him a truth about her father she hadn't planned on, and she had a right to expect some honest reciprocity.

"I've been sorting some things out, and I guess I found reasons not to make it home as often as I should." Lots of 'em. And excuses to cut phone calls short when the conversation shifted to tender topics.

A wistful smile filtered across her lips. "You'd like the trucking life, then."

"Would I?"

She nodded. "As much quiet as a person can stand to sort things out. Days and months and hundreds of miles of it, if you want."

Was that a thread of longing in that sentence? Loneliness, perhaps? "And you don't get tired of it? All that quiet?"

"No." A sliver of moonlight from under the shade brushed her face.

Convincing, almost. "Did all those miles help you? Sort your family things out?"

She cupped the mug between her palms as if it were a baby bird. The pause lingered for a moment too long. "I put things in order enough that I can keep moving."

An interesting answer. A fascinating lady.

She was picking up her mug to sip from it when the

floor shuddered, one quick jolt that sloshed liquid onto the table from both their cups. The window glass rattled and floorboards squeaked. In unison they rose and turned toward the room where the baby lay. As they reached the curtain, the movement stopped.

They froze, waiting. The fabric swished around them, until slowly, subtly, it went still.

"Small one." He didn't have to articulate the obvious questions. A precursor? The fuse burning down to Mount Ember's detonation? He realized he'd taken her arm, a subconscious reaction. He decided since she wasn't objecting, he'd maintain their connection as they waited. Was he steadying her? Or was it the reverse?

Seconds ticked by into thirty, then a full minute with no more movement.

He checked his watch. "Almost time to go. Maybe we'd better hustle things up a notch."

Archie clattered down the steps, breathing hard, carrying his boots.

"Earthquake," Cullen said stupidly as Kit renewed the space between them.

"Yeah, I got that." Archie held a wrapped bundle. "Reminded me of the earthquake kit we keep upstairs. Mostly old and degraded, but there's a couple of things included that might help. Kindling and a dozen waterproof matches. Couple of meals ready to eat that haven't expired, if your culinary tastes aren't too snooty."

"I'll add them to the supplies." Kit took the items, pulled on her boots, and walked out. She was tired, had to be, but steely with determination. He thought of her anguished expression the previous night, her wild plan to return to her rig, which meant everything to her, the satisfaction it had given him to hold her close and comfort her, his lips imprinted with the feel of her skin. What was this weird connection they had? But maybe he alone felt it prickling whenever he was near her. One-sided? She'd out and out said she was a loner.

"Cullen."

Archie's voice snapped him out of his thoughts.

"Yes, sir?"

Archie waited until the library's front door swung closed behind Kit. "You know it's a slim chance we make the evacuation zone without help."

"Yes, sir. I'm praying we encounter a friendly—National Park Service, cop, or scientist, anyone with a working radio."

Archie rubbed the back of his neck. "That would be our best hope in my view as well."

Tot rolled onto her side, and they both looked at her.

"Heck of a situation, a baby landing in the middle of this."

"Yes, sir, it sure is." It'd be one thing for him to face annihilation because of his choices, his decisions, but for little Tot, who hadn't even lived long enough to decide one single thing for herself?

So small.

Her hands were tucked under her chin, the cutest thing he'd seen in probably his entire life.

The door thumped open.

Cullen turned, but the gun stopped him.

"No moving," the newcomer said. A mild East Coast inflection colored the word. Dark hair, dark eyes, expensive haircut, neatly shaped brows. Nico, the guy from the newspaper clipping. He kicked the door shut behind him, the revolver in his gloved palm. "Hands showing and sit. Both of you."

Archie and Cullen did as instructed. How had they missed his approach? They'd not seen a vehicle. And where was Nico's partner?

Cullen's mouth was bone dry. Kit would return any moment, walk right into the ambush. *Stay where you are, Kit,* he silently pleaded.

"Didn't see you coming," Archie admitted.

"That was the idea, old man."

Cullen craned to see any sign of Nico's second in command. Was he going around to confront Kit? "Where's your buddy?"

"He's my brother, Simon. He's on another assignment."

Another assignment. Okay, so second SUV guy was Simon, the brother. Not Kyle, not the guy on the motorcycle. He was still an unknown entity. But what other assignment? Targeting the runaway Annette? Stalking Kit?

Cullen started to speak, but Nico cut him off by waving the gun at the baby. "I'm not here to chat. This has stretched on too long already. Unbelievable that Annette got you all involved in this in the first place. You stopped to help the trucker, and now here you are. Rotten for you. If everyone had minded their own business, none of us would be here right now. Where's Annette?"

Good. He didn't have her. Yet. Cullen clamped his jaws together. Not gonna get any info on Annette from him. Not that he had any. Archie's look was pure defiance too.

"Macho men, huh?" Nico waved the gun. "Not important. That problem can wait. I want her stuff."

Cullen kept his expression neutral. "What stuff?"

"Her luggage, backpack, a phone. Whatever she was carrying with her when she hitched a ride from the trucker."

Cullen kept his gaze away from the door. "What's your interest in Annette?"

Nico's eyes narrowed. "She's mine. That's all you need to know. What happens to her isn't your business."

Fury flamed in his gut. "You trafficked her, didn't you? Forced her to work for you when she ran away from home at seventeen?" Cullen could not keep the disgust from his voice. "What kind of big man entraps a child?"

Without warning, Nico slammed his fist into Cullen's cheek, tumbling him off the chair to the floor. Lightning pain sizzled through his skull. When Archie moved to intervene, Nico jammed the gun against Archie's forehead.

"She was a desperate runaway, and she would have starved to death if I hadn't stepped in. I'm perfectly willing to kill you both, but I don't have what I came for yet." He stared at Cullen. "You're going to give it to me because you don't want this old man to get a bullet in the brain. Or the girl truck driver." He darted a look around. "Where is she? Bathroom?"

Cullen felt a thrill of hope through the red-hot agony in his cheekbone as he sat up, warm blood flowing down, seeping into his shirt collar.

Nico didn't know Kit's whereabouts either. The longer they talked, the greater chance Kit would have of hearing them, becoming alert to Nico's presence. "She left." The words felt thick on his tongue, and he had to press them past the wall of pain. "Took off because she got tired of baby care. Figured she had a better chance of making it on her own."

Nico kept the gun pressed to Archie's brow. His friend's eyes brimmed not with fear but with rage. *Stay cool, Archie.*

"That smells like a lie to me," Nico said.

Cullen blinked hard to clear his vision, felt the blood drip from his chin in a steady stream. Nico's finger tightened on the trigger.

"Annette's stuff is in the rig still," Cullen said quickly. "We didn't take it. Too much to carry."

Nico shook his head. "Nope. That's not going to fly. Simon checked the semi after we fixed the tire that Lover Boy shot out."

Lover Boy? "He was going to rendezvous to help Annette escape, wasn't he?"

Nico's eyes were cold fury. "She thinks she's smarter than I am, cooking up some relationship with her john, Kyle, and arranging to meet him behind my back. Thought she'd keep me from coming after her by sending me that photo as a taste of what she thinks she has on me. Fatal mistake. I won't be blackmailed." He jerked a chin at Tot. "Baby's probably his. Little liar told me it was mine. Don't know why I let her keep it, except that she's one of my best earners. Simon figured she'd stay in line with a kid tying her down, but she wailed so hard and long about the pregnancy it gave me a migraine. Lesson learned. So where's her stuff?"

"Like I said, we didn't take it." Cullen climbed unsteadily to his feet.

Nico's gaze slid to Tot. "But there were baby supplies. You'd have taken that, wouldn't you?"

Cullen's heart thudded. No choice. "We took a duffel," he admitted. "And there was money in the bottom of it."

Nico arched a brow. He hadn't known about the money. "She stole from me too? After everything I've given her, she's been skimming off the top. How much?"

"Ten grand. It's all still there in the diaper bag. Take it and go. We'll never see each other again."

"That's the truth, because you're both going to be dead."

Cullen swiped at the blood. "Don't waste the bullets or the possible forensics trail you'll leave. Volcano's probably going to get us anyway, right?"

But Nico was fixated on Tot. He moved toward her, and Archie would have lurched at him, but Cullen pinched his arm, gripping the table edge with his other hand. Archie blinked to show he understood. If Nico messed with Tot, Cullen would overturn the table and hope to take Nico's legs out from under him. It was the only plan he could think of. His nerves iced over at the thought of Nico's gun inches from baby Tot. One reflex flinch of the trigger finger . . .

Nico looked around Tot's sleeping mat. "Where is it? The baby stuff?"

"Upstairs," Archie said quickly. "I'll get it for you right now."

"No," Nico said. "You stay. Soon as I check here, I'll go find it."

And kill us first. A shadow crossed under the door, and Cullen's gut tightened. Kit was about to enter. "Come on, Nico," he said loudly. "Not like we hid your goods on a baby. What is it you're looking for? If it's not the money, why'd you barge in here with a gun? What's so important you'd risk your own life? What was on the photo she sent you?"

"Shut up."

"No, really. Smart girl to collect evidence without your knowing. Must have been something for you to risk pursuing her here."

"I said shut up," Nico said louder.

The shadow had frozen.

Don't come in.

His heart slammed into his ribs.

Run, Kit.

But where would she find safety? Now? By herself?

Nico stared at the baby in her pajamas and poked the toe of his boot to pull up the edge of her mat. He reached out, and Cullen gripped the table. He'd have to shove it with sufficient force to topple Nico but not enough to strike Tot. He and Archie would laser in on the same target . . . Nico's gun hand. Whatever happened, bullets could not be fired in this small space with an infant lying unprotected.

Where was the shadow? Where was Kit?

Nico pawed at the small stack of supplies Kit had left for the last-minute change of clothes and diapers.

Cullen's breath caught as he saw movement, now in the front window, to the side of the "Welcome, friends" sign. Kit peeked through a dusty pane of glass.

Her eyes were wide, searching, taking it all in until she locked on him. She turned away for a millisecond, returned to view, held up her fingers in a silent count. Archie saw too. Nico tossed aside the baby clothes, kicking them into a heap. Tot stirred.

Kit held up three fingers.

Nico went for the blankets next, shaking them into disarray.

Now two . . .

Archie braced at his side.

Kit's last finger went down. It was followed by the crash of breaking glass. Something shattered the window. Tot's eyes flew open. When Nico spun toward the noise, Cullen bulldozed him, hitting him squarely in the stomach in a textbook football tackle. With a gust of air, Nico went over with Cullen on top of him aiming all his weight on Nico's right side, desperately grappling for the gun. Nico was strong, enraged. He writhed and tried to jab Cullen in the ribs, but Cullen kept hold. Archie stomped with both feet on Nico's wrist.

Nico cried out, releasing his grip, and Archie triumphantly kicked the gun away, then lowered his bony knees on Nico's arm. Cullen panted hard, immobilizing Nico.

Kit raced in. "Hold on," she said breathlessly. "I'll duct tape his wrists."

Cullen and Archie managed to hold him in place, though Nico kicked and swore. It took extreme effort to pin him long enough for Kit to loop tape around his wrists. Cullen loosened his bear hold and helped Archie prevent Nico from kicking them off while Kit did the same with his ankles.

"You're dead!" Nico spat.

"Quiet. You're going to upset the baby." Kit ripped off a piece of tape and slapped it across his mouth.

His eyes sparked vicious fire at her, but she didn't shy from it. Conversely, she brought her own face close to his and took his cheeks between the thumb and fingers of her right hand. "Are you listening closely, because this is important. I'll speak in simple sentences so you can understand." She leaned a fraction closer and lowered her voice to a whisper. "You don't own Annette. And you don't own the baby. And you never . . . ever . . . will." She shoved him away and went to check on Tot, who was whimpering.

Cullen could only stare. The strength in this woman, like a small, perfect stone standing fast against a raging current. His whole body went hot then prickled with gooseflesh, and he was certain he had never seen anything so impressive.

With Archie holding the gun on Nico, Kit bade Cullen to sit in the chair. "Your face is a mess. You need a bandage."

He looked dumbly at her and sank into the seat she offered him. She tipped his chin back with an index finger and examined him. "That looks like it hurts. A lot. Are you going to be all tough and pretend it doesn't?"

"I . . ." It was exactly what he'd been preparing to do.

She arched a brow.

"No, ma'am."

"So it hurts. How much?"

"A ton and a half."

She smiled and held a stack of gauze to his wound. "Hold this, please."

Her mouth was close to his, her satiny cheek inches from his battered one. He swallowed. "First aid skills on top of your others?" he croaked.

"In my job, it pays to be able to take care of yourself."

"Well, you took care of Nico all right," Archie crowed.

She pulled a wry smile. "Sorry I smashed the window."

"Don't be sorry," Archie said. "Your plan worked slicker than a slug on wet cement." Nico stirred, but Archie's attention didn't waver. "Not going anywhere, dirtbag, till we say so."

When the bleeding stopped, Kit dabbed some ointment over the cut, which stung, and then covered it with an adhesive bandage. He was sorry when she moved away.

"Here." She tore open a tiny package and handed him two tablets and a bottle of water. "Aspirin will help."

He dutifully swallowed it down though it hurt to tip his chin back. "The second guy's his brother, Simon. He must have dropped Nico near town. Nico said he's on another assignment. He'll come here sooner or later."

Archie poked at the phone he'd taken from Nico's jacket. "He doesn't have any service either, so his brother will be in the dark about good old Nico's situation. GPS might still be working though." Archie handed the gun to Cullen, then trotted to the break room, and there was a sizzle and bang. He returned with a grin. "Good thing I already warmed the water for Tottie. You should never put a phone in the microwave, by the way."

"I'll make a note of it." Cullen pocketed Nico's gun and the spare clips he confiscated. "If Simon catches up, we'll be ready for him."

Tot started to fuss, jamming her thumb into her mouth and whimpering. Cullen was already lacing up his boots, but he took a second to drain the dregs of his coffee. Who knew when he'd see any again? Kit grabbed his cup, hers, and another for Archie, carrying them to the sink before she started snatching up bundles, staging them by the door. "I'll load the rest."

Archie yanked on his boots and went to the tiny kitchenette. "I'll whip up that travel bottle for Tot."

"Make a couple," Kit called. "We can keep the extra in the insulated lunch bag I found. There's an ice pack in the bottom of the mini fridge."

Archie shot a worried glance at the baby.

Cullen echoed the feeling. It was one thing that they'd somehow escaped injury thus far, but there were endless risks of driving an ATV in the dark through a fire-breathing wilderness.

And Nico. Oh, but if Cullen had the chance, he was going to make sure Nico understood the error of his ways. Traffickers were the reason his career had ended, why Daniela couldn't walk, why he lived with an anvil of guilt in his heart that he could not dislodge with any amount of prayer. This trafficker was not going to win. The fatigue was replaced by a harsh adrenaline buzz.

"Shotgun, Arch?"

"Already in the car with extra shells. Mind you don't lose my weapon like you did your rifle, huh?"

"Yes, sir."

Kit darted a look at him. "The rifle's gone?"

He ducked his chin and confessed, "Dropped it when I fell off the drainpipe."

She shrugged. "At least it wasn't Tot."

"Baby's hungry," Archie said.

Cullen was going to volunteer to feed her when the ground shook, rattling the window coverings and the bits of broken glass on the library floor.

No, delaying wasn't an option.

Not anymore.

▪ NINE ▪

WHILE CULLEN AND ARCHIE rushed to take last-minute items to the ATV, Kit stared at Nico, who glared back at her from his position on the floor. She relished seeing him helpless. It gave her a rush of triumph and hope. He'd sent Simon on an assignment somewhere, so maybe that meant Annette was still alive. Again her heart lurched as if she too were running alone and scared. She prayed with everything in her that Tot's mom would keep a step ahead of Simon.

Archie hefted the first aid kit and jiggled the keys to the ATV, and Cullen entered behind him. "All set." He arched a grizzled brow at Nico. "Should we leave him here? Let his brother or the volcano get him, whichever comes first?"

Kit picked up Tot and soothed her. She wanted to leave Nico to his fate, render him helpless and victimized like he'd left Annette. Tot grabbed at her hair and tugged. She looked into the vibrant baby eyes, rimmed with thick eyelashes. So innocent.

Would she want to tell Tot someday about this man who might be her father? That they'd left him to die? Helpless and alone? That because of his horrific choices, she had the right to abandon him? As much as she longed to punish him, something deep down whispered that it wasn't right. Why that should be important now, she didn't know.

Cullen and Archie were both looking at her, waiting. "This is my decision?"

"Not completely, but you've got a say," Cullen said.

She glanced at Tot and back at the two waiting men. "How do you two vote?"

"Take him," Cullen said at the very same moment Archie said, "Leave him."

Archie rolled his eyes. "I say we leave his sorry self behind to find his own way out."

"See, Kit? We need a tiebreaker," Cullen said.

She groaned. "Take him."

"You two are simpering softies," Archie grumbled.

True, she thought, but she also felt a sense of relief knowing she wouldn't have a death sentence weighing on her soul.

Cullen scooped up Tot and delivered her to Archie, who began to coo and hum. "I know you want your bottle, love. You'll have to take it to go. It's adventure time, sweetheart."

Nico looked on in poisonous fury. Archie caught his glare and tucked Tot closer, hitching his shoulder to block Nico's view. "Not going to let my bitty girl get a case of the heartburn, having that nasty mug looking at her."

Kit checked the break room one last time while Archie shimmied a clean diaper onto Tot.

A wave of wind-born soot puffed along the ground when she joined the men. The sky was a wall of thick, gray steel.

140

It hit her that they were actually going to take an infant out into the massive roiling darkness, away from walls and any shred of protection.

A fool's errand. She felt the edges of panic nibbling at her stomach until Cullen caught her attention with a wink. The cheeky move made her smile, and he did in spite of the eye that was swollen nearly shut with an angry welt forming below it. Cullen believed God would help them make it. What if he was right? Maybe his belief could at least prop up her own.

"God's gonna watch over you, Tottie girl," Archie said.

But had he saved her mother, Annette? She thought of the young woman's newspaper photo. What had she risked to escape?

Everything. The magnitude of that thought urged her on.

Kit accepted Tot from Archie. Cullen shoved the paper map in his pocket before he and Archie hauled Nico to his feet and exited the library.

Kit followed and climbed into the rear seat with the crying Tot, whom she quieted with the bottle. Even with her borrowed clothing and trusty knit cap, the air inside felt frigid, and she had to stop her teeth from chattering.

Archie quickly unzipped one of the sleeping bags and fed it over the seat to Kit. "Bundle up. It'll help if we crash too. Extra padding."

Cullen deposited Nico in the seat next to her and buckled him in. "Can't be too safe, now can we?"

Nico was still bound at the wrists and ankles, and his mouth was taped. Cullen leaned forward until his face was inches from Nico's. "If you cause one lick of trouble, we toss you out into the ash and drive away without a backward glance." Then he gave Kit a friendly nod, closed the door, climbed behind the wheel, and cranked the engine.

"Keep the lights off till we get over the ridge," Archie said. "Don't want to alert Brother Simon."

"Easy for you to say."

Kit could understand Cullen's trepidation. The landscape was a palette of black, less black, and gray, and he could not exceed a slow creep without risking damage to the vehicle or its occupants. Even at that slug pace, he still seemed to hit every buried branch and sunken spot. Tot cried out at a particularly bad lurch and screamed so robustly Kit lost her grip on the bottle. It fell to the floor and rolled under the front seat.

Archie scrambled and retrieved it, wiping the nipple carefully on the hem of his shirt before handing it back. She pulled Tot closer and offered the milk again. The seat felt too small, forcing her and Tot to breathe in Nico's anger. He was a toxin, adding his own pollutants to the air.

It was bizarre. The man responsible for their current predicament was mere inches away from her, breathing in short bursts through his nose, brows drawn in a line. Though she did not stare at him directly, she kept him in her peripheral vision because the hatred on his face indicated he was far from done destroying lives if given the opportunity. She recoiled as far as she could, gathering up the corners of their sleeping bag so not even the fabric would touch him.

The pungent scent of smoke and ash pried its way into the vehicle. She smoothed Tot's hair. Those tiny, inexperienced lungs . . . a wilderness full of foul air. She thought suddenly of the picture in the *Your Baby, Month by Month* book of the developing fetal lungs in chapter 2 that were no bigger than moth wings, fragile as gossamer. Tot's were stronger, surely. She tried to make a sort of hood around the baby's face with the sleeping bag, though it wouldn't actually help much. She'd grabbed medical masks at the convenience store, but she didn't want to rummage around to snag them.

The vehicle plunged into a dip, and she slid against Nico. He shoved a shoulder at her, and she braced and got away from him, scalded by his touch.

"Sorry." Cullen found her in the rearview. His eyes were pained before they slid suspiciously to Nico. "Is he causing a problem?"

She shook her head.

Archie turned to glare at Nico. "Watchin' you. Give me a reason to chuck you out, buddy boy. It'd be a pleasure and a half."

Nico retorted something, but the tape over his mouth contained the vitriol.

Kit watched fixedly out the window where she could track Nico in the reflection. Through the film of soot, she tried to pick out landscape features. It was as if they were caught in a darkened snow globe, shaken and tumbled. It left them dizzy, no footing, no bearings.

She tried to discern which direction her rig lay buried. Heart squeezed, she pressed her forehead to the glass. Though she tried to convince herself otherwise, the tractor part was a total loss, even if the trailer was salvageable. Why hadn't she gone for the premium insurance package instead of partial?

Because you needed to have enough for the website, fuel, rent, and basic necessities like secondhand raincoats and food.

The last loan payment had been tantalizingly close. When she pictured her ruined truck, it felt like a death, this stabbing sensation in her chest. *You can still fix things. It's not too late.*

A plan started scrolling through her thoughts. The insurance payment would help her restart. She'd take out a new loan. Or there could be pieces to salvage. Maybe the engine, or the tires, or . . . All the custom modifications, though. The luxuries she'd scraped and saved for to make her rig a rolling home. The cupboards designed and built to her specifications, the expensive blackout curtains. The alarm system that would alert her if anyone was breaking into her rig while she slept. A memory from long ago shot to the surface, her father's voice gravelly from years of smoking.

"Kitten, you always want the same story. How about a new one?"

"No, Daddy. The one about the man and the wagon."

From age four, she'd relished turning the pages of the tattered book her father would read to her about the man who sold hats, making his way along the countryside under apple trees and along windy lanes. When the last page was turned, she'd put her cheek on his tobacco-scented shoulder, and they'd talk about what it would be like if they embarked on such journeys, rambling the roads every day, the people they'd see, the campfire meals they'd cook together under a canopy of stars.

"Someday, Kitten. I'm going to quit my bean counter job and get a trailer, and we'll go on rides together."

That would spin a whole new thread of conversation about their destinations, warm tropical places, faraway deserts, the dangerous ice roads through Canada, forests, sandy stretches of California coastline, and everything in between. When she heard the sadness creep into her father's voice, she'd hold him extra tight.

She didn't understand that he was trapped in a job he despised, a life he struggled to afford, quietly growing more desperate each day.

He'd never gotten that trailer.

He'd gone to jail after stealing money from his company to pay the mortgage after much of his salary had gone into car repairs, a new roof after theirs was lost to a storm, and to cover a series of bad investment choices he'd been certain would turn them around financially. The day it had all come out was permanently burned into her memory.

"You stole money?" Her mother had been in the process of putting on her earrings for a church meeting, and she stood there, gold circle suspended in her fingertips, staring at her husband.

"I did. I'm sorry. I told the cops everything. Took full responsibility. I'll go to jail and afterward I'll work the rest of my life to repay what I've taken."

Kit had held her breath as the seconds ticked by, stricken by the utter defeat in her father's voice as her mother answered.

"How am I going to hold my head up in this town? I'm humiliated. Completely."

She'd been too young then to understand why the comment bothered her.

I'm humiliated.

It was true, what her mother said. She'd borne the label of being married to a criminal, lost friends who'd cut her off, endured whispers of acquaintances in the supermarket. The impact on her mother had been terrible. But in the space of that single remark, her father had shifted from husband to criminal, and nothing he'd ever said or done later had changed that in her mother's mind. Kit had never thought of him that way, though. He was her father, her hero, who'd made a colossal mistake. Who'd apologized and tried to make amends like he'd taught her how to do since she was a toddler.

"You're gonna hurt people in this life, Kit." He'd pointed to her chest. *"That line of sin runs through every human heart. You gotta ask for forgiveness and mean it."*

He'd asked.

And he'd meant it.

So what did it say about the person who would not grant it? The Christian woman who'd been forgiven but couldn't forgive?

The ringing of the phone each week, her father calling, filled her grandparents small house in a nearby town where they'd moved. She'd been forbidden to answer, and the letters he'd written were destroyed before she could read them. Her mother would only speak of her father when pushed to the limit. At seventeen, Kit made elaborate plans to run away. She'd apply the pittance she earned cleaning offices after school to a trailer, get her license, sweep up her father, bolt. They'd live together on the road like they'd planned.

But she'd been a minor, and he'd grown sick by the time he was released four years later. Upon his discharge from jail, he'd worked two minimum wage jobs, rented a room in a converted garage, and died within six months, before he'd actually repaid all the money he'd taken. His dream dried up.

Kit's never had.

A feather stuck to the window, broken at the tip. She hoped the bird had flown away, undamaged, to a safe place. Moisture collected under her lashes. Cullen's gaze flicked briefly to hers in the rearview mirror as if he knew she was washed in sudden grief.

Tot wriggled and she resettled her, keeping her own gaze away from Cullen's.

He's not part of your future.

You're on your own.

Like she'd been since she was a teen.

"Left turn," Archie said.

"There is no left." Cullen gripped the wheel in exasperation. "There's only a bunch of rocks that look like the other rocks."

"Left turn there," Archie said, pointing. "See that flat spot? That's the start of the Silver Canyon trail. We turn off here and it's twenty more miles to the evacuation site."

Cullen snorted. "Practically a hop, skip, and jump."

"Don't be snarky."

"I'm entitled to be snarky."

"You're entitled to nothing whatsoever, son."

Cullen laughed. "Sorry, sir. Moment of self-pity. Won't happen again."

"See that it doesn't."

Kit smiled. Listening to the two of them bicker was the only bright spot in a dark journey.

Cullen made the turn, which put them on a slight incline, the path wide enough for the ATV and a more level surface than she'd imagined. Fortunate, since Tot was winding up for a good cry, turning her mouth away from the bottle and wrinkling up her forehead. Kit hoisted her enough to rhythmically pat her back like Cullen had done at his cabin. That did the trick, but it was a temporary fix. Tot bunched her knees up and writhed against Kit, rejecting the binky. What should she try now that the bottle and pacifier had lost their soothing powers? No way she was going to sing "Jingle Bells" with Nico sneering at her. She was mulling it over when Cullen hit the brakes.

"Would you look at that," Archie said.

Cullen whistled. "I must be hallucinating."

Kit looked through the front window and gasped.

Through the smear, she saw a filthy white truck with amber lights parked midtrail. Her whole body prickled with gooseflesh. A rescue worker, her disbelieving senses told her. An honest-to-goodness official who could get them out of there. She wanted to fling open the door and run to him, but Cullen held up a palm.

"Archie, stay in the car and watch Nico. I don't want Kit and the baby to be out in this until they have to be."

She felt something warm in her belly. Was it tenderness at his care? Self-consciousness? Impossible to decipher especially with her nerves cascading with excitement.

"Hey, Tot," she whispered as Cullen got out. "We made it."

The worker was covered in yellow neoprene overalls and wearing a National Park Service hat. His face was the same color as the grimy brim. He'd been studying something on the ground, but at the sight of the ATV, he straightened so suddenly, he dropped his clipboard. Papers fluttered loose as he took in the sight of Cullen's big frame, from his boots to his battered face and the gun tucked in his waistband. He flicked a hasty look at the ATV.

Kit didn't miss the way the man's hand flew to his holster. Obviously he'd noticed that Cullen was armed and maybe gotten a peek at Nico in the back seat with his mouth taped. He drew his weapon. Her heart beat faster.

Cullen's palms went up.

She cracked the window, desperate to hear.

"Hello, sir. My name's Cullen Landry. I own a ranch off Pine Hollow Road. We need help."

Still holding his weapon, the man cocked his head. "Stay right there. Why are you here?" He jerked a look at the vehicle. "Guy in the back seat's mouth is taped. Why?"

"He's a human trafficker." Cullen shook his head. "Let me start over. I'm with Kit Garrido, Archie Esposito, and a baby we found."

The man gaped. "You found a baby? Out here?"

"Yes, sir. Guy in the back seat trafficked her mother."

The man's expression, even in the near darkness, was incredulous. She understood why he edged toward his truck and tightened his grip on the gun. Her entire experience since she'd crashed had been completely incomprehensible. She wouldn't believe their story either if she hadn't lived it.

Cullen was still talking, jerking a thumb at the ATV, but the man's body language did not indicate he was buying what Cullen was selling. There was more talking but little progress that she could see, so she rolled down the window, Tot's cries loud and clear.

The man stared in her direction.

"He's telling you the truth. I'm Kit Garrido," she called out. "I was giving a woman named Annette Bowman and her baby a ride." She explained how they'd been shot at and she'd crashed. "But Annette ran. Something's happened to her." When the worker let his gun down slightly, she called, "I'm getting out, okay?" She ignored the warning look from Cullen and handed Tot to Archie. "Stay here, Tot. I'll be right back." When had she picked up the habit of explaining everything to an infant?

Archie thrust his chin at her. "Move slow. Guy's got a lot to absorb and he's jumpy."

That made two of them.

She eased the door open and stepped out, approaching at a snail's pace and keeping her palms up like Cullen.

"So you're the truck driver?" the emergency worker said.

"Yes. Everything he's telling you is true, even if it does sound totally bizarre."

The whites of his eyes were bloodshot, grime caking the wrinkles around his mouth.

"We're trying to get to the evac zone via Silver Canyon trail," Cullen said, "but we didn't figure on running into any personnel so soon."

"Shouldn't be any here to run into. I got an alert there was a woman spotted a couple hours from here, so I checked it out. Then I helped a guy with a broken-down truck full of goats. He's back in action, and now I'm headed out of here."

Kit froze. "Where was the woman seen?"

"Juncture of Pine Hollow and Mountain Valley Roads. I didn't find her. Only a wrecked rig."

"That's mine." Her voice wobbled for a moment. "Did you have a description of the woman?"

"Small, young, wearing a pink coat."

The memory sizzled through her, a woman in pink fleece that dripped with moisture, waving desperately for her to stop. She'd geared down her engine, halting right there in the middle of the road. "I remember."

Cullen bent toward her. "You remember meeting Annette?"

She nodded. "She startled me, stepped out into the road wearing a pink coat and ratty sneakers. She was shivering, holding a bundle, but I didn't realize at first it was a baby." She rubbed her forehead. "I can't remember anything else right now."

Cullen nodded. "Kit gave Annette and her baby a ride. Annette was running from that guy." He gestured to the ATV. "His name's Nico Phillips. He showed up to retrieve his 'property' while we were sheltering in Grandlake, and we got the upper hand."

Tot's cries grew louder. "Are they still looking for Annette, sir?" Kit pressed.

"John. Call me John." He slid his weapon into the holster.

Kit and Cullen let down their hands.

"Search has been suspended."

"No," Kit said. "You can't stop looking. She could still be alive."

"The report . . . Did it say she was injured?" Cullen asked.

"Possibly. She was spotted waving at a helicopter. Pilot said she was crouched over, holding her side."

Kit's gut clenched. But injured definitely trumped dead.

"A vent erupted and the helicopter lost visual. When they circled back, they found no sign of her." John unclipped a radio from his pocket. "I'm sorry. I couldn't find any clue to her whereabouts either."

Kit's heart squeezed. "She's got to be there somewhere. You have to call the helicopter back or bring search dogs."

John shook his head, frowning. "We can't risk any more people. I volunteered to stay for one more shift, but the agreement was I'd pull out by 8:00 a.m. No one should be anywhere on this mountain. It's going to blow. Soon."

His face was lined with fatigue. Probably the guy had been pulling double shifts. He'd volunteered, chosen to risk his own safety to return to a volatile zone to locate Annette, and it was likely not the first time since the volcano had rumbled to life. He was one of the good guys, one of the people who ran in when everyone else ran out. Like Cullen had done in his career. *And still does.* Folks who put their lives at risk to save others.

Annette had to be terrified, hunted, and now left to die? That fuzzy pink jacket . . . those frightened blue eyes. She fought a swirl of dizziness.

"John," she said. "Please. Take the men and the baby to the evac zone, and I'll go."

Cullen swung a look at her, mouth open. "Go where?"

"I'll take the ATV and look for Annette."

Cullen glowered. "That cannot happen, Kit. There's no way."

"She'll die if we don't get to her before the mountain or Simon does." Kit glared at him.

John's expression was as dour as Cullen's. "I can't let you do that, ma'am. I'll radio the info. That's the best we can do. We still have one helicopter up, and if they spot her, maybe there will be a chance for rescue, but right now, you need to follow me out of here."

"But . . ." Kit gestured to the ATV. "She risked everything to get the baby away from Nico."

"Unbelievable story," John said. "So wild it's got to be true. I'll call it in. We'll get help rolling, but with Ember's status, I have to insist you accompany me to the evac site immediately."

"We can't just leave," Kit said, her throat clogged with unshed tears.

John squeezed the button on his radio. "Ground, this is—"

A crack ripped the air.

Kit flinched, expecting to see the ground opening up.

She gasped in horror. John grunted, clutched his chest. Before she and Cullen could react, he was sliding to the ground.

His blood sprayed across his vehicle as he crumpled, a second bullet catching him under the chin and spinning him around. The shooter hit him again in the chest, making sure the lethal job was accomplished. The scream building in Kit's throat never emerged. Her body was rigid, wooden. Cullen grabbed her arm and whirled her around toward the ATV.

"Run."

She stumbled as more bullets whistled by them.

"At our eleven," Cullen shouted. "It's Simon. He's in the trees."

But even as he spoke, an SUV broke from cover, rolling

out of the wooded glade in an attempt to cut them off from the ATV.

The SUV ate up the ground between them before Simon braked and leaned out the window, preparing for another shot.

Before he could fire, Archie flung the passenger door open, knelt behind the metal, and began blasting away with the shotgun to provide cover.

Simon hit the gas and shot wildly out his open driver's window as he raced toward them.

Their saving grace was the irregularity of the ground. It caused the SUV to buck and dip. Coupled with Archie's bullets, it was impossible for Simon to get off more accurate shots.

The slimmest advantage, but it was enough.

Kit dove inside the back seat, praying no bullets had penetrated the flimsy walls of the ATV, and grabbed Tot as Archie bundled her over.

Tot cried, choking, gasping sobs.

Kit looked at the empty seat next to her.

"Cullen!" she shouted. "Nico's gone."

Archie drew back into the passenger seat as Cullen cranked the wheel. "That sack of garbage jumped out. Look. He's making for the SUV."

Simon again stopped, leaned out, and began to fire with better accuracy while Nico hopped, falling once, using his bound hands to get to his feet again. A bullet broke the passenger side glass, and she squeezed herself onto the floor, covering Tot with her body.

Cullen gunned the engine and took them in such a tight circle he almost flipped the vehicle.

"Look out!" Archie hollered.

She didn't see the obstacle, but she knew what Cullen had in mind. Their only chance was to punch their way deep into the trees, move across through ground so uneven the SUV could not follow.

Kit thought of John, the rescue worker, bleeding to death, alone.

Grieve later.

Escape now.

If they didn't, four more bodies would be added to Nico's kill list.

▪ TEN ▪

SWEAT STUNG THE CUT on Cullen's cheek as he maneuvered deeper into the trees. There was no way to prevent the three riders from being churned as if they were in a blender set to puree. Tot screamed her displeasure.

"Still behind you," Archie barked. "Losing ground though. There, drive down into that hollow. Thick trees. No way they can follow."

Cullen wrestled the ATV down a bumpy slope and plunged them into an army of pines. Some were so close together he had to detour around them, and others had branches that scraped across the body of the vehicle as it squeezed through. South, now southwest, he struggled to keep some sense of direction because ultimately they would need to make it out of their overgrown hiding spot.

If they survived the immediate danger.

He gritted his teeth. When, not if. A thicket of blackberry bushes taller than Cullen appeared, and he didn't second-guess it but buried the vehicle deep into the thorny vines, praying there was not a concealed rock that would take out the suspension.

With no headlights and only the faintest dawn sunlight, they were practically invisible.

Unless Nico caught the trail of disturbed ash.

Cullen didn't think Nico was a savvy outdoorsman. Hopefully his brother wasn't either. And their vehicle was not built for such terrain.

Archie was trying to help Kit quiet the baby. Unknown how far that piercing, shrill cry would carry in the mountain air.

Cullen grabbed the binoculars and craned every which way, trying to track their pursuers. Sporadic points of light told him Simon and Nico were moving to a higher point on the trail where they hoped to get a better view of the hollow.

He didn't think they'd spot the ATV buried in its thorny nest.

Then again, he hadn't anticipated John's murder. Cullen had been caught completely unawares, and the cost could have been even higher with Kit standing right next to him and the baby and Archie only a few feet away.

So focused on your own plans, Cul. Just like you were back then.

Daniela had tried to slow him when he'd approached the van that day.

"Wait, Cullen. Backup is ten minutes out."

But he didn't wait.

And he'd spent long, dark nights trying to figure out exactly why.

The answer stuck in his gut like a burr under a saddle.

He'd wanted to be the one.

The one who saved those women.

The one who enacted the rescue, supremely confident in his capabilities.

He should have waited.

He should have listened.

Tot's wailing broke off suddenly as she latched angrily onto the binky. The silence was so deep he could hear Archie blow out a ragged breath.

"Safe for now," he said.

For now.

Cullen picked up the SUV in his binoculars farther up the trail, moving toward a better viewpoint. It stopped periodically, the driver's side door opening, the slash of a flashlight beam gleaming as one or the other got out to help navigate the treacherous terrain and look for any sign of their prey.

Kit laid Tot on the spot that Nico had occupied and snuggled the sleeping bag around her. "How are we going to get out of here?"

"That's going to require some thinking." What he wouldn't give to trot out a plan of action, but the fact was he didn't have one. He respected her too much to offer a placating half-truth.

"We're safe for the moment, but we're pinned down here until they move far enough away that we can escape."

"Escape where? They'll be on the same trail, right? They'll know exactly where to find us."

"That leaves the second route, Flame Ridge."

She shook her head. "Farther away and parts of it are obliterated like Archie said, so we'd have to go around."

"Yes."

Pinned, with the bomb ticking down. He kept his "cop"

tone, the one that sounded calm and collected even when the scenario was falling to pieces. He'd learned a lot from his partner, Daniela, about how situations could escalate or deescalate with the cop's inflection and demeanor. He'd once seen her get a two-hundred-pound drunk guy to drop the pipe wrench he was wielding by striking up enough rapport that he'd agreed to show her photos of his nieces and nephews. Maybe if Cullen hadn't ended her career, he might have learned a ton more from her.

The silence grew heavy with despair, so he infused his next comment with as much calm as he could muster. "All right. So we wait until they move out of range and then we head for Flame Ridge. Can you find it on the map?"

"Yes." She took it from him and fanned it out.

He tried to uncramp his calf muscle. "Least we aren't on foot." Though he wasn't at all sure that wouldn't be more comfortable than maintaining his current posture.

Archie cleared his throat. "Ladies and gents, I got me a different plan."

Cullen didn't like the way that sounded. "What's that?"

"I'm going for the truck."

It took him a beat for understanding to penetrate his pounding head. "John's truck? The service worker's?"

"Yeah. Nico and Simon didn't linger, so John's keys are on him. Radio's working, more than likely. I'll sneak back there and call for help. Drive the truck to the evac site on whichever route I can manage, or catch up with you and we go the distance together."

Cullen opened his mouth to argue, then closed it. Archie's bold idea might be their best option, with a few modifications. "Better if I do it."

"Better why?" Archie's mouth puckered. "'Cuz you're a young buck and all that?"

"No, sir, but—"

"But nothing." Archie poked a finger at him. "You gotta be here to take your shots if Nico and Simon find you."

"I . . ."

Archie turned to Kit. "You know how to shoot?"

She shook her head.

Archie smiled. "No worries. I'd still bank on you winning a fight any day, gun or no gun. This musclehead can do the grunt work," he said, jutting his chin at Cullen.

Kit's expression was grave. "Archie, that's not—"

"Safe?" He quirked a brow. "I heard you back there suggesting you go off and find Annette by yourself. You're ready and able to take risks. I am too. Out of the three of us, makes most sense for me to take the trip. If John's still alive by any stretch of the miraculous, I'll do what I can for him. If Nico and Simon spot me, I'll keep them busy from the truck while you get away. It's the best option. You hafta admit that."

Cullen was frantic to find a way to refute Archie's proposal, but he couldn't land on anything except he was afraid for his friend. This stubborn, faithful, tough old bird was one of the good ones, the best example of what it meant to be a man. "Sir . . ."

Archie waited in silence.

Some things just couldn't be said. And Archie was right. There really were no other feasible options. Cullen exhaled. "Take a pack with water and food."

Archie shoved the door open, pushing back the thorny vines. Cullen did the same on his side.

Kit made a move to get out, and Archie helped her.

Cullen handed Archie the gun he'd stripped from Nico. "And this. I've got the shotgun and my handgun." When Archie reached for it, he gripped the old man's arm for a moment. The words remained stuck in his throat.

Archie smiled. "Didn't think I'd get a chance to storm some beaches this late in my life. Who'd have imagined? Wait till I tell the grands."

"Don't let it be the last beach, okay?" Cullen rasped out.

"Tell you what. If all this simmers down and Ember decides not to blast us into oblivion, we'll go fishing." He looked at Kit. "You fish?"

She nodded. "Oh yes. My father taught me, and not to brag, but I once snagged three twenty-inch rainbow trout in one morning."

Archie laughed. "I don't doubt it for a hot minute. All right. It's a fishing date. We can teach Tot too. Never too early to start the learning process when it comes to fishing."

She wrapped him in a tight embrace and then pulled him to arm's length and poked his chest with her pointer finger. "Do not get yourself killed, do you understand me? If you do, I will be furious with you. I won't even come to your funeral."

He laughed again and kissed her forehead. "You are a treasure, Miss Kit Garrido. Only one who could keep Cullen Landry in line."

"I'll get that pack for you." She pulled in a breath and made her way to the back, avoiding the thorny branches. Cullen suspected she didn't want them to see her cry.

Archie leaned inside the back seat of the ATV. "All right, Tot. Grandpa Archie's got to go. You be real good for Miss Kit and Uncle Cullen, you hear me? Give their ears a break sometimes, huh? And save all your big diaper blowouts for Cullen's watch." He stroked the fuzz of hair and kissed her. When she reached out, he pressed her tiny hand to his wrinkled cheek. "Grandpa's real proud of you. Don't you forget it." He accepted the pack Kit handed him and stretched his scrawny frame before he slid it onto his shoulders. "I'll stick to the bushes, move slow so as not to attract attention."

Cullen considered that this might be the last time he ever laid eyes on librarian Gunnery Sergeant Archie Esposito. "Sir . . ."

Archie quirked a brow. "If you try to hug me, I'll brain you. Only the ladies get away with that."

Cullen drew himself up and snapped off a sharp salute.

Archie returned it, and in that moment he was every inch the proud marine. "Don't look so serious. I wasn't finished boxing the collection of Zane Grey novels at the library. Not gonna let them get burned up, am I? I'll be back to finish."

With that, he turned on his heel and slunk off into a narrow margin of shrubbery until he vanished from sight. They watched for a while, sequestered in their thorny fort.

"Is he going to make it?" Kit whispered with the tiniest wobble in her voice.

"If I've learned one thing from Archie, it's to never bet against a marine." Cullen put an arm around her shoulders, and she turned her face to his chest. She was breathing hard, seeming to fight back tears. He was trying to swallow a lump in his own throat.

Then somehow her arms were around him too, and he found himself stroking her hair, this slender woman with a truck-sized helping of grit and grace. Was it too much? He'd barely known her a day, but she felt so right. The branches seemed to weave together around them, cutting them off in space and time from the wreck and ruin. He angled his face down toward hers, drinking in her soft profile, the pearly glimmer of her eyes.

She tipped her mouth up to his and kissed him. It seemed the most natural thing in the world to return that kiss with one of his own. Surreal. Definitely not his imagination, though, because he couldn't have conceived such beautiful warmth, the absolute perfection of that kiss. They eased apart a few inches, and he was reaching to brush her hair with his palm, moving in for another kiss, when she twitched and inched away. The moment popped like a soap bubble against an unforgiving thorn.

"I, um, I should close the doors. Keep the air clean for Tot." She climbed back in and pulled the door shut while he tried to understand what had just taken place. It felt so . . . momentous, but that could be his thumping heart spinning a tale. He'd shared a kiss with an astonishing, complicated, surprising woman because they'd been through terrible trauma and they were both worrying about Archie. It probably shouldn't have taken him aback that she clearly had some second thoughts and appeared not to want to acknowledge what had just happened between them.

Other things to consider at the moment, Landry. But his lips still tingled and pulsed from the kiss, and his arms missed the feel of her body against his. A twig caught his hair as he plowed back to the driver's seat. Tot had fallen into a quiet examination of a plastic toy Kit had given her. All right. He resigned the moment to the back part of his brain.

They hunkered down in the ATV as the morning turned from silver to dull cream. The less movement now the better. The quick glimpses he'd gotten indicated Nico and Simon had moved almost out of range, uncertain about the location of their quarry, and they were no doubt still scanning for any sign of movement in the hollow. He tried to calculate how long it would take Archie to reach the truck and radio for help. Two hours? Three, maybe, since he'd have to move stealthily.

The list of potential complications was endless.

Archie could fall, break an ankle.

Become lost, victim to ground movement, toxic gasses, heart attack, simple exhaustion, or dehydration.

Kit startled him out of his thoughts by handing Tot to him. "She needs changing and it's your turn." She followed up by passing him the wipes and a padded mat. Tot's legs bicycled as he began the process.

"Hold up, Tottie. You're not competing in the long jump here."

"Gah," Tot answered, then offered a string of syllables that sounded almost like words.

Kit looked up from her perusal of the map to check his progress. She wasn't quite making eye contact, and there were spots of color on her cheeks. He wrangled one of the diaper tabs closed and then the other, re-snapped all the access points, and cleaned his hands with a wipe. Tot grabbed his sleeve. He suspected she might be ready for some refreshments.

"Would you like to sit up and have a snack, sweetie?"

He propped her up in the passenger seat and opened one of the packets Kit provided and a plastic bowl into which he dumped the cereal. Tot wasted no time grabbing a hand-ful and cramming it into her mouth. The puffs he didn't catch spilled onto the floor and some stuck to her fingers and his when he tried to catch them, but this was clearly an experience to be enjoyed. She smiled, hamster cheeks filled.

"Gah," she said again.

"Not sure if this is playing or eating, but you're doing awesome, Tottie." He caught several more puffs before they hit the floor. Maybe his hand-eye coordination would improve along with his bowling. Delighted, he continued to field rice puffs, lost in the game.

"It's small," Kit said, startling him.

He looked at her. "What is?"

"Whatever Nico's after."

"Yes." The thought had occurred to him too. "He mentioned photos. Could be prints or a memory stick?"

"Whatever it is, it's easily hidden. You said he looked for it in Tot's things, and he was after the diaper bag. And he didn't care about the money?"

"He wasn't aware she'd taken any, and he didn't appear all that eager to retrieve it. He's looking for something else."

"Annette's phone?"

"He asked about it. Could be why he sent Simon after her and came to the library himself to find us. Cover his bases. Do you remember her having a phone on her? Talking to anyone? Dirt bike Kyle maybe? I'm thinking he's an ally of Annette's."

Kit exhaled in frustration. "No. So far I've only got that one memory of her in the pink coat." She lapsed into a moment of silence. "She was desperate, Cullen. I remember that."

Desperate. Scared, for herself and Tot. Going to meet Kyle? Escape her life as Nico's prisoner? Cullen thought about plenty of things that might be stored on Annette's phone to make Nico worry. Photos, recorded conversations, files. Tot dove in for another fistful of cereal.

"I'll search through the baby bag again," Kit said, "but if it were me, I'd have had my phone in my pocket, close by the whole time. She was trying to meet up with Kyle. It would have been her lifeline to communicate with him, especially meeting in the wilderness like this."

"Yes. My guess is it would have been on her person when she bolted." He hesitated. "But it could be that Nico might not have allowed Annette to have a phone, or he cloned it to his so he could track everything she did."

He could feel the fury radiating off Kit as she extracted the duffel bag and plopped it on the seat next to her. "Nico's an animal. If he's still looking, Annette is probably alive though, right? Or at least he's worried she is. The helicopter spotted her, like John said."

Her voice lifted with hope he didn't want to squash. Annette had been spotted hours before, according to John, and there had been no further contact. Plenty of time for Simon to have found her and killed her, while Nico pressed on to pursue the people he believed had her possessions. No point in sharing that information.

He peered through the binoculars with one hand, his other steadying Tot. No sign of them or their vehicle, but they might have purposefully moved the truck out of sight to entice their prey into giving themselves away. Much as he detested hiding like some helpless rabbit, it was the smartest choice, maybe their only one.

When he swiveled the lenses in the other direction, he could make out the timber boom of the mill in the distance, a relic from the lumbering days. Though they'd decided to reroute to Flame Ridge, they hadn't made it very far, and Silver Canyon was tantalizingly close. He recalled what he'd seen on Archie's paper map; this hollow where they currently hid was nestled at the side of a small valley through which ran a creek large enough to power that decrepit sawmill. It was in ruins now, according to Archie, only some stout walls remaining, but interesting to hikers and the odd photographer.

The trailhead was accessed near that old dinosaur of a mill, the way they might just have to go, regardless of the fact that Nico and Simon were also on the trail. Maybe they could get ahead of the two. He didn't put much stock in that idea. Nico and Simon had proved to be savvy trackers.

As soon as they moved away, Cullen would have no choice but to sneak them onto the Silver Canyon trail. Somehow. He felt better, having at least oriented himself. An illusion since they were on the brink of a geological catastrophe.

Stay asleep for a little while longer, Ember.

Tot wrapped her tiny fingers around his thumb and pulled it toward her mouth.

"No way, kiddo. You got barracuda teeth."

She burbled at him.

Kit finished rummaging through the contents of the duffel. "There's nothing in here that I didn't see before. Now I wish we hadn't taken the money along. It's too bulky."

Amusing. In what other circumstance would money be an inconvenience? Ten thousand in cool cash would certainly outshine his monthly police pension payout. But this was blood money, bought and paid for with the freedom of other human beings.

167

He checked his phone, glad he'd charged it while they journeyed away from the library. No signal, but at least the clock worked. Going on 9:30 a.m. Where was Archie? Not at the truck yet, for sure. Archie didn't expect to find John alive; he'd likely thrown that in for Kit's sake. No, he'd seen plenty of death in his day, and John couldn't have survived the amount of blood he'd lost from those lethally placed shots. His stomach muscles tightened.

There would be a reckoning. Nico and Simon would pay. He'd summon every last bit of his strength to ensure that they both went to prison for an eternity. Justice. Elusive though it was, every once in a while he'd gotten a taste of it in his career as a cop. He craved another, one last savor of it, and he'd get it when he handed Nico and Simon over with enough evidence to lock them both up.

"Cullen."

He whipped his head around while Tot tried again to chomp his finger.

"There's something in the bottom of the duffel, underneath the liner. I can feel it." She'd carefully unloaded the contents and stacked them neatly on the seat while she searched.

"Can you get it out?"

She peeled the bottom panel from the bag, putting the rigid plastic liner on top of the unloaded supplies.

He kept a palm on Tot as he watched Kit remove a small clasp envelope secured in a zip-top bag.

"Bingo," he murmured. "Good search, Garrido."

She held it up, opened the plastic bag.

So this was it, the prize that Nico and Simon were willing to kill for, had killed for. Cullen could taste it again on the edges of his tongue, the hint of justice, close and pungent. It was now in their possession.

"And there's something else . . . a lump—"

An odd sound caught his attention. "Did you hear that?"

"Uh-huh."

It was a roiling, billowing boom as if an enormous load had been dropped from a great height. The vehicle began to shudder, and the spilled puffs of cereal fell off the seat. The tremoring grew more pronounced.

Kit dropped the envelope back into the duffel. "Earthquake."

"Worse. Buckle in," he snapped. He handed Tot over into the back seat and she did so.

"This is going to be rough," he said.

"What is it?"

But he didn't need to explain. She'd looked out the passenger side window and seen the enormous belch of smoke cloaking the slopes above the valley, the roiling clouds of debris gathering into a monstrous river above the trail as the cliff above them collapsed. Landslide.

He heard her gulp.

A tsunami of timber, rock, and earth was headed right at them.

He put it in gear and punched the ATV out of the blackberry brambles. How fast could he go without hitting a tree or rock that would immobilize them? And Tot with no car seat, nothing to protect her from impact except Kit's determined hold. *Lord, get us out of here.*

In the back of his mind, he thought of Archie.

He wouldn't have had time to hike far enough to be out of range.

Cullen sped through the trees, avoiding a collision with a boulder at the last minute. Each ticking second revealed the sickening truth. They wouldn't outrun the onslaught. The edges of it were already outpacing the ATV, slithering trails of debris that would engulf the tires soon enough. Their only shot was to find something, anything that would protect them.

"The lumber mill," he shouted over the growing din.

She might have answered, but he was barely able to control the ATV.

A pile of loosened rocks he hadn't noticed slid across his path. He braked hard, corrected, and avoided the slide. Around and in between and behind, he drove frantically, riding the gas and brake pedals. Tot cried as Kit struggled to keep her in place.

The far edge of the hollow appeared, close. Movement in the rearview made his heart stop. An ocean of debris behind them, swelling with every passing moment as the fallen trees knocked over standing ones, ripping them from the ground and snapping them like matchsticks. The sheer enormity of it took his breath away for an instant.

He goosed the gas, launching the ATV clear of the hollow and onto a smoother hillside where he pushed the speed. The wheels bumped and ricocheted as they traversed the shuddering ground. Fewer trees here also meant the monster behind them would surge unimpeded.

The jutting remnant of the lumber mill appeared above the choking clouds.

Those old bones had withstood decades of punishment.

He prayed they would be enough to save three helpless people from the rage of an angry mountain.

▣ ELEVEN ▣

KIT LOST HER GRIP on Tot after a vicious slam to the ATV. With a scream, she grabbed for her, managed to catch the edge of her pajamas and hold on a moment before the baby would have hit the door. Fingers clawed, Kit hauled Tot back to her. She planted her boots against the seat and encircled the baby with both arms in a rigid embrace. All around them rocks and branches thumped against the vehicle. She didn't know how Cullen was keeping them upright. She thanked God she'd fastened her seat belt.

He yelled something at her, but she only caught "mill." His destination was the ruins of the lumber mill Archie had pointed out, probably the only structure that could offer the slightest chance of survival. The jutting timber boom was visible above the debris cloud. As she bounced like a sock in the dryer, desperately trying to deflect the force from Tot, she caught only glimpses. A corner of weathered wall and the iron skeleton of the waterwheel that had defied the centuries flashed in and out of view.

Something smashed through the rear window, and she folded into a ball with Tot at the center. Whatever it was glanced off her shoulder and sailed over the driver's head-rest in a cascade of glass flecks.

"Cullen!" she screamed.

Behind them the slide gave chase, gaining speed and volume. The ATV was being overtaken by that killer wall, and there was nothing to prevent it. Soon Cullen would not be able to navigate as the rubble swallowed the vehicle. End of the line.

She closed her eyes and held on to Tot. The baby was probably screaming, but she couldn't hear her. There was only one thing she could think to ask.

Lord, let this be easy for her.

That was all Kit could plead for, that the little baby wouldn't suffer like her mother likely had, on the run, scared, tired, hungry, and cold. Annette . . . Was she in the path of the landslide too? Dead already at Nico's or Simon's hand? If only Kit had moved faster after taking them into her truck, traveled far enough to get them to the police.

If only . . .

Her arms cramped from the desperate hold. A shadow of the mill loomed ahead as the landslide pursued them. The wheels bounced and slid. Terror squeezed every nerve to the snapping point. Would it be painful?

The ATV came to a stop so suddenly she and Tot were only reined in by the seat belt. Dazed, she forced her eyes open, uncertain if the tires had exploded or if they'd hit an obstacle. She could see nothing but filthy air swirling by the broken windows. The thundering all around them did not abate. They hadn't outrun it. Not even close.

Beyond the front headrest, Cullen drooped crookedly.

Why had he stopped? Had he been hit? Hurt? The fear was a painful punch to her middle. All he'd done for a couple strangers, for her and Tot, jumped into their troubles with both boots and a warm chuckle. *Help him . . .* But her body was frozen with fear that she would find him outside the bounds of anything she could do. Her throat throbbed with agony as the ground rumbled underneath the ATV.

She was trying to force herself to call out to him when he straightened. She heard his seat belt unclick, and he tumbled over the front seat into the back. He unfastened her and guided her and Tot to the floor, then curled himself over them as the shaking increased, the oncoming tumult rattling the ATV. A noise like the end of the world screamed through space and time. The violence was so intense she had to grit her teeth to keep them from slamming together.

How long? How much more could they endure before it was all over? But she was not alone. Cullen was with her, in it until the last.

Suddenly the roar abated, replaced by a quieter cascade of sounds.

The minutes passed in a blur, until gradually she became aware of details her ragged senses were feeding her. The sound of her own breathing. Tot squirming near her belly, her cries muffled. A soft shushing, like skis traveling over new snow. She tried to move, but a mass pressed her down. Cullen.

With a flood of terror she realized his body was a dead-weight on her.

"Cullen," she whispered. He did not answer. Did not move. She battled down the panic. With all her strength she reared back, levering Cullen's weight onto the seat.

Tot screamed out a lusty complaint, and Kit silently thanked the Lord. The baby was alive and outraged, which meant she might have escaped serious injury.

"You're okay, Tot."

After a quick shake of the sleeping bag, she spread it on the driver's seat and laid Tot there, tuning out the screaming. Tot kicked and bucked, but Kit could see no obvious blood or broken bones. Stomach clenched, she turned to Cullen. The daylight was weak and almost obliterated by the debris cloud. The meager gray was not enough to check his condition. Hands shaking, she pulled out the flashlight from her jacket pocket and flicked it on.

"Cullen." She wiped the sooty film from his face. "Can you answer?"

Even if he was conscious, he wouldn't have heard her above Tot's crying. But his eyes remained closed, his long limbs frighteningly still.

Frantic, she ran her hands over his arms, legs, head. There was a bump on the side of his skull where he'd been slammed by something, possibly whatever had flown through the rear window. The passenger side front glass was broken too.

"Cullen," she said again, her fingertips cold with fear as she sought a pulse under his chin. Nothing. She repositioned, her mind spinning frantically. How would she do CPR when he was too long to stretch out on the seat? With no hope of access to medical care anytime soon? She'd bend his knees, lay him as flat as she could . . .

But then she felt the strong, steady beat. The air whooshed out of her in sweet relief.

He was alive. That would have to be enough for now.

Completely foreign to her nature, this was a moment-by-moment situation. Not ideal for a woman who planned out her days in different-colored ink right down to the vending machines she'd visit on each of her routes.

Okay, Kit. Whatcha gonna do now?

She peeked cautiously through the broken window.

The wreckage around them had begun to settle enough that she could make out their surroundings. Cullen had somehow managed to drive them into the confines of the ruined lumber mill. The ATV had come to rest under the protective steel beams of the timber boom, and the onslaught of tree trunks, rocks, and soil had been diverted neatly around the beams, which split the flow, funneling the load on through the valley. She looked up at the aged steel that had saved their lives and then down at the still, silent man who'd done the same.

"Cullen." She stroked his cheeks and forehead. "Wake up, okay? I don't know what to do next. I need you to open your eyes and start being bossy."

And she needed his warm smile, and the kindness that came off him in waves, and the unexpected, rare gentleness that spoke to her soul. He remained immobile. She looked helplessly out the wrecked windows at the smothering moonscape of ash. What was she going to do? How would she care for Tot and Cullen? Get help? Survive?

When the panic flamed, she forced it down.

You're not a quitter. God must have saved you for a reason. Cullen would say she should leave room for the "what if."

What if God would give her the strength to survive this? What if she could figure out what to do even though there appeared to be no way out? She eased Cullen onto his side and folded his arm in front of him in the recovery position she'd read about in her first aid book. His breathing remained regular so she redirected her attention.

Tot still screamed, her eyes swollen, the tears making tracks in the ash on her skin. She'd cried so hard her chest heaved in shuddering gulps. Kit climbed over the seat to her, and with some creative seat belt and blanket usage, she managed to secure her in an upright position. With a tissue from her inside coat pocket, she wiped Tot's face. Tot was still enraged, her arms and legs rigid, but at least she wouldn't be cut or slide off, and her breathing was better. Kit remembered the pacifier in her other pocket. She fished it out.

"Here, baby girl. How about this? Just for a minute until I can help you better."

Tot turned away at first, but Kit persisted and eventually Tot accepted the offering. The sudden cessation of howling enabled her to pick up other sounds, the creaking and groaning of the debris outside the ATV, which could be an ominous predictor of what was ahead. Would they be swept away? Might the steel and brick of the lumber mill suddenly fail?

Nothing you can do about that right now, she told herself savagely. Order. She had to restore some sort of order.

Everything was a jumbled mess, the contents of the duffel bag strewn about. *The proof against Nico,* she recalled with a start. But what did that matter in the face of survival? She'd find it, though; if it was still in the vehicle, she'd locate and secure it. She spotted the arm of her teddy bear and snatched it, shaking off wood shavings and a few pine needles. The ear ripped slightly as she freed it.

"Here, Tot. You can play with this, but no chewing." Tot instantly gathered up the toy and clutched it to her. A quiet baby playing with a teddy, and Cullen resting comfortably. Good job so far.

She began to pile the baby supplies atop one another and eased them to the cleanest part of the floor, since Cullen required the whole seat. She checked his pulse again. Steady.

"Ready to wake up now?" she suggested hopefully. "No? A short nap then."

She spent a few minutes craned over the back seat to check the supplies in the rear. They seemed intact, the ATV having protected them from being crushed. God's provision. It could be nothing else.

Supplies. You've still got them. Water. Food. First aid.

The issue next on the priority list was air quality. Ash and debris were infiltrating the vehicle in spidery wisps. With a bone-cracking stretch, she managed to snag the small bag she'd packed at the library with Archie's help. Her breath caught as she thought of him. Where had he been when the mountain let loose?

She would not stop hoping and praying for Archie until she had proof positive he hadn't survived. Until then, Archie was no doubt problem solving like she was. *Do the next thing. Right now.*

She located the roll of clear plastic bags and the duct tape. Her dad would have smiled. Duct tape, in his opinion, was the single most useful tool in the history of tools. She ripped off pieces and sealed plastic over the broken places of the window. Not perfect, since some of the cracks spidered out to the far edges, but it would keep most of the foul particles out.

Until when? They starved to death?

Nope. She wasn't going to go there. They had a fragile bubble of safety, and that was her goal.

Sweat collected on her brow. She scooted over and repeated the treatment on the other window, finishing up by gingerly gathering the bigger chunks of wood, rock, and glass in the vehicle and wrapping them in a paper bag before shoving them under the seat. With a wet wipe, she sponged off all the surfaces she could reach. Done. The sterile scent made her feel better.

She checked Cullen's pulse again and found it strong. She cleaned his face and hands with a baby wipe. Then the angular planes of his cheeks, tanned, stubble speckling his chin. His fingers were long, strong, calloused from hard work.

Was his condition a temporary thing? She knew firsthand how a head injury could be a game changer. After the crash, she'd lost her entire memory of meeting Annette. What if he didn't wake up? There were no answers to her question in the formless miasma floating past the ATV, only fear unless she figured something out fast.

The one positive thing about their current predicament was that she was completely confident Nico and Simon hadn't followed them. Their best chance of escape had likely been to tear up the trail and get sideways of the lethal landslide. They might not even have made it that far. Determined not to think of Archie vulnerable and alone, or their murderous pursuers, she set to work returning the envelope she hadn't had time to investigate and the supplies as neatly as she could into the duffel bag. Tot was still relatively calm, sucking her pacifier and wriggling and stroking the teddy bear's fur.

There was nothing more she could do inside the vehicle. It was time to determine exactly how stuck they actually were. If the mill had created some sort of gap, a clearing in the debris field . . . if the tires weren't blown . . . if, if, if.

She opened a package and looped a medical mask over her ears and fit it over her mouth, then shoved open the rear door and got out. She immediately pushed it almost closed but not completely in case the door locks might malfunction. Instantly, her feet sank in several inches of debris, branches imprisoning her ankles. It was a shallow dusting compared to the massive bulk of the slide, but enough to make her unstable. Awkwardly, as if she were wearing snowshoes, she climbed to the front of the ATV. The view froze her in place.

Their position under the sturdy beams provided an oasis of clearance, a wedge of safety. Outside that defined space was a wall of wrecked trees and earth that still rose and fell as the mass continued to move downslope. It was as if they were a tiny toy boat secured by a thread in the raging ebb and flow.

Her breath caught. Cullen Landry had most definitely saved their lives.

Any other position outside the protection of the mill and they would have been crushed. Breath puffing inside her mask, she turned in a complete circle, her brain spinning and useless. They were alive, yes.

But where would they go from here? How would they

get there? The ATV, even if it was still operable, was walled up in every direction. Windblown ash stung her eyes.

She felt a wild sense of sorrow, the same sickening lurch that had flooded her soul when her father died before they could embark on their fanciful journey, and when she'd miscarried. It was twined with fury at the unnatural ending of things, a savage snip that abruptly severed a person from their purpose.

Purpose. The word felt like a taunt.

Up until the day before, she'd known her purpose absolutely: securing her independence with her truck, living her life on her own terms, interacting only with people she chose, when she allowed it. In the face of destruction, independence was a laughable goal and it crumbled away, leaving only unruly survival instincts. She'd never appreciated it, not really, God's gift of life. Each breath, every morning, the people who came and went, all gifts she hadn't savored.

One detour, one moment to help Annette . . . and everything had changed.

Now she certainly did appreciate that divine gift . . . as she stood on the precipice of losing it.

A memory flashed across her vision.

Annette, her neck craned up to talk to Kit through her open driver's window, the pink coat buttoned over a bulge that had thrashed and moved, her baby. *"His name is Nico. He kept me prisoner, made me into a . . . It's been years."* Annette's lips had quivered as she said the words, her cheap rhinestone earrings catching a beam of sunlight. *"I finally got away. I'm meeting someone, but Nico's after me, and if I don't get out of here fast . . ."*

She remembered herself saying with uncharacteristic impulsiveness, "*Get in.*"

Her moment of deviation from the plan had cost her the truck and her life, likely. But for some reason, she knew she'd make the same choice again, and she would continue to make choices to keep Tot alive until she was physically unable to do so. Because there was something more important than her goals and plans.

Infinitely more important.

A branch whirled by, flinging freezing droplets of moisture against her forehead. If she had to strap Tot to her body and climb over the cage of monstrous broken trees, she would.

But she couldn't leave Cullen. There was no way to manage them both. *What am I going to do?*

Her limbs shook with cold and fear, and sparkles danced around her. Tiny ice crystals were falling along with the ash as time slowly passed. It was going to snow? Now? How would she keep Tot from freezing? Herself and Cullen too?

She scanned the devastation, and an audacious idea ignited. There were plenty of sticks littered about if she could dry them out sufficiently. Jagged walls of brick stood not five feet from their trapped vehicle, within the perimeter of the safety zone provided by the bones of the old mill. She could make a fire within their meager oasis. The air was poisonous, sure, and there was no way she could keep Tot out in the elements for long, but maybe she could make a fire and warm them up as needed. When it got too cold in the ATV, they'd scuttle out with masks, then return to the shelter of the vehicle. Repeat as necessary.

Hour by hour, they'd survive.

There was also the slimmest chance a rescue helicopter would spot the flames.

That was probably pure delusion. Slim to no chance of rescue, and equally as slender a possibility that Archie would come looking for them.

Didn't really matter.

Unless she acted, they would freeze in that drafty vehicle, cold and exposure exterminating them, doing the job for Nico and Simon. But the brothers wouldn't get the envelope they'd risked everything for. That thought gave her a spark of satisfaction.

Back at the driver's door, she swiped a forearm across the sooty window to look inside. Tot peeked back at her over the top of the teddy bear. Safe and not screaming. In the back, Cullen had moved slightly but remained unconscious, crammed in the fetal position on a seat a couple feet too short for his frame.

To minimize the exchange of bad air for good, she edged to the back, quickly reached in and grabbed her pack and the bundle Archie had insisted they bring along, and then closed it again.

Archie's foresight would be a lifeline: a plastic-wrapped pile of logs, a neat firewood bundle, dried and ready.

Thank you, Archie. She prayed again that he was not suffering, wherever he was.

She moved slowly along, gathering some torn-away branches and chunks of wood that had tumbled into the vicinity. Hopefully they'd dry out enough to burn when Archie's supply ran low. How long? How many hours, days could she remain with limited supplies, a makeshift shelter, no medical care for Cullen . . .

Teeth gritted, she tossed the wood down in the brick corner and cut away the plastic wrapping with her pen-knife. She'd read plenty of articles about wilderness survival but nothing specific about the proper way to start a fire in the middle of a volcanic eruption. In a suitable spot she laid down a latticework of small pieces of wood and lit a match from the waterproof canister. It fizzed and flickered and flamed out before it caught the wood.

She added a few pine needles and tried a second match, but they did not ignite either. A third and fourth attempt reduced her to eight matches, which she was terrified to waste. Her pocket yielded nothing flammable but the map, and she couldn't commit that to the flames. *Come on, Kit. You have something that will work. Think.* She pawed through the pack until her fingers found a crinkly bag.

Doritos. She grinned.

A bit of ridiculous information gleaned from her father rose to the top of her jumbled memories. She pulled out the Doritos they'd taken from the store in Grandlake.

"Because who doesn't need some crunchy, salty cheesiness when you're outrunning a volcano?" Cullen had said to Archie while they meandered through the abandoned store.

Her fingers were cold and clumsy, but she managed to rip open the bag and arrange the chips in a precarious pyramid. The waterproof match shook as she struck it.

A flame sizzled to life, and she held it to the bottom of the chip pile. Just like the time her father had proudly done the same in their backyard barbecue, the edges of the chips blackened and sizzled and . . . to her immense delight . . . ignited. The odor of roasting corn seeped through her mask as she crouched to protect the flame from any wayward breeze.

Quickly, she fed in the smaller sticks from Archie's supply, and they reluctantly caught. When the fire appeared to have taken hold, she slowly added two bigger logs. The yellow flames danced in the gloom.

"Yes!" She thrust a fist into the air. "Do you see that? I did it. I made a fire out of corn chips. I am woman. Hear me roar!" The words were muffled, and there was no one around to hear them anyway, but she put her palms close to the fire and let the warmth seep in. She'd produced heat and they could survive, at least for a while until she figured out the next step.

Tot's thin wail carried over the sound of the crackling flames, bringing her down to earth again. The baby would need a bottle and a diaper change. And when the clean bottles and diapers ran out? The formula? She carefully rolled the top of the bag of chips and zipped it inside her pack.

"I'll figure it out. You just keep burning, fire." Now she was talking to flames. Swell.

Tot was working up to a painful volume when Kit returned. It was a relief to climb in and pull off the mask before she secured a premade bottle. It wasn't warm, not even close, since it had been in an insulated pouch. Tot turned her face away from the milk when Kit offered it.

"Please try, baby. It's all we have for now." Kit stroked Tot's cheeks. Cold, too cold.

Kit's stomach lurched.

She extracted the baby from the belt, unzipped her own jacket, and nestled Tot against her chest like Annette had done. She tucked the bottle in too, in one of her sleeves, hoping to take the chill off enough to tempt the baby. Tot cried, but as Kit's warmth spread, she settled into a pitiful whimper and mercifully closed her eyes.

Kit snuggled her close and kept vigil as the baby slept. Her own body floated in and out of a doze, and she lost track of time. Maybe it had been an hour, maybe two, when Tot started to fuss again, refusing to be placated by anything Kit could come up with. Kit swayed on the seat, side to side, trying to create a soothing movement, but Tot's crying intensified.

"You want your mommy, don't you?" Kit whispered. It struck her again that Tot and Annette might not be reunited in their lifetime. Annette could already be dead. Maybe Kit and Tot and Cullen weren't far behind. The freezing air seeped in through the taped windows.

Was Annette a good mother, she wondered? That young woman in the pink coat who looked so small holding her baby and the duffel bag, frantically waving down Kit's truck. She'd been willing to risk everything to get her and her child away from Nico. Annette doubtless knew all the tricks to comfort her child. Kit remembered her own mother reading Bible stories and showing her funny finger plays about steeples and the people inside. So much talk about loving and forgiving.

And so little evidence of it where her father was concerned.

Maybe some hurts were so grievous that only God could crack open the walls and let his forgiveness bathe the hearts inside. But wasn't it then the obligation of those people to forgive others?

A thought startled her. Wasn't it Kit's responsibility to love her mother in the meantime?

Tot rubbed her nose against Kit's collarbone.

Kit swayed and patted, looking in the rearview mirror at the rise and fall of Cullen's chest.

"Cullen?" she called. "Ready to wake up?"

Silence.

Tot whimpered.

"It's okay, baby." She looked out the window at the small orange glow from the fire she'd kindled. A few moments before she'd been crowing her satisfaction at the skies. Now the fire seemed pitifully insignificant in the sprawling ruins.

Tot started to scream.

To prevent herself from doing the same, Kit summoned the song that popped into her addled mind. It was the one her father had sung when they'd gone to see the local minor league team on blazing hot summer days when the bleacher seats were nearly free and they'd smuggle in their cheap bag of peanuts bought at the nearby grocery.

"*We gotta spring for the ballpark sodas, though,*" her father always said. "*There's nothing like a ballpark soda.*"

And there wasn't. The cheap cups sweating in their overheated hands, the ice melting into wafer-thin particles that crunched between their teeth.

"Take me out to the ball game," she sang softly to Tot. Tot didn't appear to like the song much, but Kit continued on about peanuts and Cracker Jacks. When she came to the finish, the lyrics evaporated from her brain.

Tot cried, and Kit tried again to recall the words. *Let me root, root, root for the home team . . .* But as she looked out into a day as dark as night, watched the toppled tree trunks sliding and locking together around their tiny oasis of safety, she simply couldn't remember the next line.

Why couldn't she finish the silly song?

Because you're alone with a stranger's baby and you're cold and hungry and scared.

And no one's coming.

No one.

And Mom will never know what happened to you.

A lump lodged in her throat, and her head began to spin.

Tot cried louder.

Tears blurred her vision, and her breathing came and went in irregular gasps. "Let me root, root, root for the home team . . ." But her throat locked away the rest as despair took its place.

A rumbly baritone started up in the back seat. "If they don't win it's a shame . . ."

Her mouth dropped open, heart slamming into her ribs as she twisted to look into the back seat.

Cullen was lying on his back, arm over his head, face bruised and swollen, one brow arched as he grinned at her.

"For it's one, two, three strikes you're out at the old ball game," he finished and then coughed and groaned. "Man, I love that song."

■ TWELVE ■

CULLEN HEARD CRYING as he finished the song. His voice was raspy and his entire skeleton felt cracked, but his soul caught fire.

Crying. Two people crying. Proof of life. Kit and Tot. *Both. Thank you, God.*

Head spinning, he was attempting to get himself to a seated position when Kit crawled awkwardly over the seat with baby Tot bundled in her arms.

She landed half on his shins and promptly kissed him full on the mouth.

"Cullen." Her voice was breathy with tears, the baby wriggling between them.

Sparks danced up and down his agitated nerve endings as she kissed him again, on each cheek and once more on the mouth. "You're alive."

He forced himself to push words past his clouded brain. "Never has my singing been so appreciated," he managed.

She laughed and cried, blushed, and scooted over so he could straighten on the seat. His head pounded and his vision spun, but he steeled himself. No way was he going to conk out again. Her chin was smudged with soot, her swollen eyes red from crying. But she was smiling, and there was a world of emotion in that smile, including a genuine fondness. Or maybe it was simply her relief that she wasn't stuck in an ATV with a corpse. Or simply his own hallucination.

Positive thinking, Landry. What if she actually cares about you? He was so happy to see her and Tot that he had to force the goofy grin off his face. Not the moment for it, surely, considering the circumstances. He cleared his throat. "How . . . are you? Hurt?" He held out his arms and willed them not to shake as he took Tot.

Kit wiped her eyes. "No serious injuries that I can tell. Tot certainly hasn't lost any of her spirit. But you . . ." She worried her lower lip between her teeth. "You were out for hours. Are you . . . wounded somewhere?"

More like everywhere. But he joggled the baby, melting as she snuggled herself under his chin, and considered what to tell Kit. "Shoulder's kinda messed up and everything hurts, but I can move my arms and legs, and I'm breathing. Don't see any blood on the seat, so I guess that's a good report, considering."

She offered a shaky nod. The confusion in his skull was clearing slightly. He babbled to the baby, filling up the silence, giving Kit time to steady herself since she wasn't the kind to air her emotions. His own stomach turned into a mass of knots as he looked past the baby to the ruins surrounding them. Nico and Simon weren't the most significant problem anymore. If he and Kit couldn't figure a way out, those two would never be an issue again.

And what of Archie? Her swollen eyes told him she'd

probably considered that too. Best not to bring it up. An orange glow caught his attention.

"Is that . . ." He peered out the window. "Is that a fire?"

Kit nodded. "Made it with Doritos." She explained her plan for keeping warm.

He shook his head.

"What?" she demanded.

He looked at her silhouetted there against a backdrop of pure catastrophe that would have overwhelmed many other women and probably most men too. Yet she'd tended to a screaming infant, taped over the windows, and made an actual campfire. "You are the bee's knees, Kit Garrido. Archie would be proud of you, and I am too."

She wrapped her arms around herself and looked away, her lips trembling. He couldn't tell if he'd pleased or embarrassed her.

"Thank you," she said quietly.

Pleased. She was pleased, and that pleased him, but not enough to dispel the worry. There was no way they were going to drive the ATV out of there. And minimal chance they'd be spotted by any search and rescue teams. It was as if they were blockaded by the tumbled logs framing the edges of the lumber mill that had saved their lives.

Trapped, sure as anything.

Could they hike out? He didn't think so, but he'd reserve judgment until he got better eyes on the situation. Tot squirmed against him. He felt her hands and feet. She was cold. Kit, too, by the looks of her pink nose and the way her breath turned to visible vapor.

His arms were too full to consult his phone. "What time is it?"

"Almost 2:00 p.m."

Practically a half day he'd lost. "Got any more masks? I think Tottie girl needs to warm up at the corn chip fire."

She provided a large one for him. With another she managed to knot the ear loops and slide it over Tot's mouth, which did not please her but at least it muffled her outrage. Kit took her while he unfolded himself and stepped out. His muscles spasmed so strongly he almost collapsed, but he balanced himself with a palm on the roof, and the worst of the pain passed.

Together they made their way to the soft glow. She rocked Tot and gave Cullen the bottle, which he held close enough to the flames to take the chill off. He didn't mind the warmth on his face one bit. Tot still cried too loudly to afford any conversation, which gave him space to try to think of an escape plan.

He scanned the shifting logs that still moved like a wooden river down and around the slope, diverted only by the sturdy walls of the mill. No driving out. Check. Hiking? It would be like trying to navigate a minefield. There was no way they could avoid broken limbs or worse with the unsteady pile all around.

Wait for it to settle? Then they'd somehow be able to climb over the massive logs and not sink into unseen holes and gaps. Kit was watching him, so he kept his expression neutral, though his heart was plummeting with each passing minute. The steel beams of the mill had somehow kept most of the walls intact and deflected the flow. Otherwise, the whole structure would have been swallowed by the landslide.

Funny how old craftsmanship could withstand what

modern buildings couldn't. Archie would have enjoyed pointing that out. He prayed his friend had somehow gotten clear.

Archie's gravelly voice replayed in his memory.

"Used to pretend I was one of Snow White's dwarfs when I'd pop out from behind the waterwheel and scare the workers."

The tunnel from Archie's childhood that connected his hometown to the mill . . . Was that even a possibility?

"You've got an idea," she said over Tot's outrage. "What?"

He decided to keep his thoughts to himself. No sense disappointing her with an option that was as flimsy as paper. But when she cocked her head and looked at him in that way that got right inside him, he knew he wouldn't disrespect her strength. Not after what she'd done, how she'd pounced like a lion on their difficulties instead of turning tail.

Kit patted Tot, who continued to wail, and waited for his explanation.

He stowed the bottle, took Tot, and pointed back to the ATV. Their boots crunched over the stone floor, accompanying the sound of Tot's screaming. Kit sat in the front seat, turned with her elbows over the headrest, and watched as he contained the flailing limbs long enough to change the diaper. Two dozen or so remained of the stash they'd taken from the store. Tot didn't appreciate the cold air on her exposed tushy, but he completed the mission and offered the warmed bottle. She clamped on, grabbing the bottle with both hands and sucking with all her might.

He chuckled and so did Kit. "Way to work that bottle,

Tottie. Don't let a little thing like a landslide slow you down."

"You're really getting good at the bottle and diaper thing," Kit said. "I think you should be given the job full-time."

"It'll look good on my resume."

Her smile vanished, and he knew she was waiting for him to share his plan. If it even was a plan. "Archie said that as a kid he played in an underground tunnel that the workers dug between the town of Twinfork and the mill. They used it to get to work without having to drive around the mountain, remember?"

Her eyes widened. "Yes."

"He said he'd get in trouble for popping out from behind the waterwheel."

She brought out the map. "Twinfork is here, or it used to be. Maybe it's far enough east that the landslide didn't take it out. If we could get there, find help . . ."

"Or even shelter, a phone signal, a working vehicle . . ." Pretty much anything would be an improvement over their current situation.

He loved the spark kindling in her expression, and he dreaded the thought of it being snuffed out again. "There are a lot of variables. The entrance might be sealed over or blocked. Even if we find it, the tunnel could have collapsed or the other end become impassable, and—"

"A dicey escape plan is better than no escape plan at all," she said firmly.

He couldn't argue with that, unless it got them dead quicker. "Soon as Tottie is done with her bottle, I'll go have a look."

"I'll help. We can take turns on baby duty."

"You'll be safer in the vehicle." He immediately recognized his mistake. "But you're in this as much as me and you cooked up the rockstar corn-chip fire, so why don't I treat you like a fully vested partner and not the babysitter?"

"Exactly."

The way her mouth lifted at one corner reminded him of Daniela. Two determined women, tough and self-sacrificing. He drifted into the past, to a moment when he'd been laughing and joking with his partner.

"Because I'm the best uncle," he'd said. *"And one day I'm getting Mia a pony."*

"You'll have to run that by my husband. He doesn't even want a house plant."

"Okay. Compromise. I'll keep the pony at the ranch I'm going to buy someday. She can come ride whenever she wants."

"Done. And you scoop the poop."

He realized Kit was looking at him. "Lost in a memory?"

"Oh. Yeah. My partner had . . . has a baby. Not a baby anymore. She's going on two now. I used to be real close, sort of an honorary uncle."

Each word of that conversation they'd had before their last traffic stop was etched in his brain. On that sweltering summer day, the temperature topping 102, they'd arrived first to examine the cargo truck abandoned on the side of a road, the rear tire flat. The plates came back reported stolen. He'd been content to wait with Daniela in their air-conditioned squad car until backup arrived, but something made him get out and approach the vehicle.

He found himself unspooling a story he'd refused to

discuss with anyone since the incident debrief. "I heard a sound, like fists pounding on the door, muffled, high-pitched screams." People. There were people inside that truck. He felt again the flood of adrenaline, the way his pulse had slammed into high gear as he'd run to get the battering ram from his vehicle.

"Daniela told me we should wait, help was only a few minutes out, but I didn't listen. I grabbed the ram to knock the padlock off the door handle. She was right behind me, backing me up even though she'd wanted to wait. I didn't examine the scene well enough. Guy had an explosive wired to the lock, and it blew. I got knocked out, but . . ." He breathed long and slow. "The ram flew backward and hit her, severed her spinal cord. She's a paraplegic now. Thanks to me."

Kit continued to look at him, but he couldn't maintain eye contact.

"Does she blame you?"

"No. The opposite. She has invited me to stay in Mia's life, sends me texts and cards, invitations to Christmas and birthday parties. Her husband feels differently, though. Caught me outside last time I visited and made his position crystal clear."

He'd stood on their front porch, knuckles raised to knock and a stuffed giraffe under his arm when the door had swung open. Ron was waiting for him, staring him down. He kept his voice soft so Daniela wouldn't hear, but each word clanged like a gong.

"Cullen, I don't care what Daniela thinks. You're not welcome here. You went all cowboy on that call. You had to be the hero, and now my wife can't walk. She's got to

take care of our baby from a wheelchair. Everything in our life has gotten exponentially harder because you couldn't wait five minutes."

He looked at Kit and let it loose. "Ron said, 'You're not the hero anymore, not in our story, so butt out. Daniela may not fault you, but I do, and I don't want you around my kid or my wife.' He slammed the door before I could respond. But there was nothing I could say anyway. So that was that."

He'd never told Daniela about the encounter with her husband, in order not to cause any more stress or pain in their marriage. Besides, deep down, he knew every word was true. Five minutes. He'd changed all their lives in five minutes.

Kit broke into his reverie.

"You didn't go back to being a cop because of what happened?"

He blinked, looked at his lap and then at her and finally at Tot. "Could have returned, but . . ." He let the comment trail away, tapped the bottle to get the last of the milk into Tot's mouth. "They got the women out of the truck, six of them, some barely into their teens. Several were injured from the explosion but not severely. One died later of heat exhaustion. They were being moved out of state for trafficking purposes."

Her nostrils flared. "Disgusting."

"Yes. The truck driver vanished, and whoever hired him wasn't caught either. Nobody got what they deserved." *Nobody.*

"Cullen, I'm sorry. That's a horrible thing to live with."

He didn't answer. What was there to say?

Kit's gaze drifted out the fractured window, roving over the devastation. "Do you think Nico and Simon escaped?"

He tried to peer through the sifting clouds. Though they couldn't see past the walls and the hideous pile beyond, he had a feeling deep in the marrow of his bones that the two had made it up trail before being caught in the landslide. "If they did," he said quietly, "I will spend the rest of my days hunting them down until they're locked away."

"I wonder what's in that envelope." She pulled it from the duffel while he put the baby to his shoulder. Gingerly, she removed the contents and scanned them.

"It's a series of pictures, ten, twelve, fifteen of them. All photos of young women, some very young. They all look so scared."

His gut began to burn.

"And . . ." Her voice pinched off. She tried again. "Nico's in each one, his arm around them, grinning as if he's taking a selfie with his girlfriend. It's vile."

They were silent a moment as she pulled the bottom photo loose. She gasped.

"This one is Annette. I know it is. I remember her face now, big eyes, high cheekbones. She's younger in the picture and she's terrified. Nico's smiling and she's scared to death." She flipped it over. "On the back of each one is a date, a name, and a location."

"Probably where the women were picked up."

Tot seemed to grow heavier on his shoulder, and he felt his soul sink. Annette had been snatched away by a monster, and she'd risked everything to save herself and this baby. What were the chances that they'd survive, Tot and her mother, to be reunited? The chance of a happy ending was plummeting with every moment.

That mental path wasn't helpful. He resettled the baby. "All right then. Tot's just about out. Allow me to take the first shift and hunt for that tunnel. I'll stoke the fire while I'm at it. You can keep my phone in case there's a satellite that happens to zip over in the next few minutes and beam us a signal. Fair?"

"Fair." She repackaged the photos with care.

He eased Tot gently to the seat and laid a blanket across her legs. Her earlier rage had left her tuckered out. She was cold, yes, but not hungry at least, and not wet. Best they could do.

"Here," she said.

He took what she offered. "Peanut butter cups?"

"You haven't eaten all day, right?"

"Have you?" he countered. "Eaten while I was enjoying my refreshing nap?"

She shook her head. "No. When I finally managed to get her to sleep, I was too afraid the crackling wrappers would wake her."

"Let me." He took the sweet from her. "My mom didn't allow candy in the house, so my brothers and I developed a massive black-market business trading our hidden loot. I honed some pretty good skills opening wrappers silently." He eased open the package a millimeter at a time and solemnly delivered one of the peanut butter cups.

She giggled. "I'll add 'stealth unwrapper' to the list of attributes I have for you."

"How long's the list?"

She ducked her head suddenly, shy. Well, well. Maybe

there was an actual list after all. He could certainly rattle off a lengthy set of her positive qualities at the drop of the proverbial hat. They clinked the candies in a mock toast.

"To you, Kit Garrido, founder of the feast and maker of fire."

She laughed. "And to you, Cullen Landry, crafter of escape plans, changer of diapers, remover of wrappers."

Amazing that they could joke, considering the enormity of what they were facing. He was still chuckling as he slid on his mask, snuck out, and closed the door softly. The chocolate and peanut butter tingled his taste buds and provided the burst of energy he needed as he picked his way across the littered stone floor. A quick moment to add another dryish log to the fire and then he moved directly to the waterwheel. Archie had been specific in his description, and the tunnel entrance would be near a wall, he figured, so the access wouldn't impede any of the machinery. Back corner?

Doubts began to assemble themselves in short order as he exhaled frigid puffs of air through the mask. In the decades since the mill had been abandoned, it was completely likely that it had been sealed up, cemented over, or collapsed. He cinched the rising hopelessness and tamped it down. Kit and Tot were alive and unharmed, and he wasn't going to throw that blessing away in the face of despair. He'd search until God made it clear there was nothing to find. He set to work.

The process was easy in some places where the walls and floors were clear of debris. On hands and knees, he shone his flashlight over every seam and crevice, going so far as to tap on the rock every few inches to check for a hollow sound that would indicate a tunnel. Shin bones aching, he turned his attention to the shorter side of the structure that abutted the waterwheel. Most of it was covered by piles of fallen bricks, particularly in the place where a massive trunk had landed, partially collapsing the wall. Everything would have to be cleared to get a proper look.

His hands were cold and stiff, and the work of removing the busted brick was arduous. A sprinkling of snow began to sift down, collecting on his shoulders as he worked, but he kept at it. The rough bricks bit at his palms. Work gloves. Why hadn't he packed a pair? Even knitted gloves would offer some protection. He had a pair of those in his gear, but it wasn't worth stopping to retrieve them and he didn't want to wake Tot or give Kit any false hope that he'd found a way out.

As he burrowed closer to the corner, flinging debris behind him, a squirrel shot out from the twisted branches of a shrub. He jerked back with a muffled holler. The animal raced up to a higher position and chittered at him. He blew out a breath. At least it wasn't a rat.

He wiped the sweat from his brow. "Sorry, squirrel. Didn't mean to mess up your den. I know we're all just trying to work with what we got at this point."

The squirrel continued to berate him from its perch. Poor thing had probably fled to the mill like they had, running for its life, but the lively critter was plump and bright-eyed so it must have access to shelter and a food source. He looked around to see if the squirrel had a family somewhere, and when his attention returned, the animal was gone, the ultimate vanishing trick.

"Where'd you go, buddy?" He moved closer, pushing

the branches aside and narrowly avoiding being poked in the eye.

"Progress?"

He jumped, turned to face Kit. "You scared me."

She peered at him over her mask. "Sorry. It's boring watching Tot sleep, and I got nothing with the phone. There's not enough sunlight to use the solar charger either. I figured it was okay to risk a quick progress check on you, since she's completely conked out."

Once he'd stopped moving, his nerves informed him that his back and knee were killing him and the headache clung tighter than ever thanks to his busted cheekbone. Plus he had no concrete progress to report, which hurt most of all. "You could have at least brought more candy," he quipped to cover his fatigue and discomfort.

"I did." She handed him another peanut butter cup and a bottle of water.

He arched a brow. "Already ate the other?"

She shrugged. "Like I said, watching a baby sleep is boring and I didn't bring a book to read."

He quickly crammed in the candy and gulped the water before slipping the mask on again and gesturing to the pile. "I've moved stacks of bricks and a cubic ton of rotted planking. So far I've uncovered a squirrel, and yes, I screamed like a preschooler if you must know."

She laughed, but her gaze was on the floor, roving the walls, scanning every crack and crevice she could find. Something snagged his thoughts. "Where did it go?"

He hadn't realized he'd spoken aloud until she answered. "Where'd what go?"

"The squirrel."

"I'll protect you if it comes back," she said.

"Ha-ha." He waded deeper into the ash-coated branches. At the back, the part of the mass that skimmed the brick wall, the leaves were protected and whole. It wasn't a bunch of blown-in foliage, as he'd first thought, but an actual shrub sprung up from the ground that had been there prior to the slide. That didn't make sense. There was no fracture in the stone floor here that he could tell, so where had the plant found soil to plunge roots into? Same place into which the squirrel had vanished?

Pulse thumping, he burrowed into the branches, found the slender main trunk of the shrub, and followed it. As he scrabbled his way to the source, his fingers found the answer first. At the base of the plant was a metal square, four feet by four feet. It was bolted into the stone, but a softball-sized spot in the corner had rusted away. Some opportunistic seed had tumbled into the crevice, set down roots, and headed for the sky. Plenty of room for the rodent to find shelter below as well and use the trunk as a highway to come and go as he pleased.

He whistled. "Would you look at that?"

Kit crowded in next to him, her shoulder soft against his. "Archie's tunnel?"

He put a palm over the compromised corner. "Feels cool, like there's air coming up from below."

Kit squeezed his forearm, and he clapped a hand over hers and returned the pressure, allowing her excitement to mingle with his own.

"The tunnel. It's gotta be," she whispered. "Oh my gosh, you actually found it."

He relished the admiration in her tone, but his optimism

was tempered. Finding a tunnel was a step, not a solution. He pointed. "The bolts securing this thing are solid iron. It's going to be a task to knock them loose."

"Then we better get on it." She was already prowling, snatching up a brick, shoving aside the branches that covered the trapdoor. Brick clanged against metal followed by a yelp as the brick broke to pieces in her grasp. "Well, that's not going to work."

He joined in her searching for something with more heft. The snow began to fall more steadily, and they were both shivering when his foot encountered something hard in a patch of slimy pine needles.

"All right," he cheered, grabbing up a rusted sledgehammer. "Back in the day, tools were built to last, that's for sure."

She watched, wide-eyed as he lugged the hammer over. "Sorry, squirrel," he called. "Fire in the hole! If you're down there, take cover." He swung the hammer like a golf club at the exposed top of the bolt. He felt every millimeter of the impact that ignited the pain clear to his skull and relayed it to every nerve and sinew.

The bolt stood firm. He clanged away again and again until it finally sheared off enough that he could kick it free with his boot heel. If he could get the other three bolts to do the same, he could lever the lid away from the opening. He was already sweating and puffing like a steam engine when Kit gestured for the hammer.

"My turn."

He opened his mouth, closed it again, and handed over the tool. She slammed away until she, too, was sweating. He thought she would give up when the bolt head sailed off and ricocheted against the bricks. Two down. Two to go. They took turns slamming at the third, but it remained stubbornly set.

He bit back a groan as he set down the sledgehammer. "Let's check Tot. Have some water and something besides candy."

"But . . ."

He shook his head, held firm. "We're both sweating and it's freezing. That's not a good combination." He checked his watch. "Almost four. We'll have two more hours of sunlight, if you can call it that."

Reluctantly, she assented, and they returned to the ATV to find Tot stirring. Kit tucked in the blanket around Tot while he tried to rest his quivering muscles before he rooted around in his pack.

"I'll make dinner. Should I fix up a bottle?"

"I already have a few premixed in the cooler, but maybe we should try to give her solid stuff when she's a little more awake. The bottle would be good later before bed, right?"

He pursed his lips. "Makes great sense to me."

She looked happy that he agreed.

"Back in a jiffy." At the campfire, he used his penknife to slit open the meal pouches and splash in some water before he nestled them near the flames. Probably not exactly to specifications, but he wasn't picky. Never, ever again would he take indoor heating for granted. Or running water. Or roads. Or mattresses.

When the packets were blackened, he yanked them free with a stick and let them cool until he could carry them by the corners. Snowflakes collected on his cap, so he shook his head like a dog before he hopped back into the ATV. Tot was sitting up in the front seat, gumming a graham cracker. He leaned over and kissed her on top of the strawberry cap Kit had managed to get on her head. It remained to be seen how long it would stay there. She chortled something at him that probably meant, "You look like a man who's on the verge of collapse."

He felt it too, in every complaining rib and joint. The fatigue was getting more difficult to ignore.

Kit joined him in the passenger seat, and he delivered his foil packets, full of steamy noodles that were still slightly crunchy. She provided two plastic spoons, and they dug in.

"Delicious." The steam from the packet curled around her cheeks. "Reminds me of the days . . ." She trailed off.

"Keep going," he said lightly, hungry to know more about her.

"I was married, briefly."

He hid his surprise. "Really?"

"We went backpacking a few times and ate camping food. Mitch was a whiz at cooking on the trail."

"A handy skill. How long were you married?"

"Six months."

"Ah." He was desperate to know more, to be the person she could confide in, but he knew enough not to push.

"I was young, just before I turned twenty-one." She ate another spoonful of crunchy noodles and stared into the gooey mess. "After a couple months, I found out I was pregnant."

Pregnant. Another surprise. Again he waited to see if she would continue.

"I didn't want the baby." She said it a shade too loudly, chin up and staring at him, reading his reaction. When he simply nodded, she took a breath. "Mitch had been acting distant, not coming home some nights, which he said was due to late business meetings, but I guess I knew the truth even if I didn't want to acknowledge it. In my fantasy world, I was hoping when I told him about the baby he'd light up, hug and kiss me, and say, 'Honey, this is the best news ever. You're going to be a great mom.' And then I'd believe it and start to feel happy about it too. I'd suddenly want to be a mother. All those feelings I was supposed to have would emerge." She twirled her spoon. "Does that shock you? That I wasn't filled with maternal feelings like other women? That's bad, right?"

She watched him intently. It was both a question and a statement, and he heard the well of fear in it, that he would condemn her as she'd condemned herself for years, he suspected.

He said a silent prayer that his words would be gentle, godly, true. "Not bad, Kit. That's honest. You were young. Scared and uncertain. How did Mitch take it?"

She grimaced. "That whole fantasy thing crumbled right quick. He told me he didn't love me anymore, that our marriage had been a mistake, and the baby was my problem to deal with. That was the second time I saw love fizzle like a blown-out match."

The second time. "Your parents?"

She didn't answer for a minute, lost in a memory. "After Mitch left, I went back to my mom's. I didn't have much choice since I couldn't manage the rent for our apartment by myself. She let me stay, but clearly she was disgusted. She'd never liked Mitch, told me as much. Said I'd regret marrying him, and though she wouldn't come out and say it, I knew that was how she felt about Dad. She rued marrying my father and I could tell I'd disappointed her every bit as much as he did. So I didn't tell her about the baby. I pretended there wasn't one. Worked. Slept. Ate. I saved up like a fiend and moved into a one-room rental as soon as I possibly could."

"You didn't have any contact with your father at that time?"

She shook her head. "Dad was convicted when I was seventeen. He'd call from prison and Mom would let it ring. Once I ran to get it, and she grabbed the phone from me and slammed it down before I could say a word. 'He's dead to me,' she said." The pain rippled across Kit's face. "I couldn't take it. I started yelling, throwing all the Christianese back at her. 'You say we're meant to forgive because God did, but you won't.'"

Cullen reached for her hand, and she let him take it. "That must have hurt so deeply."

Kit closed her eyes and dropped her chin. "Dad begged her to forgive him. I'd heard him crying and pleading before he went to jail. She told him he was going to get what was coming to him." Tears shone as Kit refocused on him. "This woman, this Christian woman with Scriptures on the walls and pillows and who never missed church . . ."

He squeezed her fingers, urging her to get it out, to relieve herself of the burden.

She sniffed. "On my eighteenth birthday, I packed and left. She didn't try to stop me. I was engaged three months later to Mitch, my high school sweetheart. After he dumped me and I left Mom's, I worked two jobs, grocery clerking during the day and cleaning hotel rooms at night. A regular grocery store customer owned a trucking business, and he said if I got my credentials in order he'd hire me. I studied, got my commercial driver's license, and started a training program. All the while I hid the pregnancy from everyone, even myself. I just kept saying, 'Work today. Worry about that tomorrow.' It was the only time in my life I didn't have a plan for what was going to happen."

Tot dropped her cracker and fussed until Cullen handed her a fresh one and she settled back into the seat.

"Dad got sick, had a stroke a short while after he was released from jail. He died in the hospital before I could get there. Mom forwarded his life insurance check to me. She didn't go to his funeral."

"Any contact with your mother now?"

Kit's expression softened. "I've tried hard, and she's done the best she can, I think. There's always . . . awkwardness when we talk on the phone, as if we both can't wait to finish and get off the line. It's a work in progress. Maybe she would have eventually forgiven him if he'd lived longer, but . . ."

He paused, weighing the question. "Your baby?"

She shrugged. "I miscarried in the second trimester."

"I'm so sorry."

She looked bewildered as she shook her head slowly. "I was, too, which came as a huge surprise. I didn't think I wanted the baby anyway. I was flirting with plans to put it up for adoption, so why would I be sad?" She hunched her shoulders. "I have this sense of guilt, that the baby died because I didn't want it enough."

"I'm not an expert, but miscarriages happen, Kit. They just do."

She looked at him, wanting more.

He prayed again because he suspected she'd never had this conversation with another living soul. "People lose babies all the time, people who are 100 percent sure they want them right alongside the ones who don't. Things happen on earth. It's messed up down here and that's certain. God knows that."

After a long pause, she nodded and blew out a breath. "Thanks for saying that."

He let go but leaned forward, holding her gaze. "Tell me the rest of the story, Kit Garrido."

"What rest of the story?"

"How you came to be the owner of that stylish rig?"

She smiled. "Nothing glamorous. Old-fashioned hard work. I invested what was left of my dad's insurance money. Ate ramen and beans for months and even lived in my car for a while to save money for the down payment. After I got the truck, I hung out my shingle and started my own business, which I've been building for years."

"Hard work and sweat equity."

"Absolutely. I did it right. Even if all that work is covered by a pile of lava by now." She blew out a slow breath. "Wish I'd . . . I dunno. Done some things differently. With people in my life, I mean. Tried harder with Mom. Let more friends close who wanted to be. I hurt some people by pushing them away."

He stroked his thumb along her wrist, soaking in the sadness that drifted like the falling snowflakes outside. "God forgives you for all that, Kit."

She arched a brow, as if she were trying to solve a logic puzzle. "You're not credible to say that though, are you?"

He goggled, straightening as he lost touch with her. "Not credible? Why would you say that?"

"Because you don't believe what you say, deep down. You don't live like it anyway."

Now she had his full attention. How had he communicated *that* message?

She didn't sound angry, only sad.

"I don't know what you mean," he managed.

She wiped the spoon and put it away. "I shouldn't have said that. Never mind. Too blunt. I have to work on that."

"Please. I want to know." He *needed* to know.

She exhaled. "Well, you say God forgives, but you don't forgive yourself, for what happened to your cop partner, I mean."

"I, uh . . ." How had the spotlight shifted so abruptly to him when they'd been talking about her life? "I know it wasn't completely my fault."

She wasn't buying it. "You tell yourself your actions gravely injured your partner and ended her career. You punish yourself by leaving a job you love and moving somewhere away from your friends and family. You are your own judge, and you've decided you're not forgiven. You. Not God."

The statement landed like an ember thrown onto a bed of parched grass. He felt the fire burning through his flimsy walls, the sweep of flames cleansing away the chaff. She was right, this intense woman bound to him in a surreal moment in time. He had refused to accept the gift God offered, his clutched fists holding on to guilt. The realization shocked him into speechlessness.

She shifted uneasily. "It's . . . probably not the moment, but after Dad died, I spent a lot of hours thinking about this. Long road trips with no one to talk to will make a person introspective. That's what I had to learn, with my mother. Whether she forgave my dad or not, that's on her soul. If a person can't accept forgiveness themselves, or refuses to give it to someone else, it puts them in the place of God, doesn't it?"

Puts them in the place of God.

Her face was gentler than he'd ever seen, and her tone was sweet, almost loving.

He wasn't ready to put it all together, but he knew in the quiet of his heart he had some reckoning to do. "You've . . . given me a lot to think about."

"I apologize if I offended or hurt your feelings." She cleaned her hands with a napkin. "Are you sorry yet that you jumped in to help this trucker with her wrecked rig?"

"Not for one single second."

The connection shimmered between them. Not for an instant would he choose to be with anyone else, anywhere else. He wanted to say more, to reach out and bring her to him, kiss her even, but she drew back, packing the trash away, agitation showing in her movements. He leaned against the door, wondering at his feelings. *Trauma bonding, Cullen. Remember that.*

She avoided looking at him. "So, um, Tot's finished her graham cracker and she's snoozing again. Better see what's in that tunnel because the peace isn't going to last."

The past few moments and hours were going to last, though. The truth, the kisses, the bubble of comfort amid the ruins. He'd nestle them deep.

Warmth radiating through his bloodstream, he followed her again into the whirling snow.

◼ THIRTEEN ◼

AS SHE AND CULLEN moved through the debris, Kit reeled at what she'd shared with him. She'd never told anyone about her miscarriage, or the complete story about what had happened with her parents. Even Mitch had only gotten a cursory version of the events that landed her father in jail. Certainly, she'd never had a deep conversation with anyone on the topic of forgiveness. Actually, she hadn't had many deep conversations with anyone about anything for as long as she could remember. Yet it had all come tumbling out. Now. With him.

And to top it all off, she'd actually expressed her opinion about his lack of self-forgiveness. She shivered at the recollection, and a cold stone lodged in her stomach. What was wrong with her? She'd overstepped, no doubt, and she wondered why it bothered her so much. Why was it important that Cullen refused himself forgiveness? And why did it comfort her to hear him say aloud what she already knew, that her baby hadn't been lost because she wasn't ready to be pregnant? Somehow, it felt comfortable and right to share her most vulnerable thoughts with him a few moments ago. Their struggles were common ground, and she'd been so eager to join him there.

Common ground. Surreal. She tried to shake off the prickly realization as they reached the tunnel hatch, where he picked up the hammer and whacked away at the remaining bolts. They had a job to do, and Mount Ember was in her death throes.

Collected soot streaked everywhere from Cullen's blows, and her eyes burned and teared above her mask by the time the third bolt gave way. The last stubborn one held on through fifteen strikes. At the moment she offered to take over, it broke loose with a ping. Elation blasted away her fatigue.

She could tell he was grinning behind his mask as widely as she was as he bumped his fist to hers. They reached for the edges of the metal plate and pried it loose, levering it aside. The effort took all their combined strength and left them panting. Together, the two of them stared at a black void punched into the earth. Could it be an escape?

Cool, musty air wafted up from below as they peered in. Kit held her breath. The darkness was impenetrable. Was the passage clogged with earth? Collapsed and impassable? Had all their efforts been an exercise in futility?

Cullen freed a flashlight from his pocket, laid on his belly, and shone it into the maw. She flopped down next to him, adding her light to his. The beams revealed a ladder, rusted in places but appearing intact, bolted into the walls faced in stone. The ladder vanished into the darkness, where their light could not reach.

Still no answers. Was it a passage to survival or a temporary delay until the final destruction of her fragile hope?

She'd been terrified all their hard work would reveal only a small storage area, but this was certainly more than that, yet the development held no promises, only uncertainty.

Cullen lit a match from their remaining supply and held it in the gap. The flame wavered. "There's some air circulating down there so it's gotta have room to move, right?"

She frowned. "If you say so."

"Please, I saw this in a movie once. Guy only had a match and an air sick bag, and he handled the wilderness tunnel like a champ." He fired that cocky grin at her. "I'll climb down and take a look." He was already sliding over the edge and two rungs in when she began to protest.

"I'm lighter. Maybe I should—"

"I'll ignore that rude comment about my girth," came his muffled reply. "You're the one that keeps plying me with candy."

"I'm not . . ."

But she was talking to no one. She couldn't even see the top of his baseball cap anymore.

Uneasily, she darted a glance around the wrecked mill. It was almost completely dark, the snowflakes mingling with the ash that dropped through the gaps in what had been the mill's roof. The only noise came from the leaves scuttling over the ruins. In the distance, the ATV was barely visible, and she felt every inch of the distance between her and the sleeping baby. Soon she'd have to hurry back and get Tot to the fire to warm her up. The solitude ate at her, and for a moment she considered what it would be like if Cullen didn't come out of that tunnel, if he fell and died or got lost in a subterranean labyrinth.

Then it would be you and Tot and no way out. Terror

214

churned her gut. "Kit, you have to keep it together," she scolded aloud. For herself and for Tot and for Cullen, whom she prayed would appear any minute with a thumbs-up and a hopeful report.

Seconds ticked into minutes. She hadn't heard a yell or thud. Surely he'd make noise if he fell, wouldn't he? *And then what exactly would you do, Kit? Climb down and carry out a six-foot man on your back?*

She jogged in place to keep her circulation going and the fear under control.

Something rustled in the logs outside. Maybe branches settling, wild creatures struggling to find their own shelter in the devastation, the wind tearing the remaining leaves from the fallen trees.

When she couldn't stand it anymore, she thrust her head into the tunnel entrance to call out just as Cullen crested the top rung. Their foreheads bumped, and she staggered back.

"Sorry," they both said simultaneously.

To cover her relief, she flicked on her light and held it steady while he crawled out. Her legs were rubbery. He stood, panting slightly, and she could not resist reaching up to brush a dry twig from his shoulder. The gesture turned into a tight hug, his embrace as needy as her own. She held him close, spilling out silent gratitude to the Lord that Cullen had returned in one piece.

"You were gone a long time," she managed, finally letting him go.

"Middle-aged knees." His tone was reassuring, as if he knew of the fear she'd tasted while he'd been below.

She steeled herself for his report, unable to read his expression.

"Good news. Tunnel was clear for the fifty feet or so that I explored. No indication it's blocked. Air's good too. Much cleaner than up here."

She heard his hesitation. "What's the bad news?"

He rolled his shoulders and exhaled. "Not bad, exactly. Cautionary. I mean, there's a reason the tunnel was sealed off from the public. This is risky business, Kit. Very risky. Climbing down with a baby's not going to be a picnic. If we manage that feat, we could travel for hours and come on a blockage we can't breach. The passageway is old and unmaintained. The walls aren't in great shape and there's water pooling, which appears to grow deeper from what I could observe. No telling what will happen down there."

"We're going to die if we stay, Cullen," she said flatly. "You know that as well as I do. We can't hike out of this place, not with Tot, and no one even knows we're in this area except Archie and a couple of killers." She held her voice steady. "I know we're both praying that Archie's safe and on his way to get help, but he might be trapped too, or . . ." She closed her mouth, unwilling to say the rest. "No one is going to find us in time."

"There's another option, Kit."

"Like what?"

"I can go alone. Try the tunnel by myself or trek out of the landslide area on foot."

She felt as if he'd shoved her, as though she were falling down that dark and treacherous tunnel. "You'd leave us behind?" Her voice quivered. He tried to take her arm, but she pulled away.

He shook his head. "I would go for help, while you stay safe here with Tot."

"Safe? Here?" She tried to moderate the shrill edge that crept into her voice. "Even if you do find someone crazy enough to be in the evac zone besides Nico and Simon, it might be weeks before you could get back to us. We're already running low on water. We won't survive until you return." *If* he returned.

His forehead furrowed. "It's not what I want either. Rock and a hard place."

She barely heard. "Plus there's the poisonous ash, unstable ground, venting gasses, any or all of which could kill you before you ever clear the landslide area." She ticked off the items on her fingers. "I hate your idea. It's . . . it's . . . silly."

He chuckled, and that made her angry. "Don't you dare laugh at me, you big galoot."

He did laugh then, but his expression was pure tenderness, and it melted her rage away. She swiped at a tear she hadn't realized had slipped down her face.

"I've been called a lot of things, but big galoot is a new one."

She let him reach for her now, pulling her into the circle of his arms. He felt warm, his embrace strong and steady against her trembling. For a moment, she let her cheek rest on his chest, listened to the steady beat of his heart.

"I know this is scary," he said.

She buried her face into his chest. "The only way we survive this is together." She squeezed his biceps. "Together, do you hear me?"

His embrace tightened, and he cradled her against him. "Kit, I'm not sure that's the best idea, but if that's what you want . . ."

She could not quite make herself say it to his face, the

raw truth that left her vulnerable. "That's what I want," she murmured to his shirtfront. "You, me, and Tot." They'd survive together, or they'd die together.

His ribs expanded in a massive inhale, and then his body relaxed. He put his mouth close to her ear. "I didn't really want to leave you two. The only reason I'd ever do it is if I thought it would save your lives. You know that, right, Kit?"

She stayed quiet.

He kissed the crown of her head. "Together. I got it."

She clung to him, realizing how much they now needed each other. Thrilling and terrifying at once.

Stop this foolishness, Kit. This emotion isn't real. She pushed away and shoved her hair back behind her ears. "All right, then. When do we leave?"

A flicker of disappointment crimped his brow, or maybe she was imagining it. He'd wanted something from her, an indication that he was more to her than a fellow survivor. "Wait until morning or go now?"

He considered. "No one's going to get a wink of sleep in that ATV tonight 'cept maybe Tot, so we might as well shove off. I can make a carrier out of her blanket and ferry her down on my back. We'll have to put all the supplies we can carry in the duffel and our two packs, prioritize water, food, my external phone battery, Tot's stuff."

They walked back to the ATV. All was still and quiet, save for the sporadic movement of the debris. Every few minutes there was a crack from a trunk snapping under the massive weight of the flow. The noise sounded like the breaking of bones. Cullen set to work on fashioning a sling, and she perused their supplies.

The redistribution of the goods soothed her nerves,

though there was so much they'd have to leave behind. With concentrated effort, she managed to include all of the food and water and some of the extraneous supplies, but there was simply no room for extra clothing to supplement the meagre bundle she'd already squirreled away. To be on the safe side, she stowed the proof against Nico in a second plastic bag fastened around the first and slid it into the waterproof pocket of her backpack. The packs were heavy, too heavy, thanks mostly to the bottles and pouches of water, but there was no guarantee when they'd be able to resupply. Tot's duffel was filled to the brim as well, and she couldn't think of anything else to eliminate. What would happen when the clean bottles ran out? The formula? The water with which to mix it? Her fingers grazed the stuffed bear.

She pulled him to her chest, suddenly fighting tears as she fingered his torn ear. *It's just cloth and stuffing. It doesn't even smell like Dad anymore.* She rubbed her cheek against the toy.

There was only space for the absolute essentials. She laid him in the ATV, blinking hard against her foolish tears. She felt movement behind her.

Cullen reached in and plucked the bear out and handed him back to her.

"We're taking the bear."

"No space," she squeaked. No room for silly sentimentality. The toy was useless, and they had not a square inch to spare.

When she didn't move, he edged her out of the way, unzipped the duffel, shoved the neatly packed contents over, and crammed in the bear. He had to hold the sides of the bag together in order to zip it closed. "See? Fits fine."

Tot chattered from the front seat. "Uncle Cullen's coming, Tottie girl." He hastened off.

The tears did slide down her cheeks then, while he was busy fiddling with Tot. He'd packed her bear. If she was going to love any man on this planet, she was certain it would be Cullen Landry. But that thought, and the pinballs of emotion whizzing around her insides, would have to wait, maybe forever. She went to Cullen's side.

"Project strap-on-the-baby begins now," he said, holding out a blanket that he managed to tie around his waist. "Hold her up to my back while I hitch the corners around my shoulders. I'll need both hands to climb down. It's about thirty feet to the bottom."

She used the blankets and some zip ties to tether Tot to Cullen in a sort of reverse kangaroo pouch before she wrestled the baby inside. He did a few knee bends. "Feels secure."

"It better be."

Tot screamed, not comforted by the offered pacifier.

"I'm going to lose a whole range of hearing," Cullen said, wincing as Tot wailed on. A graham cracker offering didn't work either, so Kit brought out the big guns.

"Tot." She waved a wafer cookie in front of her button nose. Tot's hand shot out and grabbed it. The screaming turned to satisfied sucking.

Kit laughed. "You're going to be covered in cookie mush very soon, but at least she's not hollering in your ear."

"An acceptable trade-off," he said. "How about we dally for another few minutes to warm the bottle by the fire before we go? I can stick it in my pocket to at least maintain a bit of heat if she's not ready for a while." He tugged her foot, chubby from the two pairs of socks Kit had put on her. "Princess Tot, will you take to that better? Warm milk to go with your cookie?" he asked over his shoulder.

Tot let out a gurgle of pleasure, grinding her tiny teeth into the gummed cookie. She should probably be wearing a mask instead of snacking, but Kit didn't see how she would be calm enough to leave it on. They had to keep her as still as possible while he climbed down.

He gave Kit a thumbs-up. "While you were changing her, I fixed up two meals we can carry with us, warmed them on the campfire. They won't stay hot, but maybe the noodles will actually cook this time. I guess it'll be our breakfast later since . . ." He trailed off.

Since they might not be able to cook any more food in the foreseeable future. Since it was possible they were about to climb down to their deaths.

She stuck the meals in the outside pocket of her backpack before she gave Cullen the warmed baby bottle. Tot grabbed for it.

"Well, okay, a drink before we hit the trail," Cullen said. Kit offered her a few gulps.

Tot let out a loud burp.

He laughed. "Don't yak on my shoulders if you need to spit up, Tottie. I don't have an extensive replacement wardrobe, now do I?"

The duffel bag and backpacks bulged with supplies. Cullen shouldered the duffel, and she lugged the others from the cargo area. She felt a pang as she closed the ATV's doors for the last time and gave the vehicle a pat. The metal contraption had kept them alive, along with Cullen's expert driving and the shelter from the lumber mill. She imagined it almost had a personality of its own, like her truck. She turned away resolutely.

The tunnel would be their safety now, she prayed. It had to be.

As they trudged past the campfire, she scraped a layer of dirt with her shoe and kicked it over the flames.

Cullen chuckled. "Because you're worried about starting a forest fire?"

They both scanned the landscape for a moment, the sprawl where there had once been a majestic army of trees. Now it was a pulsing moonscape of desolation. It would take decades, if not centuries, to regrow what Mount Ember had wiped away in a blink. How many lives had it taken already? Archie's? Annette's? Was poor John still lying in the dirt, face turned to the sky he could no longer see?

She smothered the flames because she could not walk away from a burning fire, no matter what the circumstances. As she turned to follow him, something flickered up the slope where the slide had originated. She froze, staring through the dust-thickened air.

Cullen turned and joined her, instantly alert. "What did you see?"

She squinted. Snowflakes and cinders dampened the feeble light until the sun vanished fully behind the hills, leaving them in an eerie gloaming. "I don't see anything now. I thought I noticed a flash is all. A dot."

"Where?"

She pointed.

"Could it have been from a flashlight?"

Her heart thudded. "Maybe, or it might be a figment of my imagination." Her senses were addled, her body tired, nerves stretched to the breaking point. Had she seen something? Her eyes were as overwrought as the rest of her.

He gestured for her to turn and pulled the night vision binoculars from the pack she had slung over her shoulders. He scanned while she held her breath.

"Anything?"

He shook his head. "Nothing I could make out."

An idea made her breath catch. "What if it was Archie? He made it and came back to search for us." She scanned frantically, praying she'd see the old soldier signaling them of his presence. Cullen's next comment burst her excitement.

"He was headed in the opposite direction. He wouldn't have had time to turn around and come back looking for us by now. Not to say it couldn't be someone else, though."

The someone else would be two determined killers, relentlessly pursuing them for the envelope she'd tucked carefully in her pack. The thought of them made her blood simmer. "Nico and Simon would've given up by now," she said firmly. "They'd have to be insane to risk their lives out here when it's practically a guarantee that the volcano will do their dirty work for them."

Cullen's eyes narrowed. "Unless Nico saw that we made it to the mill. They were already looking for us in the hollow when the slide happened."

"But even if they did, they wouldn't know about the tunnel. That's certainly not visible to anyone outside these walls. It's tucked back behind the ruins and a bunch of foliage. As far as they know, we're stuck and we'll die before help reaches us."

His expression tightened. "Guys like that will watch

to make sure. They don't leave much to chance, and they don't like waiting around."

"Cullen, this is the worst motivational talk ever," she snapped.

He cocked his chin. "Sorry. Probably there's no one out there. And anyway, they can't take a vehicle down here to get us with the fallen trees and debris everywhere. They'd have to hoof it, and that'd take a long time. We're safe."

From pursuers, maybe. What lay before them was most certainly the polar opposite of safe. Climbing into a dark tunnel without knowing for sure where it led or what conditions they would experience was the definition of reckless in any other circumstances. It made her skin crawl to think it through.

They lingered for a few more moments with no further indication that anyone was watching. If it was indeed a watcher she'd seen, she prayed it was Archie, safe and sound, and he'd have the good sense to give up the search and get himself up the trail to safety. Just because Cullen didn't think it could be Archie didn't mean she had to agree.

But if it was him and he'd made his way up the trail to try to find them in the debris field, wouldn't that lead him to the exact position Simon and Nico would have taken to escape the landslide? Would they run into each other? Thoughts chased each other around in dizzying circles.

Maybe we don't add onto the worry stack right now, okay, Kit?

Cullen took her hand. "We have to go. Tot's started on the second cracker I handed over and I need her to be relatively still while I'm on the ladder."

She nodded and followed him to the tunnel hatch. Tot

remained mercifully quiet, graham cracker jammed in her mouth, snuggled against Cullen's back. She was probably comforted by the warmth of his body in addition to her sweet treat.

"Do me a favor, Kit?" Cullen pointed. "Wrap the sledge-hammer in one of our shirts to cushion it and drop it down, would you? Soil at the bottom is soft. We'll pray it doesn't break."

"But we've got so much to carry already, why . . ." Her question died away. "Oh. Because the tunnel is likely bolted shut on the other end too."

He nodded.

Unless they could wrench loose the barrier on the distant end, they'd be stuck in the dank passage, worse off than they were at the present moment. Her throat was suddenly constricted as she wrapped the sledgehammer and dropped it into the abyss. Again, she held the flashlight while he gingerly turned around and started down the first few rungs.

"When I get to the bottom, I'll get clear and yell. You can lower the gear. If you get stuck or need help, whistle and I'll hustle up the ladder again to assist."

She huffed. "I'm fine on a ladder, Cullen."

"No question, but the rungs are rusty and there may or may not be an angry squirrel on the premises."

It was the smile she needed. *Bring it on, squirrel.* "I'm not scared of rodents."

"Okay. Just saying."

Soon a halo of darkness wrapped around them both as he descended. Tot's half-moon cheek caught the meager flashlight beam, smudges of graham cracker streaking her mouth. So small, so impossibly young, strapped onto

Cullen as they sank farther and farther into the gloom. Kit's heart squeezed as she considered the list of things that could happen.

Cullen could fall.

Their makeshift baby carrier might come unknotted.

The rungs could give way or Cullen could step down onto an angry animal.

Breathe.

Teeth gritted, she watched until the crown of his baseball cap was all she could see. One, two, three seconds more and it was all inky blackness.

After he'd been swallowed up, she pressed herself to the ground, ear to the edge, and listened to his movements growing fainter, the scuff of his boots against the aged metal. Her fingers ached, and she realized she was gripping the flashlight way too hard. With a deep breath, she relaxed as much as possible, her ears straining for Cullen's signal.

When her neck and shoulders began to cramp, she crouched instead. Through the fractured mill wall, she sought the horizon, a black zigzag against a lighter charcoal wash. No more flickers of light. The daytime was finished, and they'd survived it.

Anyone out there?

She wasn't sure if it was more comforting to think the answer was yes or no.

A rustling sound floated up to her. "I've hit bottom. Give me one minute." From far below came the tiniest glow. Cullen had turned on the small lantern. Not much help, but a comforting target for her, which was probably his intent. "Baby's out of the way. Lower down the gear."

She tied the rope to the bags, hitched it around a sturdy

column of bricks and lowered the backpacks one after another using the plan they'd discussed. They couldn't risk dropping the gear and having the precious water bottles explode.

"Okay. Cargo received. Head on down, Kit."

His tone was cheerful, as if he were inviting her to stop in for a movie or coffee. To keep her mind off her perilous descent, she figured. How would that be, to spend time with Cullen in a nice, civilized environment where they weren't fleeing an erupting volcano and human traffickers? Would she still feel such a magnetic attraction to him? A week ago, she wouldn't have so much as entertained the notion. The truck, her business, was her sole focus, and relationships would only be a distraction. Now, she could not ignore the appeal. She liked Cullen. A lot.

Her knee knocked against a bent steel rung. *You'd like anyone who was helping you survive, wouldn't you?*

She wasn't convinced. There was something about Cullen—his mixture of goofy and gallant, silly and serious, his honest struggles with his faith and his foibles— that whispered to her heart.

The rungs grew damp in her grip. Even the air around her felt heavy with moisture, as if the walls themselves were weeping. A rhythm, that was what she needed, one that left no room for thinking. Foot, hand, foot, hand. Repeat. The small light Cullen had activated appeared impossibly far away, though she had to be getting close.

The metal groaned and creaked. The aged rails she clutched as she descended felt sturdy enough. Probably just noise.

She continued on. Foot, hand, foot, hand.

"You're doing great," Cullen called up.

Ladders were child's play. She'd been climbing them since she was six years old, helping her father pluck the ripe peaches from Mom's precious backyard tree. The climbing wasn't worrying, it was the small tremors she detected. The ground moving? Her body shivering from the cold? The metal giving way under stress?

Peaches. Think of the peaches. She could practically smell the enticing aroma of those succulent fruits, bursting with sticky sweetness from their fuzzy skins.

The perfect one, to your right there, Kitty Kat. You got it, baby. Yes, sir. That one's a beaut.

Because she wasn't strong enough to balance a basket of heavy fruit, she'd pluck the peaches and drop them carefully down into her father's waiting hands. If he missed, there was hilarity as he danced as if trying to avoid exploding peaches.

Laughter. She remembered laughing so hard she had to cling to the prickly trunk to avoid losing her balance.

It was her mother's voice she heard in her memory then, a glimpse of her full-cheeked face laughing at her husband and child. *"That's enough for ten pies."* No anger then, her expression was soft and loving, not hardened into bitter lines of disappointment. It had been a long while since she'd enjoyed a happy memory of her mother.

Next time I call, we'll talk about the peaches, Mom.

If there was a next time.

Foot, hand, foot, hand.

The groaning grew louder, rising into a squeal of metal that became a shriek.

"Kit!" Cullen shouted up at her as the rungs gave way under her feet.

◼ FOURTEEN ◼

HE TORE OFF HIS MASK. "Hold on! I'm coming!" he shouted. The ladder trumpeted its failure in a scream of twisting iron as the lower portion gave way. His nerves were electric. Kit swung by one wrist in a desperate clutch. Caught by his lantern light as he surged forward, she flailed, fighting to grab the section still fixed to the wall and succeeding, but a moment later that rung split too.

She clung tight. He thought he could reach up and snag her, prevent her fall, but the distance was too great and the entire ladder yanked free from the wall, crumbling, pelting him with rusty flecks.

Amid the shower of material, he tried to position himself to catch her. Too late. Too slow.

She cried out as she catapulted toward him. He had no other thought than to keep her from striking her head or breaking a leg, but she was turning and twisting as she toppled and he couldn't judge the angle properly in the gloom.

She hit him like a cannonball in the center of his sternum. Unable to compensate, he careened over backward, forcing the breath out of his lungs and sending his hat flying. Pain sparked through him. Fortunately, she'd only fallen ten feet or so, but they still wound up in a tangled pile on the earthen floor.

He cranked his head up to see her, sprawled half on top of his chest, the crown of her head inches from his chin. "Are you okay?"

She breathed hard, hair swept over her eyes so she peered at him from under a curtain of bangs. "I was about to ask you that."

"Totally fine," he said in utter disagreement with his screaming ribs and protesting spine. Her elbow had caught him in the cheekbone, but since he already had a blackened eye from Nico, it hardly mattered. She eased off him and got to her knees, took stock a moment, then stood before offering him a helping hand he was not too proud to take. It was a long way to standing, but he managed with only a brief groan.

"You didn't hit your head?" Last thing they needed was another injury on top of the concussion she'd likely received in the truck crash.

"No." She peered more closely at him. "Are you sure I didn't hurt you?"

He forced himself to straighten. "No worse than high school football double sessions."

"I'm glad. And relieved." She spoke shyly. "Thanks for breaking my fall. But I would feel really bad if I hurt you."

Her earnest comment eased the aching places. He brushed the debris off his pants, hiding his face, which would no doubt betray his pain level. Years of wear and tear from police work and his four decades were beginning to catch up with him. His pride spoke up. *Nothing a hot shower, a double cheeseburger, and a quality mattress won't erase.*

She scuffed a broken ladder rung aside with her boot as she looked around. "Where's Tot?"

Tot answered Kit's question before he did. She released a long, plaintive yowl that bounced and echoed from a yard or so down the tunnel where he'd laid her in a spot of relative dryness. No doubt the cold was seeping through the thin fabric of her blanket. He was still trying to restore his lungs to full working capacity, grateful when Kit busied herself scooping up the baby and holding her close.

"Dark down here, isn't it, Tot? But the air is so nice and clean." Kit pulled her mask down. "Let me warm you up, okay?" She kissed Tot's furrowed brow, which quieted the hollering and seemed to please Kit. "I'll carry her for a while."

He didn't argue. Those two had created quite a bond. All of them had. Kit had deep feelings for her two traveling companions, even if she wasn't the type to speak about it. *"I would feel really bad if I hurt you."* He was more and more convinced that the warmth he felt from her wasn't simply due to the incredible circumstances. Archie would have winked at him and said to quit "jimmy jacking around already" and pin her down on the subject.

Patience, he told himself. The right moment would present itself. *Tunnel, remember?* They had a long, scary, uncertain passageway to traverse.

Maneuvering the baby into the blanket carrier on Kit's back gave him more time to take stock and conclude that none of his major body parts had been broken, lacerated, or cracked. When Tot was properly cinched, sucking on her binky, he collected the two backpacks and the duffel and shoved the sledgehammer in his pack, trying not to give too much attention to the extra weight that yanked on his bruised ribs.

"I hope we don't have to use that."

"Me too, but if we have to bash our way out of anything, it'll be worth it."

Kit pointed to the outside pockets of her pack. "Look in there."

He didn't ask for what, simply rooted around and pulled out two head lanterns on elastic straps.

"From Archie's supply. Batteries already in them," she said. "Thought it'd be easier than handheld equipment."

He smiled. "Remind me to take you along next time I'm trapped in the wilderness, Miss Kit."

She didn't reply, but he thought she looked happy at the compliment. She deserved it. The woman had survival skills, a quick mind, and enough grit for a dozen people, and they were going to need all the fortitude they could muster between them. He strapped the elastic band around his baseball cap and turned it on. She did the same with hers. For a moment, neither one of them spoke as they took in their surroundings.

Ahead stretched what looked like an endless conduit, a highway of unrelieved black. There was no sound save a distant dripping. The ground was rutted in places, and he could imagine the hardworking men who had tromped their way to and from the mill, calloused fingers, muscles strong as iron, uncomplaining about the bone-chilling damp they must have endured. Pockets of moisture glittered in the distance, water seeping in from parts unknown.

"It has to lead somewhere," she murmured.

It had led somewhere, once upon a time, likely to Twinfork where Archie had grown up. Was it still a viable route? He double-checked the blanket knots tethering Tot to Kit's trim waist.

Satisfied, he squeezed her shoulder.

She twisted to look at the spot where the ladder had been.

He knew what she was thinking, but she spoke it aloud anyway, her voice oddly dampened by the closed-in space.

"I guess climbing out and returning to the ATV isn't an option anymore."

"No, it's not. Simplifies things. We only have one choice now. Go forward and get to the other side."

He wasn't sure if it was a ripple of determination or fear that made her lips quirk before she turned away. The thread of illumination from her lamp marked their path, and he joined his beam to hers.

He checked his watch—a few minutes after 7:00 p.m. He remembered when he'd babysat Mia that she didn't get put down to bed with bottles because of tooth decay, but Daniela made sure to change and offer a snack or milk before bed for optimal sleeping. Did the bottle they'd provided before they left count as her pre-bed bottle? Did she need more snacks than the cookie that was still smeared on the shoulder of his jacket?

He longed for Archie's advice, or at least his Marine Corps ingenuity. He'd possibly have some sort of notion about how to climb back up to the mill regardless of the

busted ladder. But would that be the right choice? Returning to the ATV? What was happening to the Cullen who
instinctively knew the best way to proceed?

He firmed up his steps and edged a pace in front of Kit.
The ceiling was low, but he could still move fairly comfortably without slumping too much, so he was confident Kit
and Tot would not hit their heads on anything.

Tot was surprisingly quiet as they marched along, seemingly fascinated by the play of lights in the dark. Not a
worry in the world, he thought, completely unaware of
what they were risking to keep her alive.

He was happy that she didn't understand their present peril, or what had happened to her mother. God had
somehow kept Tot safe to this point. *And he'll help us see
this through, Tater Tot. Don't you worry.*

The noise of the dripping grew louder as they walked,
and the ground began to slope upward, ever so slightly.
He prayed it meant they were traveling toward the surface.

A sudden tremble shook the passage, and he grabbed
for Kit's hand, pulling them against the tunnel wall. Not
much protection if the thing caved in, but something.

A fist-sized rock flung itself loose and landed near his
left boot.

Her body was as tense as his.

Life or death? Which would it be?

Faith, not fear. He fought the urge to close his eyes. No
way would he flinch. He'd stare into that darkness and
defy it, for all three of them, until God decided it was
over. He held her close and they waited, a strand of Kit's
hair tickling his brow.

Imperceptibly, the movement died away.

He released her and chucked Tot under the chin. "A little shake, is all." Her skin was cool. "Another half hour, and we should stop for snacks. Try to warm her up."

Kit sighed. "Traveling with a baby is slow."

"Particularly in an underground tunnel." The passageway narrowed in some places, pinched down to the point where he walked with his neck bowed and guided Kit through sections with his palms on her head and Tot's to prevent injury. They squeezed through a particularly narrow juncture, and his lungs tightened as he considered.

What if the way becomes too narrow for us to pass?

He mentally scoffed at the idea. If full-grown lumbermen could do it, so could they.

Unless it had become blocked.

He thought of the fury unleashed by Mount Ember, the landslide that almost killed them. Wasn't it probable that had unsettled the tunnel too?

The way was definitely damper now, fissures forming irregular ridges in the stonework. He flicked a look high up at something that had caught his eye and nearly convulsed. "Did you see that?"

Kit stopped, staring at the place where he pointed. "Where?"

"Above us. Something crept along that ridge up there where the water's dripping."

"An animal something? Your squirrel?"

"Nah." He beamed the headlight and clenched his jaw. A scream bubbled out of him in a decidedly unmanly volume. "It's a rat." He grabbed her forearm and swiveled her in line with the exact spot. "There. There's a rat right there, big as a cat."

She looked closer, squinting. "Oh, I see it now. I'd say it's more hamster size, though."

He now understood what it meant to have your skin crawl, because his was writhing in disgust. Spiders, snakes, even scorpions he could handle. But rats . . . The scaly tails, silent paws, yellow teeth. *Defense*. What could he do? He snatched a fallen rock. "Don't worry. If it comes close, I'll take it out with this."

"The rat is not interested in us, Cullen. It's got a nest up there, which means we're probably getting closer to the surface. They'd have to live near food and water, right? Nothing grows down here for them to eat." She paused. "The rat is a good thing."

He pulled in a breath through his nose. "A rat is never a *good* thing." He realized she was giggling at him, and he tried to force himself to relax a notch. "What? So I'm not a fan."

She was laughing harder now, both of Tot's hands clutching fistfuls of her hair. "A big, strapping ex-cop is afraid of rodents? Yelping like a kid?"

He did not slacken his grip on the rock. "Tons of individuals would agree with me on this point, Kit."

"You're overstating to distract from your terror."

He chose to ignore the word. "I'm not. That thing probably has hundreds of relatives waiting in the wings. Who would be okay with that situation? No one. No one at all."

She continued to giggle.

Miffed, he went on. "List for me the people who would be fine traipsing along a tunnel filled with creatures that live in sewers, probably teeming with rabies. It'd be a short list, I'll tell you."

"It's actually pretty rare statistically for a small rodent to have rabies," she said, between spurts of chuckles.

How much did the woman read, exactly? She was a walking encyclopedia. "Rodents are vermin," he said as calmly as he could. "Haven't you ever heard of the black plague?"

"The plague was transmitted to humans by the fleas on the rodents, technically, not by the actual rats themselves."

"That's hardly a comforting factoid, and anyway, the rats might scare Tot." Well, now he'd lost it. There was no saving his ego.

She held up a palm, her giggles subsided. "All right, Cullen. Whatever you need to tell yourself to get through this. I'll go first with Tot, and you can keep watch for a rat ambush. Can you live with that?"

He opened his mouth and closed it. "Now I'm coming off like a chicken."

She smiled and tugged the brim of his baseball cap. "Totally, but a really handsome, six-foot-tall chicken."

He could not stop the grin. "You think I'm handsome?"

"The best-looking chicken I've ever met."

"Thanks." Ego thoroughly checked, he flattened himself against the tunnel wall. "You two go. If it makes a move, it's going down."

Her giggle bounced and echoed in the passageway, and he was sure he was never going to hear the end of his cowardice. Rock in hand, he smiled. He didn't mind being the source of merriment for Kit, but he fisted his weapon tight anyway, shoulders to the wall so he could keep the rats in his field of vision in case of a rear attack. He didn't fully exhale until he'd edged by with no incident.

Rats behind him, he moved closer to Kit and Tot. A gradual bend brought them into a damper area where they had to tiptoe around small puddles that trickled into larger ones. Water oozed through cracks in the stone walls. Ominous? Or did it indicate they were moving in the right direction?

Minutes bled into hours, or so it seemed to Cullen as they trudged through the void. The clammy chill felt ever more oppressive the farther they traveled. It was almost ten when Tot began to fuss.

They had to continue on for another fifteen minutes before they came upon a stretch that was relatively dry with the added benefit of a couple of rocks that could act as seats.

Cullen lifted Tot off Kit's back. The bottle in his pocket wasn't warm, but his body heat had at least kept it tepid. With a painful effort, he eased down on a stone and offered the milk, which Tot took after a couple rejections, swallowing only a few ounces before refusing any more.

"Oh Tottie. You're tired of this dark place, huh? Me too." He asked Kit for a handwarmer, then wrapped it carefully in his spare knit cap before he nestled it near her tummy. She wriggled, but he distracted her with a graham cracker. There was no way he was going to risk cereal bits falling all over and enticing the rat brigade. His ribs throbbed with a steady pain now that he was stationary, the muscles tightening with the cold.

Kit unwrapped some protein bars and gave him one, which he ate with his free hand. She followed that up with a water bottle. His throat was parched, and he would have happily downed the whole thing, but there was simply no way to tell how much farther they'd have to travel. A couple sips would do.

Kit turned off her headlamp, and he did the same after activating the handheld lantern, which did little to dispel the heavy darkness. They listened to the steady rippling water and the quiet shushing, which he sincerely hoped wasn't caused by rat activity.

She gazed at the way ahead of them. "Feels like we've been hiking for days. Did Archie mention how long it took him and his friends to get home through the tunnel? Or how many miles it extended?"

"If he did, I sure don't remember." He tried to shift to one side on his rock seat to ease his aching bones.

Kit sighed. "I wish he was here with us."

"Me, too, only I'd be in trouble about the rat thing."

"You're still in trouble over the rat thing," she said with a laugh.

He enjoyed the way her laughter surrounded him, enveloped him, cheered him even in this dank place. "Yeah. Might just ruin my whole rep."

With Kit holding Tot and him the diaper, they managed to change it and get her dressed again. He draped Tot over his shoulder with the handwarmer sandwiched between them. A tight circle of patting and walking did the trick, and she grew heavy in his arms. Kit tied her on Cullen's back, and they set off again, headlamps on. He didn't feel too refreshed, and he was still thirsty. Kit must have been too, but she didn't complain.

"There was a culvert type thing near my middle school, all damp and dim like this place," he said. "We used to climb around and slide down the sides and such. Thought we were hot stuff, impressing the girls to get them to go out with us."

"Did it work?"

He chuckled. "Nah. I eventually grew up and figured out it took more than teen bravado to get a date." He paused, feeling the moment opening up before him. "Do you date much?" Slick, the way he'd brought up that topic. His palms grew sweaty, as if he were an eighth-grade boy again.

"Me?"

"Of course, you. Tot's decades away from entering the dating pool," he joked.

"Not much."

He ignored the defensive shell that coated her words. Sometimes people needed to be coaxed. He didn't think they'd have many more opportunities to walk so close together, momentarily safe from threat, literally treading on common ground. Besides, the idea of growing closer to Kit drew him like a moth to a porch light.

"Why not?" Did his comment read as rude or interested?

She tipped her face away from him, sending the light from her headlamp running from his. Darkness piled in between the beams. He tried to think of what to say to smooth over the awkwardness he'd obviously created, but he couldn't come up with anything.

"That's kind of personal," she said finally.

"I thought we'd already gotten personal." He thought of their conversation about her family and his. Wasn't that personal? He shrugged off the frisson of alarm. "I'm curious by nature." Especially about her.

Her light separated a fraction more from his. "It's because of work. I don't stay in one place too long since I started my trucking company. I don't have time for relationships. I have a business to run."

Her strides grew longer, faster.

He suspected she probably hadn't been immersed in another person's life intensely since her marriage dissolved. Yet here they were now, with no one but each other, and they hadn't landed in this spot by coincidence. God worked in mysterious ways. He pointed out a glimmering puddle, large as a hubcap, which they skirted single file before he plunged in again. "But you control your schedule, right? And where you'll be? Where you drive and how you stack the jobs? So if you met someone interesting—"

"Yes," she interrupted, the clipped word echoing slightly in the dank space. "I am in charge of my schedule, and like I said, my focus is business, not relationships. What about you? How's your dating life?"

He smiled at the way she'd turned the tables. "I like dating. I like interacting with people in general, women in particular."

"Anything serious?"

"Nothing that's stuck." He'd dated as an on-duty cop and before. He'd even fallen in love once or twice, but it was never the challenging kind of love that made him want to be a better version of himself, not the type that made it all worth the struggle and sacrifice. To his mind, God gave every serious couple an empty box, and each person had to be prepared to put more in than they took out. In some of his relationships, it had been him doing all the filling. In others, he wasn't sure the woman welcomed what he'd added.

"You don't want to put down roots?" Kit's tone was more curious than offended, and he took courage.

He ducked under a low spot to avoid a whack to the temple. "Opposite, actually. I do want to put down roots with the person God meant for me, deep roots that will last as long as I do."

Several beats of silence followed. "How do you know God didn't mean for you to be alone?"

She was really asking the question of herself, he knew. He took her hand, cold and soft, and held it firmly. "'Cuz I'm not built that way, and people are better together."

She cocked her head at him, like a bird, thinking. Considering, maybe? His heart thudded faster. The air in the tunnel grew colder and stickier under his boots. Far away came a rumble and roar, and the tunnel shuddered around them.

He stepped forward, but there was suddenly no solid surface under his feet.

Kit cried out and grabbed his belt which kept him from falling outright, but he still plunged forward as the tunnel floor dropped. An ungraceful stagger step prevented a faceplant, but he landed in frigid water up to his ankles.

The water rushed in from somewhere, passed his shins, and surged to his knees. Kit snatched the baby from the carrier.

"We have to go back!" he shouted, but a roar swallowed his comment as a fissure appeared high in the wall, gushing water and vomiting stone. Within seconds the fissure widened to a crevice that dislodged the stones around it, sending rock bombs raining down around them. They could not retreat through the deadly hail.

They splashed ahead through the swirling water. Kit held Tot as high as she could. He wanted to take the baby, but he didn't dare stop to make the transfer or they'd risk being struck by the falling stones. Icy waves slapped at them, and Kit surged on with Tot held level with her shoulders.

"Look! There. Right there!" she screamed. Unable to point, she gestured with her chin. His heart leapt. Through the thundering swirl, he realized they'd made it to the end of the tunnel.

Half swallowed up by the water was a ladder similar to the first, gleaming in the light of their headlamps. A metal plate shone at the top with the familiar bolts.

The exit. They'd actually reached it.

He splashed toward the ladder. A rock ledge about half-way up jutted out a few feet. With no time to explain, he held out his arms and helped Kit and Tot from the rising water, settling them onto the ledge. He heaved the soggy bags up next to them. The flow was lapping only eighteen inches below their perch and steadily rising.

He grabbed the sledgehammer from his pack and charged up the iron rungs. As soon as he was within reach, he started slamming the protruding bolts. This time he'd have to knock off the underside and hope it would be enough to prize open the trapdoor. One bolt sheared away immediately. Excellent. Maybe the damp had corroded all four bolts.

He continued to bang, the rushing water and his own frantic breathing loud in his ears. The second bolt clanged loose. He spared a glance down to see that Kit was crouched on the ledge, her shins swallowed up by the water, Tot clenched to her shoulder. They had moments left before it would be too late. The third bolt gave way, then the fourth. Elated, he applied his shoulder to the metal plate.

It didn't move.

He whacked each corner with the sledgehammer until he thought the impact would shatter his wrists. The plate inched up on one end, the feel of fresh air bathed his face. But the metal refused to give farther.

More. He needed to move it more. Again, he shoved against the metal and pushed until his bones were about to break.

"Cullen!" Kit yelled. "What is that?"

He paused, scanning wildly, sweat stinging his eyes. "I don't see anything."

"Listen."

Listen? He caught it. An electronic chirp he couldn't place at first.

"It's your phone," she said incredulously.

He blinked, lashes spangled with droplets. He yanked the phone out.

Below him, Kit raised the baby as the water crept higher. "Hurry, Cullen."

"Gideon?" he shouted in his cell. "Stop talking! We're in a flooded tunnel somewhere underground near the town of Twinfork. I can't talk or we'll drown. I'll keep the phone on. Track us if you can." He shoved the phone in his pocket, which muffled his brother's oaths. "And stop swearing! You promised Mom," he roared as he slammed the sledgehammer again. "We got two ladies present, you big galoot."

A frantic glance told him Kit was inundated to her torso. Water began to toy with the edge of Tot's socks. Once she was cold, hypothermia would set in. How would they warm her? Save her?

"She's getting wet," Kit called frantically.

Gideon's muffled interrogation continued.

"You have the worst timing ever, Gideon!" Cullen hollered in time to his sledgehammer blows. "Most . . ." *Clang.* "Annoying . . ." *Clang.* Before he got to the next adjective, the gap widened a few inches more. Cullen braced against the metal panel and strained, pushing and grunting. Another inch, then another until one more sinew-snapping heave levered the metal plate clear.

Praising God, he shoved the barrier out of the way. There was no time for delicacy. He bent, grabbed Kit around the waist, and half-guided, half-launched her and Tot up and out. Kit banged her knee on the way and let out a cry of pain. He followed with the gear, barely able to summon the strength to haul himself free.

On hands and knees, he blinked the water from his eyelashes, panting. It was dark, but less so than in the tunnel. Immediately he turned to take Tot from Kit's trembling arms. The adjustment in his vision came gradually, and the baby swam into focus. "Tottie girl? Talk to me."

While he jostled Tot, he became aware that they weren't outside as he'd expected. Instead, they were inside the remains of what had been a wooden structure but was now a collection of rotting beams. Where was the town? Help? People? Some kind of shelter?

As he rocked the baby, he took in the surroundings. The broken building sat at the edge of a sprawl of rusted junk, discarded washing machines, and car parts, gleaming dully in the glare of his headlamp. They were in some sort of salvage yard. Every surface was covered by volcanic ash. No sign of human activity. Anywhere.

"Where are we?" Kit whispered.

He snapped out of his own shock as he fumbled in his pack and pulled out a silver emergency blanket, slipped a mask on Tot, and handed one to Kit. He peered closer at Tot.

"She's not crying," he said desperately, chafing Tot's shivering body. They had to get somewhere warm fast. He wrapped the blanket around Tot and Kit before he got his night vision binoculars and surveyed.

"Past the junkyard about a mile or so there's . . . something." He squinted, adjusting the lenses. "Sheds? No, trailers. I think it's a trailer park."

"A mile?" she said weakly.

But Cullen was focused on the phone he'd temporarily forgotten. "Gideon? Are you there?" He shook the device with increasing agitation. "Gideon?" He smacked the phone against his thigh. "Unbelievable. Lost him."

She shook her head, and he realized she was struggling to speak.

They were all cold, so cold, and Tot was growing ever more still.

Kit tried to stand, but her injured knee gave out and she sat down hard.

Desperation felt like a river rushing through his veins. He bent at the waist. "Get on my back. Leave the gear. We'll get to shelter and I'll retrieve it later."

She shook her head. "A mile's too far and my knee's

not cooperating. I'm too heavy. Take Tot and come back for me."

"We stay together, Kit, remember?" he said savagely. "Get on my back. Right now."

Stiffly, she rose. He helped her stuff Tot inside her jacket before he crouched, and she climbed on. His joints cracked and he struggled to get upright, but he did it, then staggered into motion as she clutched him around the neck. She tried to aim her flashlight and help him avoid the obstacles. He skirted piles of scrap until they emerged on a flat acre that must have been a lovely swatch of grass before the eruption. The trailers seemed impossibly far away, tiny specs.

Don't think about the distance. He wouldn't fail. Couldn't.

Each step, foot, yard was torture. He clomped onward, straining under the effort, past a fenced tarmac. At the far end was a blur of yellow.

"Cullen, stop."

He couldn't imagine why she wanted to stop, and he wasn't sure he'd be able to continue on if he did. Momentum was the only thing keeping him in motion. "I don't . . ."

But she dug her fingernails into his bicep to the point of pain.

He wiped his eyes and blinked. The faint yellow objects came into focus.

He wasn't hallucinating.

"Buses," she said. "School buses."

And the gate was wide open.

■ FIFTEEN ■

KIT TOOK IN THE TIDY ROW OF BUSES, clutching Cullen around the shoulders as much as she dared while keeping the baby sandwiched between them. They'd stumbled upon a transportation lot for the school district. The management must have been unable to relocate the vehicles before the expanded evacuation. In their hurry they'd left the gate unfastened, or maybe they'd intended to move more out but had run out of time. Not much of a theft risk. A stolen school bus was not a prize for looters.

Tot was frighteningly still, and Kit wanted to urge Cullen on, but the man was already likely near his limit, as was she. Her arms felt numb, her fingers barely able to hold on to Cullen and the baby. If conditions didn't change quickly, there would be no saving any of them.

Cullen carried them to the nearest vehicle and set them down. It was a shorter one, a small mini bus that seated ten or fewer passengers. The paint was chipping and there was a massive dent in the side, so it was probably awaiting repair. Her arms trembled around the baby.

"Tot?" she whispered. The baby's eyes were closed,

and she thought she felt the slight rise and fall of her breathing, but Kit was shivering so hard she couldn't be sure. Before she'd even considered how to gain entry into the nearest vehicle, Cullen had found a strong stick and pried open the double doors with some remaining store of strength. He supported Kit and Tot inside and laid Tot on the first passenger seat to examine her while Kit struggled to keep the light from her penlight steady in her tremoring fingers. Her headlamp had disappeared during the tunnel escape.

"Tottie, it's okay now, sweet pea," Cullen said. "We're in a nice toasty bus. We'll get you warmed up in a jiffy, and I'll find more cookies for you, okay? As many as you want." Tot lay silent, though her face was puckered as if she would cry.

Please cry, Tot.

He stripped off the baby's damp clothes until she was naked save for her diaper, and then pulled off his own wet jacket and T-shirt. His muscled torso was rippled with goosebumps, but he drew her to him, chafing and rubbing the child to warm her.

"Come on, Tottie. Let's hear a scream, huh? Blow out my eardrums, why don't you?"

From the corner of her eye, Kit spotted a sweatshirt draped over the driver's seat.

"Here." She pulled it over both Cullen and the baby.

He continued to rub and coo at Tot, edging up and down the aisle to help generate some warmth. His worried gaze found Kit. "I can hotwire it, maybe. Get some heat going?"

The comment broke through her sluggish brain. She

limped to the driver's seat, and her heart skipped up to a joyous rhythm as she spied what she'd hoped for.

"No need. The keys are in the ignition." *Small town. Small-time security.* She jammed the key forward and cranked the engine. It rattled and wheezed, then died after a moment or two. She swallowed the panic. "Come on, baby. You can do this." The second attempt yielded no better result. Teeth ground together, she forced herself to pause, wait, and relax her stranglehold on the wheel before she tried again.

The engine coughed to life. The most beautiful sound in the world. She swallowed the lump in her throat and flipped on the heater to maximum. Her muscles would hardly obey.

Cullen's massive sigh echoed her own relief. They'd been spared yet again. But there had been no sound from Tot. Had she gotten too cold to recover? "How is she?"

Cullen continued to joggle. "Moving a little more, I think."

She nodded. "Give it a few minutes to warm, then come sit up front and I'll blast the vents."

When he did move to the first-row passenger seat a few minutes later, she angled the heat to blow directly on them. It took a long while before the warmth penetrated her own frozen fingers and toes, painfully overcoming the chill. She couldn't feel her hands, arms, nose. Her face was wooden where it wasn't stinging and throbbing.

They sat in silence, absorbing the blessed warmth, Cullen murmuring endearments to Tot. Still no crying, but the movement gave Kit hope.

She took the phone he passed to her. Her hands responded as if she were wearing oven mitts, and she almost dropped it. "No bars."

He huffed. "Unbelievable. Figures the moment we get a signal, my brother calls while we're fully occupied trying not to drown. Typical Gideon. He has the worst timing of anyone I've ever met."

She chuckled. "Do you realize you called him a galoot?"

"A well-deserved title in his case."

She was still too cold to engage in much conversation as the bus engine rumbled. The transportation yard was silent and eerie in the shrouded moonlight.

A soft burp from Tot made them both smile. Cullen looked down at her through the neck of the sweatshirt. "You good, Tottie?"

Tot reached a hand up through the gap and grabbed his chin.

Kit felt like cheering, but her battered senses wouldn't allow it. "I have an idea."

"I'm all ears."

She thought it over again. What would it hurt if it failed? They were barely alive as it was. But if it succeeded . . . "Buckle up, Cullen."

He raised a brow. "Can you drive this thing? Oh wait. Dumb question."

"Yes, it was, but you're forgiven, and yes, I can drive this. I can drive anything."

"Your knee?"

"Painful, but it's better now that I'm warmer." Despite the heat beginning to seep into her frozen flesh and Tot fingering Cullen's scruffy chin, they were still far from safe. The bus was only a respite until they could find more significant shelter. She put the vehicle in gear and eased it across the lot and through the gate, then turned left in the direction of the tunnel.

"Retrieving our gear?"

"Practical, right? Before we check out the trailer park?"

He gave her a thumbs-up. "Beats me having to hike back and do it."

No doubt his body was depleted after hauling her and Tot to the transportation yard, but new hope laced his tone. She felt it too. With heat and wheels, they had a slim chance. Gratitude buoyed her spirit as she forced her bruised legs to work the gas and brake.

The bus rattled along the grass, kicking up rocks and clouds of ash. When they arrived back at the salvage yard, Cullen extracted Tot from under the sweatshirt and delivered her to Kit while he retrieved the supplies.

She propped Tot on the seat next to her since her jeans were soaked, thrilled that Tot was more her animated, baby self. "You are a tough customer, Tot. Like your mother." Annette was a survivor. Maybe she'd been able to elude Nico, find someone to help her, someone who wouldn't turn away when things got hard.

Someone like Cullen. That she depended on Cullen was scary. That he might have come to depend on her was terrifying.

He interrupted her thoughts with his return.

"It's all wet, but the duffel bag's contents are okay." Cullen removed an outfit from Tot's supply and slid the bag underneath one of the seats before he took over her care. "I'll change her while you see if you can find something dry for yourself."

She wanted to say she could wait, but he was right. Wet clothes in these circumstances could be a death sentence. With the engine running, she pulled the last bagged items from her pack, sweats and a long-sleeve tee, a pair of undies and socks.

Cullen sat next to Tot and waved Kit down the aisle. In the wider back seat, she managed to pull on the clothes. Honestly, was there anything more comforting than dry clothes and socks? It made it palatable for her to ease on her wet boots again.

"Your turn," she said to Cullen as she returned to the baby.

She heard his stifled groan as he pulled on his clothes in the same rear area.

"If this bus had a hot shower, I'd pay rent to live in it," he said.

"That's why I have a sleeping setup in my rig." *Had*, her brain silently corrected with a slice of fresh pain. "I'll start over again," she muttered savagely.

"What?" Cullen said.

"Nothing. I'll drive us to the trailers, see how far we get. There's a solid half tank of gas, thank goodness."

He fiddled, one handed, with his phone.

"What do you think Gideon caught of your conversation?"

"Enough to know I called him a big galoot."

She giggled. "And he heard our location. That's a biggie for a galoot." Someone knew where they were. One other living soul, but it was enough to comfort her, somehow.

Cullen sniffed. "So now that we're out in the open, we got no signal. I will never understand all these invisible

Wi-Fi and satellite beams. At least the bus runs without ethernet technology or whatever they call it."

"Yes. Give me a good old-fashioned combustion engine any day."

"Hear! Hear!" He buckled his seat belt and held Tot to his shoulder. "All right, Kit. Full speed ahead."

"Full speed" was barely a five-mile-an-hour crawl since she had to avoid obstacles both visible and cloaked by the ashen blanket. The bus headlights did an adequate job, and she only had to leave the asphalt twice to skirt large rocks that blocked the way. The town Archie had told them about extended in the distance to a cluster of houses on the ridgeline, far enough away that she dared not attempt it with the bus. As far as Cullen could tell, no lights shone in those residences anyway, indicating they'd been evacuated.

Nearer was the trailer park Cullen had spotted, at the end of a swooping gravel path that ended in a half-inundated parking lot. The water swirled and pooled, thick with floating branches and sludge. No vehicles.

Beyond that were several rows of well-maintained trailers that backed up to a woody hillside. All dark. The ones closer to the parking lot were partially submerged, but the remaining dozen had been spared. No cars here either that she could detect.

"Looks deserted. Some of the windows are boarded up." Had her voice betrayed her disappointment? *What did you expect, Kit? That a resident with a working phone would come running out to help?* It was exactly what she'd hoped for, anyway.

Cullen frowned. "Doesn't matter. We're looking for

shelter and warmth, and one of those trailers is our best option."

"I can't get the bus into that lot."

"We can leave it there." He pointed to a wooded shoulder near a refueling station and garbage area. "I don't suppose you want to—"

"Wait here while you scope it out? No. I'll help, and if she starts to get cold again, I'll bring her back here to warm her up." In truth, Kit was still cold, but she didn't want them to split up for any reason. *Who's dependent on whom?* The thought made her shiver, but she followed him and Tot. She hauled the duffel over her shoulder, and they left the other supplies in the bus. Her spine and legs reminded her of the trauma she'd subjected them to escaping from the tunnel. Cullen was walking stiffly, in obvious pain as well.

"Look for one with a hooked-up propane tank," he said. "That's our best chance at heat."

Dark, cold, empty, surreal. *Indescribable* was the best word she could think of to capture the moment as they walked through the desolate area. Wet, hungry, desperate for shelter. Ready to enter someone else's home. In other circumstances they'd be breaking and entering. Legalese meant zilch to her at the moment. They'd explain everything if they lived long enough. Right now it was quite literally a life-or-death choice.

She tried to keep away from the deep pockets of mud. Cullen focused on the units farthest from the sludgy water, three nicely tended trailers with potted plants and shades drawn over the windows. He selected the middle one, leapt over a rippling stream, and approached the door while she watched. With a sheepish look, he rang the bell and tugged on the doorknob, locked of course. She joined him as he made his way around to the side, shaded by a cheerful, striped awning. The back door was locked also.

"Wish I still had the sledgehammer, but this will do," he said.

He picked up a cement gnome from the step and whacked the handle off, stuck his hand inside, and opened the latch manually. "I'll leave another note and my contact info," he said with a wry smile. "I'm going to owe people all over this state."

She was too cold to smile, too weak to do anything but enter the trailer with her precious bundle. She laid Tot on a worn plaid sofa and wedged her in with some pillows. Tot accepted the binky, staring with wide, unblinking eyes at her new surroundings.

Cullen disappeared to fuss with the propane tank while she took stock of their new shelter. The sight of an old coffee machine made her mouth water. A faint scent of flowers perfumed the air. The tiny table and bench seats were part of a minuscule kitchen. On the counter was a vase of stargazer lilies, dry and shriveled, and a small card propped next to it. *Happy anniversary, Thelma. All my love, Frank.* She desperately hoped Thelma and Frank had gotten away safely and would have their home to return to after Mount Ember was finished self-destructing.

The fridge was covered with magnets advertising everything from pickles to national parks. It opened to reveal a jar of olives and a package of string cheese. The cupboard held a half-empty container of peanut butter and some wheat crackers and bottled water. What would be suitable for Tot? She could eat bits of the cheese and crackers. It wouldn't be a complete diet if they ran short of formula, but it would keep her alive, at least for a while.

If only Thelma and Frank had some formula stowed away for visiting babies.

A narrow hallway led to a bathroom, glorious with its pink crocheted tissue box cover and the glass dish of potpourri next to the fancy hand soap pump. She imagined Thelma and Frank snug in their cozy home, and she hoped they were the kind of people who would welcome desperate strangers. Certainly no one could begrudge shelter to a vulnerable infant with a missing mother.

The compact bedroom on one end of the trailer held a queen-sized mattress topped with a handmade quilt. At the opposite end of the rig was another smaller room that had an overstuffed sofa, TV, and a table set up with a half-finished jigsaw puzzle depicting a bunch of picnicking rabbits.

A soft hum and click indicated Cullen had been successful and the heater surged into action. Her heart leapt. Did that mean they would have hot water too? She didn't allow herself to imagine such a delicious outcome and returned to Tot as Cullen let himself back in and went to the porcelain lamp on the side table. He switched it on.

The flood of buttery light was so startling and lovely, she felt herself tearing up. Cullen might have too, because he turned away, plopped his baseball cap on the table, and busied himself closing the blinds tight.

"Precaution," he said.

It was enough to check her euphoria. Nico could not possibly have tracked them. Still . . .

He checked his phone and sighed. They put their wet

boots by the heat register to dry. She was content to settle next to Tot by the lamp, as if it were a crackling campfire. Better than a campfire. *Electricity.*

"Still no signal?"

He shook his head. "All right. Tomorrow we do some recon. For tonight, we're okay here."

"Better than okay. We have a heater and a lamp and a flushing toilet."

"And in a couple hours"—he leaned forward with a delighted grin—"there will be hot water for a shower."

She pressed a palm to her chest. "I may explode from the sheer joy of that."

He chuckled and pulled a chair next to Tot. "Little lady, it's near 1:00 a.m. You're supposed to be asleep."

"She's a little off schedule."

"She's entitled, considering what she's been through. Think she's hungry?"

"Doesn't seem so."

"Well, I am. And thirsty. Tap water's not safe to drink, maybe, though."

"There's a dozen water bottles in the cupboard above the sink."

"Perfect. How about we use what's here and save our supply? If we get the stove going, we can boil some and refill ours." He started to get up, but he groaned aloud, his face creasing in pain.

She put a hand on his shoulder. "I'll get it. My knee's feeling a lot better."

A soft expression washed over him in the lamplight, and he reached out and fingered a strand of her hair, tucking it back behind her ear. She froze, not breathing.

"Thank you," he said. "You're amazing, in case I forgot to tell you that."

And what exactly flooded over her just then? A mixture of warmth and worry that left her wanting to move closer and run in the other direction. She yearned to kiss him, but she knew that would only lead to more pain later. *Don't need me too much, Cullen,* she wanted to tell him. *I don't want to be anybody's safe place.* The trauma they were enduring was creating a fake intimacy that wouldn't exist in the real world.

She went to the kitchen, grabbed bottles of water and the scant contents of the fridge and pantry, a couple paper plates and napkins, and brought it all to the small side table so he wouldn't have to move.

He uncapped a bottle and drained it before opening the next. She, too, gulped the clean, cool liquid. Utterly delicious. She opened the olive jar and forked some out on a paper plate, then pushed it toward him.

"You help yourself to the olives." He dipped a cracker in the peanut butter and ate it with an eye roll. "Oh man. I can't even believe how good this tastes." He fixed several peanut butter cracker sandwiches and slid them over to her. "Have some before I go face down in this pile of crackers."

Again, she offered the olives.

He shook his head.

"You don't like olives?"

"Oh, I like the taste fine. I . . ." He waved a hand. "Confession. I'll eat anything on the planet except for two things, one of which is green olives unless they're chopped or sliced up or something."

"If you like the taste, why not eat them whole?"

"I'm not going to say, on account of it tarnishes my macho reputation." He mimed zipping his lips and tossing the key.

She grinned. "Oh, your macho reputation is already suffering from the rat incident."

"Unkind to throw that in my face, ma'am."

"I'll forget all about it," she said mischievously, "if you tell me about your olive hang-up."

"It's not a hang-up or anything. I just can't get past the fact that . . ." He groaned. "You're gonna tease me."

She arched a brow, waiting.

"They look too much like eyeballs."

Her laughter came out so exuberantly, Tot jerked her head over to look. "Eyeballs. Really."

"Yeah, like they're all squishy and the red thing in the middle is like some sort of horror show. Creeps me out." He shivered and devoured another cracker.

Still laughing, she stuck a fork into the jar, speared two olives, and stuffed them into her mouth. "Lucious," she said. "An amazing, gelatinous texture."

He sighed. "You're enjoying this, aren't you?"

She laughed some more until he was chuckling with her. It felt precious, refreshing, natural, to be sharing a laugh with him in spite of everything the world was throwing at them. The tingle of unease remained, a faint murmur that urged her to get on the road and keep moving.

"Tell me what the other food is that you can't stand."

"For my own protection, I will decline to state. Enjoy your eyeballs while I finish the rest of the crackers."

They rested, ate, talked, and savored the comforts of the tiny trailer. Cullen plugged the sink drain, and together they gave Tot a bath. Tot chortled and splashed everywhere, playing with the plastic measuring cup Kit had found in the drawer while they checked her closely for any wounds or bruises.

It took both of them to rinse off her hair without getting water into her eyes. When Tot was clean and redressed, Cullen fixed her a fresh bottle, warming it in the microwave, which felt like the height of luxury. Kit eyed the powder, estimating they had enough for about six more. The count unleashed a flood of fresh worry, but at least they had snacks to keep her nourished. They sat shoulder to shoulder on the couch while he fed her.

Cullen rolled his neck and exhaled. "I love this place."

She sighed. "I live in a trailer, and there's nothing better."

"Yeah? Maybe I'll look into getting one on my property."

"What about your cabin?"

"Probably not going to be there when I get back. I'll rebuild, but it will take time. This is a sweet setup. Cozy, right? White-picket-fence worthy."

She let herself imagine it for only a moment. A white picket fence meant safety and belonging. The way he was looking at her made that tingle of unease flare higher.

"Is your trailer like that?" he said casually. "Some place snug and scenic where you come home between your trips, I mean. A place to set down roots?"

"It's a place to live," she said quietly. "I don't want any roots."

He flinched. She'd struck a nerve, and it grieved her, but she had to still the wild thrumming of her pulse, had to hold on to the slender string that knotted her insides together. "That's not the life for me."

He paused for a moment. "May I ask why not?"

Nothing would do but the truth. "I don't want anyone to depend on me. It's too much weight, and I'm not strong enough to sustain anyone else."

"But you have been. Me and Tot, this whole time."

"These circumstances"—she waved a hand—"aren't real."

"It's as real as it gets."

She shook her head. "Not to me. In the day to day, I don't want the commitment of relationships, to know someone's waiting for me to come home."

"Do you feel that way because of what happened to your dad? Because he let you and your mother down by breaking the law?"

She stiffened, got up, arms wrapped around herself. "There were too many expectations, financial and emotional, from me and mom. He did what he had to do."

Cullen shook his head. "No. He did something he knew was wrong for the right reasons."

Fury clawed at her. How dare he pass judgment on her father? "Don't talk to me about Dad."

He didn't shrink from her emotion. "Then let's talk about you. You avoid relationships because you don't want to fail someone else like your dad and your ex-husband did. So you cut yourself off and limit your future because you're scared of hurting or being hurt."

Scared? Hadn't she recently survived a crash, a landslide, and nearly drowning in a tunnel? "You don't know what's best for me, Cullen."

"Maybe I do."

Her breath went shallow, irritation sparking to anger. "You've known me for a couple days. Stop trying to be some sort of hero in my life, okay?"

His face fell, the softness vanishing behind a mask of hard lines bracketing his mouth. He looked away from her, and his pain was hers, because she'd caused it. Because she'd probably ended whatever might have been between them with that one remark.

"I'm sorry," he said. "Not the first time I've heard that."

She knew. She'd just used his reluctant confession of what his partner's husband had said to push him away. Misery clogged her throat.

"I thought we had something between us." His eyes were incandescent in the glow from the lamp. "But like you said, not real. Shouldn't have assumed or tried to come off like I was an expert about your family. I apologize."

"I . . ." But she could not think of a single thing to say to erase the hurt she'd caused because it had accomplished exactly what she'd wanted—severing the bond growing between them. His expression remained shuttered, his body curved in, as if he was losing the battle against physical pain.

She mumbled something and escaped to the shower. She cranked the hot water until it was almost painful. Using the berry-scented shampoo and conditioner, she washed the grit and ash from her hair, repeating until she was sure every atom had been rinsed down the drain. Thelma's pink towels were plush and pillowy, and she helped herself to one for her body and wrapped another around her hair before she redressed. She should have felt on top of the world, but there was an ache in her stomach that wouldn't quit.

"You look like you've solved the mysteries of the universe," Cullen whispered when she emerged into the kitchen. He was joking, but the animation and ease were missing.

She forced a smile. "Pretty sure I have. You might want to wait an hour before you shower because I used up all the hot water."

He gave her a thumbs-up, no smile. "Tot's asleep on the floor in the room with all the jigsaw puzzles. I'll bunk there with her."

She nodded. "I can take over baby watch in a couple hours."

"Sure. And first thing in the morning, I'll climb up that trail past where the bus is parked to see if I can get a signal. I'll bring back our empty bottles so we can refill them with boiled water."

"Do you think we can drive to the evac zone from here?"

"We'll look at the map together. You'll have to see if you think the bus can take the terrain."

She yawned. "Will you and Tot be warm enough? There's an extra blanket in the hall closet."

"We'll manage." He disappeared into the back room.

"Good night," she said faintly, but the only reply was the sound of the door closing. She trekked to the bed and climbed in, snuggling under the quilt.

She slept fitfully, waking often with a sense of panic, reminding herself where she was and that they were safe, temporarily. Her own words replayed in her mind again and again.

Stop trying to be some sort of hero in my life, okay?

Shame licked at her. Surely there must have been some other way of explaining why they wouldn't be a couple than wounding him like that? In spite of her worry, she drifted off to sleep once more.

Sometime later, a tap on the door made her sit up. Cullen brought Tot in.

"What time is it?" she whispered.

"Four thirty. Sunup in an hour. I'm going to try for a signal." He settled Tot on the bed next to her. The baby didn't even stir.

Kit watched him go as he closed the door quietly. Her eyes were gritty, her body still sagging with exhaustion, yet there would be no more sleep as she waited for Cullen to return. For a while she watched Tot's breathing, the steady rise and fall of her small chest.

She rested until she heard the squelch of boots crossing the wet ground. Cullen must have gotten a signal. Excitement surged through her. She jumped up and pulled on her shoes. Best be ready to go quickly if he got info on a nearby rescue crew or a place where a helicopter could fetch them. It would be over soon, she could feel it. She was turning to Tot when it struck her that Cullen wouldn't approach the front of the trailer. They'd left the main door locked and used only the side door.

So if it wasn't Cullen out there . . .

Terror ignited her muscles. She quickly locked herself in the bedroom with Tot. No phone. She couldn't contact Cullen. The curtains were closed. She eased a corner up the tiniest amount. It was still dark outside, and she couldn't spot anyone, until . . .

Nico moved along the alley created by this trailer and

the one next door. He was no more than six feet away, his profile clear. She shot a desperate look at the baby. If Tot woke and cried out, Nico would hear.

What do I do?

"I know you're in one of these trailers, Kit. Your bodyguard has left you alone, right?" Nico called out.

He'd been watching, tracking, waiting. She felt the panic slowly smothering her.

"He won't get back before I'm done with you. My brother and I, we're very, very good at getting rid of women who don't tow the line."

Her heart seized. Getting rid of women . . . like the ones he'd enslaved? He'd murdered them for resisting, for trying to break free. And there was only the flimsy envelope in the duffel bag to use against him. That wasn't going to save her now.

Fear made her breathing shallow out, her head spin. Paralysis began to overtake her body until she shook it off. Nico wouldn't win. No way was that happening. She ran to the bedroom closet and eased open the door. There had to be something she could use to defend herself and Tot. A baseball bat? A walking stick?

But there was nothing in the closet except for clothes and a pile of pillows.

"Where are you, lady?" Nico said, louder now, tone wheedling. "I didn't mean what I said. Frustrated is all. Sick and tired of all this nature. I'm a city boy. If you come out, I won't hurt you. I'll take whatever Annette left you, the stuff she used to threaten me. She thought telling me would be enough to keep me from coming for her. Big mistake, but not your fault, right? That's all I want, the photos and whatever else. Not you or the kid. No need for any bloodshed."

Liar.

He was moving toward the back of the trailer now, where he'd find the broken door that no longer locked.

She grabbed a hanger from the closet and began to untwist the sturdy wire. The end was not terribly sharp and it wouldn't do much damage, but it was her only weapon and she would use it.

Nico's voice was close now, directly under the window and moving toward the side door. "I'm going to find you, and you know what's going to happen when I do."

She did.

She and Tot would die.

Fingers ice cold, she finished untwisting the wire and prepared to defend them both.

◼ SIXTEEN ◼

CULLEN'S BODY COMPLAINED loud and long as he hiked up the path past where they'd parked the bus. His heart lamented too, as he considered Kit's very clear brush off.

"Stop trying to be some sort of hero in my life, okay?" Her words burned like battery acid. Was that what he was doing without even realizing? Trying to be the big man and set her world to rights the way he thought it should be? *"You've got a hero complex, always thinking you know the best way."* Again he heard the echo of the explosion that ruined Daniela's legs.

He hiked faster, defying the thought. "Forgiven," he whispered. *I'm forgiven*. And he had started to accept it now, thanks to Kit. Ironic.

The ash glimmered in the dim light, sparkling with bits of the mountain it contained. Wreck and ruin everywhere, but the beauty on these slopes would return someday. He'd seen it, riding his horses over fire-blasted fields where the green eventually broke through, planting a flag where there had been only destruction. God would have the final word here, too, after the fury died away.

Higher he climbed, his aim a pyramid of rock that jutted out over the valley where he could see the trailer park and the swollen river that was doing its best to keep flowing in spite of the fouled waters. Over, under, around, the waves surmounted all the obstacles. His thoughts rolled along too, untidy and tumbling, until he had an epiphany.

Yeah, he was still bossy and probably had overstepped with Kit, but he hadn't wanted to change her course or direction, her character, rescue her from some perceived hardship. He merely wanted to be with her, near her . . . love her? That stopped him in his tracks.

Did he love Kit Garrido? The introverted, independent, way-too-honest woman he'd known only since Wednesday? No, it wasn't possible.

His heart argued with his brain. But the days had been intense, as if they'd been in a crucible, subjected to the highest heat that had melted away all the extraneous. They hadn't put up any fronts, rallied any posturing or pretenses. He'd seen the truth of her, unfiltered, and she'd seen the same in him. He'd witnessed it in his police work, people bonding during traumatic experiences because that's how they survived.

His boots thudded heavily as he plodded. Kit's essence made him yearn for something permanent with her . . . but she did not seem to feel the same way.

He caught a glimpse of a wide glittering lake beyond the trailers. A prime location for fishing once the river recovered, which might take decades. As he climbed a foot farther up the messy slope, the bars on his phone lit up. He whooped and immediately dialed Gideon, pulse revving.

"It's Cullen."

"Where?" Gideon demanded without preamble. "Don't clutter up the line with extra words. Tell me your location ASAP."

He did, jaw tight as he prayed the connection wouldn't drop off again before he got the information out.

"Copy that," Gideon snapped. "I got the story on Nico and his brother. Understand the threat. When I lost your signal . . ."

"My phone's working sporadically. So far, no sign of Nico here, but . . . there are three other friendlies in the area. Kyle, Annette Bowman's boyfriend, we think. Archie Esposito. He was in the area of the lumber mill before the slide. And there's a worker, John something. Shot. Dead." He couldn't rattle off the information fast enough.

"I'll come to you. Stay there."

"We need a chopper. We're transporting a baby."

Gideon said something, but the comment was lost in a wash of static.

"Gideon?"

He heard only one phrase before the connection died.

"Don't move."

Cullen squeezed the phone tight and breathed a heart-felt prayer of gratitude. Finally, their location was known. Wait for rescue, that was all they had to do. Better yet, there was a warm, comfortable trailer in which to do it. Awkwardness with Kit aside, they would be safe, which was infinitely better than climbing through tunnels.

And the cherry on the sundae? No more rats.

He chuckled to himself as he carefully maneuvered his way back, eager to tell Kit the news. When he was ten yards from the bus, the ground rattled and quivered. Earthquake.

The movement rocked him back and forth, and he spread his arms for balance.

Not now, Ember. Keep your cool. The shaking stopped and another tremor started, smaller but longer lasting. He didn't wait, moving as carefully as he could over the shifting ground to the bus.

The vehicle's windows were a mess, coated with muck from the dripping branches overhead. He felt a swell of affection for the battered bus as he pried open the doors and climbed aboard. Maybe this was similar to the love Kit lavished on her rig. If there was any way he could help restore her dream, he decided right then and there, he'd do it. Even if he wasn't going to be a part of her life in the post-eruption world, Kit would have a truck, no matter what he had to do.

Since he was alone, he didn't muffle the grunt of pain caused by his throbbing ribs. He had some aspirin in his pack. Might as well take some now and put a few more in his pocket for subtle access later. He didn't have to advertise how beat up he was, did he?

As he pulled his supplies from the back seat and bent to retrieve the tablets, he saw a metallic gleam from the bushes at the edge of the flooded parking lot. He froze. What was that? With the binoculars yanked from his pack, he focused on the spot, and his pulse slammed his throat. Barely, he made out the rear of a white vehicle.

Nico's.

How had he found them? He could not conceive of an answer as he dropped everything, grabbed his handgun from his pack, and leapt from the bus. He sprinted toward the trailers and skidded to a stop at the sight of boot prints stamped in the mud. One set, one brother. The other was probably providing backup.

Cullen ran closer.

The prints stopped at the trailer to their right and then . . .

His throat closed.

They continued around the side of the unit where he'd left Kit and Tot. He forced himself to move carefully, slow his speed so he didn't give away his position. The image of Kit and Tot unaware of the approaching murderer made him break out in a cold sweat. The side door was slightly ajar. Nico or Simon was inside.

Lord . . . please don't let me be too late. He entered, crouched low, listening.

There was a crash, the sound of a boot smashing in a door. He ran to the bedroom in time to see Nico kick his way through.

Cullen plunged after him.

Inside the bedroom, Kit stood in front of Tot, who stirred on the mattress behind her. Cullen whipped his pistol into position as Nico yanked Kit to his side, the gun swiftly put to her temple.

"Put it down, cowboy," Nico said.

"Don't think so." Cullen tried to get a clear line of sight, but Nico shrank behind Kit. There was no way he would take the shot, but he wasn't about to let Nico believe it.

Her eyes were wide with fear and something else. He caught a glimpse of the wire in her hand, a coat hanger twisted into a point.

He swallowed hard. A few inches of separation, that's all he needed.

"How'd you find us?" he asked.

Nico didn't fall for the stalling tactic. "Your gun. On the floor now, or I kill her."

When Cullen did not move, Nico cinched his arm around Kit's neck and swiveled the gun toward Tot. "How about the baby goes first?"

Kit burst into motion. She arced her fist around and buried the tip of the hanger in Nico's thigh. The point stuck in muscle or bone. He screamed, dropped his gun, ripped the wire from his body, and threw it aside in a spray of blood.

Kit dove for the gun before it vanished under the bed. Cullen fired, but the shot missed as Nico surged forward. He shoved Cullen backward and barreled for the door. Cullen grabbed his ankle, and he went down. They grappled, rolling and twisting, banging into the walls. Cullen worked desperately to keep Nico from imprisoning his gun hand. A round fired wildly would be disastrous in the confined space. Cullen thrust Nico away and put some distance between them, scrambled to his feet, aimed . . . but his heel skidded on Nico's blood and he went down on his back with a thud.

Nico raced past him and sprinted outside as Kit jumped from her knees with his gun clutched in her palms.

"Get Tot," Cullen said as he regained his footing and ran outside after Nico. He emerged at the end of the path, scanning. He knew where his quarry would go. He headed for the flooded parking lot and was proven right as Nico leapt into his vehicle and sped around the water, heading straight for Cullen.

Cullen fired into the windshield. Once, twice, but Nico kept coming, the whites of his eyes gleaming as he bore down. Inches from impact, Cullen dove out of the way.

Nico plowed into a wooden post, sending the mailbox flying. As the SUV passed, Cullen scrambled up and fired again, but the bullet deflected off the rear and Nico drove clear. Undoubtedly he was going to fetch his brother and return to finish the job.

Cullen about-faced and almost ran into Kit as he returned to the trailer. "We have to go," he said.

She handed him Nico's gun, then immediately raced to the bedroom for the baby and duffel bag. There was no time to gather further supplies except to snatch the package of water bottles they hadn't drunk.

She slung on the duffel and hoisted the baby. "How did he find us? Did he spot the bus?"

"Uncertain." It was more than happenstance how Nico kept zeroing in on their location. "I'm thinking he's got a tracker on us somehow, but we'll deal with that later. He'll have to stop the bleeding. Get another weapon and his brother." He grabbed the water and shoved a sleeve of crackers into his pocket. "We can't go out the way we came in. Too easy for them to stop us. We're slow in the bus."

"Thelma and Frank had a trail map in the bedroom, and I took a look at it. There are a couple of routes out of the valley, one road winds past the lake. Nico probably won't expect us to take that one."

They'd still be painfully slow, but what was the alternative? His gut quivered at the thought that once again they were on the run, away from the location where Gideon would arrive to save them. They could hide somewhere close, if possible. Desperation plucked at his nerves, but he elbowed it aside. "I'll go first and check. Stay in the trailer until I signal you."

She nodded. Tot's hair was sticking up in clumps, and she reached for Cullen.

"Later, Tottie girl." When he thought of how easy it would have been for Nico to kill her or Kit, his fear turned to fury. He hurried across the road, scanning, but he saw no sign of Nico having doubled back. He signaled to Kit, who sprinted with Tot across the road. He took the baby and buckled himself in while Kit did the same in the driver's seat.

Once again it required several moments of patience on Kit's part before the engine throbbed into action. He watched her profile, face set with determination. Though love wasn't an issue for him and Kit, he could not battle back an enormous swell of admiration. He wasn't certain he could've come up with the idea to use a hanger as a weapon. Courage under fire.

He kept hold of Tot as the bus jostled back onto the road heading in the opposite direction from the trailer park. "There's a lake access this way," Kit said. "Hopefully it will be wide enough to accommodate the bus."

It'll have to be, or we'll be on foot again. The morning was frosty, glimmers of ice showing in shallow pockets on the ground. He wished they'd had a minute to warm some formula for Tot or even change her into heavier clothes. He wrapped his jacket around her, keeping her down well below the windows in case Nico or Simon was in a position to take a shot at them.

It was a point in their favor that Nico was likely bleeding with an injury that had to hurt like nobody's business. He'd need to address that immediately before he passed out. Unfortunately, Kit was forced to keep their speed to a slow creep to avoid areas of thick mud. Twice she had to back up and navigate around fallen logs, an effort made harder due to the fact that the sunrise didn't actually penetrate the thickening gloom. Once they stopped for him to clear an obstruction, which took longer than it should have. Back aboard, he wondered if the movement he felt was purely the wheels searching for traction or more earthquakes. Or maybe it was his growing angst that they were moving away from the rescue location he'd given Gideon.

They rumbled up the slight slope, trees crowding in on both sides of the path. Below and to the right the lake rippled, pushing debris across its surface as if it were trying to cleanse itself. Kit slammed on the brakes as they came upon a log stretching the length of the road. A log. Odd.

Too neat, too precise. "Turn—" he started as Nico drove from behind a screen of shrubs, stopped on the other side of the log, and hopped out, using the door as a shield to protect himself.

He smiled grimly as if he'd been expecting them and raised a rifle.

Cullen lowered Tot onto the floor, where she immediately started to cry, and pulled his own weapon, breathing hard. *Escape options. Now.*

Movement by the lake below caught his eye. Simon was in the distance, wrestling with an enormous branch near the water. Cullen discerned their plan. Simon would lug it behind them while Nico covered them with his gun. They'd be boxed in. How could they have emerged from one ambush directly into another?

Should Kit reverse before Simon got the branch into position? If anyone could steer a bus backward down a hill it was her.

Kit's hand hovered on the gearshift. Cullen glanced from Nico to Simon down by the water. A shorebird pecked at the sandy soil near Simon's feet, snagging whatever it could find to eat. Nico pointed his gun at the bus windshield, holding the weapon with both hands.

He'd shoot the moment she began to back up.

Cullen wouldn't have time to draw and fire his own weapon, which Nico fully knew. The moment he showed his gun, Nico would fire a round through the glass and kill Kit, then Cullen and Tot. A standoff if there ever was one.

Nico jerked the weapon toward the bus door. The message was clear. *Get out.*

And he'd shoot them dead on the spot and take the duffel. Simon succeeded in hefting the branch from the sticky shore. No more time.

Cullen kept his eyes on Nico. "I'll go meet him. Soon as I step down, you reverse out of here."

"No." Her jaw was clenched so tight a muscle danced and twitched.

"No other choice, Kit. You done real good getting us to this point." There were so many more things he wanted to say, but it was game over. He slid the gun behind his back and tucked it into his belt before he raised his palms slowly and pointed to the door, indicating he was getting out. As he turned, the tires began to bump up and down on the ground, the windows rattling. Another quake.

Nico felt it, too, and grabbed his open door, but he didn't lose his concentration on his target. He was leaning on one foot, favoring the leg with the wound Kit had given him. Satisfying, but not enough. Neither was the heaving ground sufficient to distract Nico.

The interior of the bus rattled louder. Not a massive quake by the feel of it, but the lake demanded his attention, suddenly boiling and bubbling like a massive stewpot. He peered in disbelief. Kit gasped.

Simon straightened at the shore's edge, arms still around his dripping bundle.

Nico shot a half look, trying to spy his brother and maintain his aim on his prisoners. A pungent smell of sulfur drifted into the bus. The bird took off flying crookedly as if it had lost its equilibrium. Without warning, Simon collapsed, sprawled spine first on the damp ground, the branch falling on top of him.

Cullen gaped. What had he just witnessed?

Nico's mouth opened as he shouted for his brother.

"It can't be," Kit murmured.

"Can't be what?" He darted attention between the fallen Simon and Nico, trying to understand what he was seeing.

Nico goggled, eyes wild as he tried to comprehend.

"Down!" Kit yelled as she ripped the bus into reverse and hit the gas, scrunching low. He grabbed for Tot as she slid around the floor. Nico fired a series of bullets shattering the windshield and spraying them with glass.

Cullen held Tot tight, struggling to keep them from being tossed about. Twenty frantic yards of full-speed retreat and Kit stomped the brakes, swung the bus into a turn. He managed to crawl into the seat, curl over the baby with one arm and hold on with the other. They were moving at top speed, the trees and bushes flashing by.

A risky glimpse told him Nico had run toward Simon but changed his mind and dove into his SUV instead.

Leaving his brother?

She passed the flooded parking lot by the trailers.

"Exit road," Cullen said. "Maybe we can outrun him."

"No," she said frantically. "We need to go up."

"Why?" he shouted over the squeal of tires, but she didn't answer. Several steep routes spidered up and away from the trailer park. The first he spied was a twisting horse trail, a wooded hillside path with places where they could hide—which might be her plan—but it was rough and rutted. He grimaced as she rammed the gas and surged ahead. Would the bus be able to take the grade? Boots braced against the floorboards, he held steady as she zoomed up the hill.

The path was tight. The bus sprayed debris from its wheels as it struggled to keep traction. She swerved into a turn, then another. Why had she chosen this way?

There was no chance to ask her about it as they sped upward for one mile, then two. He'd lost sight of Nico. Behind them? Had he taken a different route? Gone back for Simon? When she finally guided the bus to a stop behind an enormous rock pile, overgrown with stringy bay bushes, he handed the baby over and grabbed his binoculars. "I'll check."

She triggered the door to open for him. He slipped out and climbed atop the rock pile to scan the routes leading up the slope to their position. He didn't see Nico's truck. He zoomed in on the lake, still uncertain about what he'd witnessed. What he saw there confirmed she hadn't been overreacting.

He returned to the idling bus, and Tot lay against Kit's shoulder watching a leaf on the windshield caught in a bullet hole, her fist wrapped in Kit's hair.

"Didn't spot Nico, but I could see the lake." He hesitated.

She freed her hair from Tot's tugging fingers and waited for him to continue.

"Simon's . . . still lying there. Looks dead." His stomach felt queasy as he took Tot from her. "What happened, Kit?"

She chewed her lip. "I'm not sure."

"Yes, you are. Explain it to me, please."

She darted a look at the spinning leaf. "I think it was a limnic eruption."

Tot grabbed for the binoculars hanging around his neck. He let her toy with the strap. "What's that, exactly? I've never heard of a limnic eruption."

"It happens when magma builds up under a lake and the carbon dioxide dissolves into the water until it becomes saturated. It's like if you shake up a soda can. Some trigger pushes the gas upward, probably the volcanic activity, and there isn't enough pressure to keep it in solution. It explodes and discharges the gas into the air."

The gas. He stared at her. "Carbon dioxide causes suffocation."

She nodded, resting her shaking hands on the wheel. "Yes."

He reeled. Simon had suffocated, along with anything else in the vicinity that required oxygen. If Nico hadn't put enough distance between himself and the lake, he might very well be dead also.

"And you drove up instead of down because carbon dioxide is heavier than air."

"Yes."

He let out a long, low whistle. "Kit, thank you for not doing what I told you."

"You're welcome."

His gaze remained on her until a pink flush crept up her cheeks, and he realized there must be out-and-out admiration in his expression. "How did you know all that?"

"I read a lot."

"I think I need to renew my library card."

"Uh-huh."

"And the driving. In reverse. Evel Knievel couldn't have done better."

She shrugged, looking away. "Where's Nico, do you think?"

"If he changed his mind and went back for Simon, he could be dead too. If not, he may be somewhere close. Won't take him too long to figure out he bypassed our hiding spot, especially if he's got a tracker on us. Guy has more lives than a cat."

"But his brother didn't."

"No." They fell silent for a moment.

His pulse still thundered in his ears. They'd just watched a man suffocate. And they'd been moments away from doing the same.

Cullen paced the narrow aisle, distractedly patting Tot as she gummed the strap of the binoculars. "The only item of Annette's we've been carrying is the duffel bag."

Kit's eyes went wide. "The lump. I felt a lump when I discovered the envelope. I completely forgot about it with everything that's happened. You don't suppose . . ."

"Hold her a minute, would you?" Cullen handed off the

baby and snagged the duffel from under the seat where it had settled. He unzipped it and dumped everything out.

"I packed that up carefully," Kit said, disapprovingly. "You're making a mess."

He ignored her and ran his hands over the lining, checking the pockets, turning them inside out.

"Bingo." He pulled out a small rectangular device for her to see. "It was between the lining and the outer fabric. Explains how they found us at the library too."

She groaned.

He felt like doing the same.

Nico and his brother had been tracking them the whole time.

■ SEVENTEEN ■

"IT'S A PERSONAL LOCATOR BEACON. Satellite fed and activated." He stomped on it with the heel of his boot. Kit opened the door, and he pitched it. The device sailed away onto the slope below, kicking up puffs of ash as it tumbled down.

Without a word, she delivered Tot into his arms and guided the bus back onto the path, bumping along until she found another, wider one that would still maintain their elevation but take them in the opposite direction from the spot where Cullen had tossed the beacon.

"I feel terrible. If I'd remembered it earlier . . ."

"You were busy trying to keep us all alive. Nico must have had a suspicion Annette was going to bolt, maybe saw her packing the duffel and slipped it in." He rested his cheek on Tot's head.

"He was on to her the whole time. She never had a chance." Kit's throat closed.

"Yes, she did," he said quietly. "She met you. You gave her a chance, but it also put you and Tot into the crosshairs."

"And you."

"And me," he agreed.

The sky grew darker, and a swirl of ash and wind whipped branches. He told her he'd gotten through to Gideon before Nico's arrival, watched her shoulders sag as she wrapped her mind around the situation.

"And now we've left the pickup spot."

"I've been thinking about that. Hear me out." He took a deep breath. "I could drive around, be real obvious about it. If Nico's close, he'll follow me. You and Tot stay back at the trailers and wait for Gideon. It's the best option."

A wild idea formed in her brain. "I have another plan."

"Why do I think I'm not going to like it?"

"Wait and see." She drove the bus back down the way they'd come, stopping at the spot she'd noted earlier, a precarious bend in the road with a precipitous drop on one side. She parked. They walked to the edge and peered over into the chasm below.

"Yeah, my bad feeling's getting worse." Cullen nestled Tot in his jacket as she finished explaining.

"It'll buy us time, if nothing else. We're almost out of gas, anyway. The bus goes over the side, maybe we set it on fire first. If Nico's nearby, he'll hear the crash, see the smoke. He'll assume we're dead or he'll have to hike down to the bottom to check, which will take hours if not a full day with his leg. Gideon will reach us by then. We'll have to reimburse the district for a new vehicle, but hopefully they'll take installments."

"My plan's better."

She crossed her arms. "You're a big galoot, so your plans are not even close to being better."

He paused for a moment, then laughed heartily. "Okay, but we're racking up quite a bill in this region."

"We'll split the tab. Small price if it saves our lives."

When he wiped his eyes, she could not ignore the delight in them, the tenderness. For Tot. For her. And her heart lurched in response. He moved as if he would kiss her, then hesitated, backed up. She was glad, wasn't she?

It's what you wanted, Kit. There's nothing real between you. Go set something else on fire, why don't you?

"All right," she said brightly. "Let's get to work then."

They tore pages of the bus's emergency manuals to use as fuel and put them in an empty cardboard box they'd found. Since he'd eaten all the corn chips, they used hand sanitizer from Tot's duffel as an accelerant. When the papers caught, Cullen added sticks until they had a respectable fire . . . in the back seat of the bus.

This had to be the craziest thing she'd ever been party to.

Cullen insisted on being the one to position the bus a few feet from the precipice. She found a suitable log to wedge down the gas pedal.

She touched the cheerful yellow vehicle that had saved their lives. "Sorry, my friend," she said, blinking back tears. Silly. But she thought of her truck, crushed and ruined, and knew that in a strange way that vehicle had saved her life too.

And here she was, without the future she'd planned on, vulnerable and in danger . . . but somehow not alone. Strangest of all, it felt the tiniest bit comfortable to be that way. Scary, but comfortable too.

For now.

Cullen put the bus into gear, jammed the log in place, and once the vehicle began to lumber toward the drop-off, he jumped out. The wheels churned as the flames crackled inside. With a screech, the bus catapulted out over the lip and plunged down the slope, picking up speed.

Her fear had been that it would get caught on a hidden obstacle, too close to the road, but it continued on, faster and faster until they heard a faraway crash, saw a faint streak of different-colored smoke in the clouded air.

They remained quiet for a moment, Cullen's arm draped around her shoulders. The gesture felt warm and right, and for the briefest of moments, she leaned into him. He was just as banged up and depleted as she was, but together they were strong. Soon her brain reminded her. Another day, maybe hours, and that would be the end of things. Of their partnership.

She cleared her throat and pulled out the blanket that had finally dried from their tunnel excursion. "Who wants to be horsey first?"

He did, so she tied Tot onto his back. With his backpack and the duffel, they began the long trudge to the trailers.

The air was foul and thick, stinging their skin and eyes in spite of the medical masks they pulled on. There was no way to get one to stay in position on Tot. Though they'd taken a spare jacket and tied it over the top of the blanket sling, Kit worried that the stench was permeating Tot's improvised bubble. The baby did not help the situation, crying on and off, batting at the fabric from the inside.

Kit kept up with Cullen, but her feet were sore, her lungs burning. Her bones ached with a deep and penetrating exhaustion. Only one thought kept her trudging on.

Almost over.

Help was on the way.

Nico could not find them without his tracker and his brother.

The proof against him was still safe in her pack.

God would give her the strength to finish what they'd started an eternity ago when she'd stopped to let Annette into her rig. Had they shared much, she and Annette? Her memories remained largely blank. She wondered if she'd ever recollect their exchange, the minutes that had bonded them together much more deeply than they'd each realized.

After two arduous hours, they arrived back at the trailer park. There was no point in securing a different trailer, so they reentered Thelma and Frank's. The expanding floodwaters had gobbled up two more homes until only a few remained dry. Nico might manage to return and figure out their deceit.

But they'd be gone long before that happened. Hopefully.

Cullen led them through the same side door and insisted that Kit shower immediately. "Going to pop Tottie in the sink and wash her off."

She didn't argue. Her own skin was on fire. The warm water was a straight-up blessing. She had to put on her dirty clothes again, but she took a damp towel and wiped away some of the debris first.

When she finished, she found Tot squirming on a blanket and playing with her toes in the living room. Cullen was on his knees, wiping Nico's blood off the hallway floor. He looked chagrined. "Oh. I thought I'd be done before you got out. I, er, didn't want you to have to look at a big bloodstain."

Her mouth rounded in a circle of surprise, but the response stuck in her throat.

He cocked his head. "What's wrong?"

"Nothing, it's . . . I mean, that's very thoughtful, is all."

He ducked his head and shrugged. "Be done in a minute. Tot probably wants a bottle."

She padded away and fixed Tot's milk. Only a few servings of powder left and a handful of diapers. Tension tightened her stomach until she reminded herself that Gideon was on his way. They were safe.

And there's a man who cares so much about you that he's mopping up blood to protect your feelings. She'd gotten the occasional gift in her life, flower bouquets, Valentine chocolates, and even a tiny diamond chip necklace, but no gesture had ever meant as much as what Cullen had done.

For her.

Even though she'd basically told him there would be no future between them.

Tot's squeal broke her reverie, and she offered the bottle. The wind howled around them and the shower pattered softly as Cullen took his turn. Tot yanked her mouth away, winding up for a good shout. Kit offered the pacifier, which Tot allowed for a moment before ejecting it. Kit rested the baby across her knees and took a close look. Was Tot flushed? She pressed her cheek to the baby's with a tingle of alarm. Feverish? Or perhaps Kit was simply warm from the shower.

She fished through the duffel and retrieved a graham

cracker. Tot cried, and her alarm grew. Cullen appeared. He too had to put on his dirty clothes again, but he appeared much more comfortable.

"Cullen," she started, but he held up a finger.

"One second."

She didn't understand what he was up to when he went to the bedroom, until she heard him hauling a dresser to block the kicked-in door from opening.

So he didn't believe the Nico threat was neutralized either.

When he finished, he joined them.

"Tot's really cranky. Does she feel hot to you?" Kit watched anxiously as Cullen inspected the baby.

"Not sure. Won't eat?"

"Not even the cookie."

"Could be a lot of things: teething, she's tired . . ."

Poison in her lungs, dehydration, she'd gotten too cold, been injured somehow in their crazy mad escape . . .

"I'll walk her around for a while. You rest."

She yawned. Yawned again, and the fatigue pressed down on her.

"Go ahead. Take a nap," Cullen said. "Tot and I will hang out."

"If you need me . . ." To do what exactly? If Tot was sick, how was she going to help? "I'll walk her in an hour, let you rest."

He winked. "I know where to find you."

Maybe she should have argued more, insisted on a time-table where they could each get some sleep, but she was simply too depleted. With a grateful nod, she plodded down the hallway and flopped onto the bed. Never had she felt a more comfortable mattress, a cozier room. Sleep might not have been immediate, but it was nearly so.

A minute, or an hour, or several might have passed when a draft caressed her cheek, and her brain remarked on it while her eyes remained firmly closed. Sleep. There was nothing her body required more than that. But the fear that had been coiled in her chest since the moment she'd crashed sprang loose. She heard the stealthy tread of a man's heavy boots.

Nico. He'd found them again.

With a shriek, she leapt from the bed, swinging.

Someone caught her, and she thrashed to get free.

"It's me."

Cullen.

She stopped wriggling and jerked the hair from her face. Cullen stood wide-eyed in front of her, his huge palms cradling her fists.

"Why . . . why are you in here?" She gulped.

"I heard you cry out. I was worried. Came to check on you. You must have been dreaming."

Her jaw was clenched tight. "So Nico hasn't come back?"

He shook his head. "All buttoned up tight. You don't need to worry."

"Tot . . ."

"She's sleeping at the moment. Super fussy, but I let her have your bear. Hope you don't mind."

"Is she sick?"

"Don't think so, but our little pookie is sprouting another tooth, so probably everything is okay."

"Okay?" She tried and failed to make that statement ring true. "The volcano's imploding and Nico is out there still and we experienced a limnic eruption and wrecked a bus."

"Well, yeah, but we're still kicking, aren't we?"

Whatever retort she'd meant to give him dissolved in a humiliating gush of unexpected tears. "I'm tired of being tired... and scared . . . and hungry and cold . . . and lost."

With a bemused look, he nodded.

She sobbed, hiccupped, cried some more. "And I'm angry that I'm crying. I don't want to cry."

"Understandable."

She held up a palm. "Don't say anything sweet to me right now or I'll cry harder," she said severely.

"Um, okay." He shifted from one socked foot to the other. "How about I get you a drink of water?"

She forced breath in and out, wrestling for control. "No. That's sweet too."

"So I'm thinking a hug's out?"

"Definitely."

He thought for a moment. "All right. Nothing sweet. Come on, Garrido."

He left and she found herself following a moment later.

"Sit there," he commanded, pointing to the sofa before he went back to the bedroom and returned with a pad of paper and two pencils, then slapped them down on the cushion. "Tot's still asleep. Plenty of time for me to whoop you at tic-tac-toe."

She blinked.

"What's the matter?" He thrust a pencil at her. "Embarrassed to be trounced?"

"No."

He dramatically licked the pencil lead and dashed off a

game square. "Then try to unseat the Tic-Tac-Toe Master, why don't you?" With a roguish flourish, he scribbled an *x*.

And all of a sudden she was playing a ridiculous game in an unreal situation and deriving an inordinate amount of comfort from it. Five games later, they'd each won twice and one was a draw.

"This is humbling," he said, appearing crestfallen. "The Tic-Tac-Toe Master should make a better showing. I blame dehydration and the distracting smell of those vile green olives for messing with my skills. Another game?"

She smiled. "No. I'm ready for some sleep now, I think, even though it's still afternoon."

"Excellent. I'll lay down with Tottie girl and get some shut-eye too." He leaned forward, moving closer, and then stopped. "I'll, um, see you later."

She quickly closed the gap and kissed him lightly on the cheek. "Thank you."

"Anytime," he said softly.

The bed felt more comfortable now, her tension drained away after the tic-tac-toe match. She pulled up the handmade afghan and patted the envelope with the incriminating photos she'd zipped in her pocket, appreciating the heft of it. Eventually her eyelids grew heavy. As she edged closer to sleep, a roar split the silence. She leapt from the bed, sliding, the floor suddenly sloped at a forty-five-degree angle.

"Cullen!" she yelled, grabbing her pack and running to the living room, where the walls were emptying themselves of decorations, photos and paintings flung to the carpet. Books tumbled from the shelves, but she could not take her eyes from the floor splitting apart before her eyes. It was as if a giant hand was tearing an envelope in two.

Cullen appeared in his doorway, Tot and the duffel bag in his arms. The kitchen side of the trailer broke off, a crevice forming between her and Cullen. Terror twisted through her. She'd be cut off from them.

Without hesitation he ran and vaulted over the gap and skidded to an abrupt halt next to her. Their side of the floor was tipping, leaning into the crevice, and taking them along with it. Cullen grabbed the door frame, and she clung to his outstretched arm. The effort made his forehead furrow as he reeled them back into the hallway, where she got her balance.

He thrust Tot at her and wrestled the wardrobe he'd placed as a barricade out of the way. A lamp crashed off the side table, a piece of the flying ceramic nicking Kit's cheek. She hardly felt it. Only one thought pulsed through her being.

We're going to be swallowed alive.

They'd outrun the wrath of Mount Ember, but the minutes had ticked away.

Run or die.

Or maybe it was run *and* die, but they'd decided together they would hang on to every precious moment of life, and she felt in Cullen's strong grip on her shoulder that his determination was as great as hers.

Shrieks of ripping metal hurt her ears. They stumbled, slid, fell out of the structure and landed outside. With a last bit of optimism, she'd hoped to see a miracle, a helicopter, a vehicle with Gideon behind the wheel, anyone . . .

But there was only the heaving ground, split by the deepening chasm that she now saw was filling with molten lava spilling into the riverbed with a monstrous hiss. Some of it hardened into blackened chunks that floated atop the incoming lava. The orange goo was rising, bubbling up at a pace that would rapidly overtake the channel.

Cullen looked wildly around. She pulled Tot closer to shield her from the whirling particles, the acrid vapors stinging her nasal passages and making her eyes tear. Cullen pulled them along the gap between the collapsing trailers and the riverbed, heading for the road where they'd previously parked the bus. Should they climb up? Away from the rising lava? It was likely their only chance to keep from burning to death, if the poisonous air didn't sear their lungs first. They'd made it a few lurching yards when Cullen stopped short.

Through her blurred eyes, she made out a vehicle and her heart leapt.

Until she realized who was stepping out.

◼ EIGHTEEN ◼

NICO AIMED THE RIFLE AT THEM. "Sheer, dumb luck wins out sometimes, doesn't it? Found that little crash site you engineered, and while I was at it, the road collapsed right in front of me. I almost died. And who do I find down here when I switch direction? The people who got me into this mess."

How could Nico have done it again? Cullen's gut clenched with outrage.

Kit pulled Tot closer.

Nico extended a palm. "You know there's no more chances. Toss Annette's stuff to me, whatever it is. Now. I'm done with this."

Behind them, a fissure opened between them and the river, belching noxious gasses. The lava rose inside, hissing steam and surrounding Nico in a vaporous corona. He shot a terrified look behind him. "Hurry up!"

"You're not gonna drive out of here after what you've done," Cullen snarled.

"What I've done? I'm only looking out for myself, and I've lost my brother in the process." His face twisted. "He

295

was the only one I could trust on this whole lousy planet. We've had each other's backs since we were kids."

Cullen shrugged. "You didn't work very hard to save him."

Nico's mouth trembled. "I didn't understand what happened. You took off so fast and I followed, figured Simon was passed out or something and I'd get back to him after, but . . ." He shook his head. "He's dead because of you two."

"It was an eruption of carbon dioxide from under the lake," Kit said. "We didn't have anything to do with it."

Nico cocked his head. "Doesn't matter. You got involved where you had no business."

"We didn't—"she started.

Nico fired three rounds in quick succession, the bullets plowing the ground in front of them. Kit cried out. The baby wailed.

Cullen's jaw clenched tight, and he jerked Kit and Tot behind him. "Wise up, man. We're on an exploding mountain in case you haven't noticed. The ground is literally going to swallow us up. There's no point in wasting lead by shooting anyone."

"It'd be a way to honor my brother's memory." Nico swiped an arm over his sweating brow and gestured to Kit with the gun. "Open the back of my SUV. Take a look inside."

"Kit . . ." Cullen warned, but Nico swiveled the gun to him and Tot.

"Shut up," Nico said. "She'll do what I tell her."

His muscles were wire taut as Kit walked to the vehicle, opened the rear hatch, and looked in. "A rolled-up mat, so

. . ." Then she stopped and peered closer, her expression sick with horror. "It's Annette."

No. His heart dropped. Not Annette.

"Simon caught her just after the landslide. She was practically dead anyway. When he pressed, she told him the proof against me was with the baby stuff in the duffel. I know she was telling the truth because she thought it would save her life." He shrugged. "Turns out, she was wrong. You two have it. And you're going to give it to me now."

Cullen's brain spun. There had to be a way out. Something.

Nico's finger tightened on the trigger, his face paling. "The proof, now. You can give it to me or I can cut you down and take it off your dead bodies."

Kit looked at Cullen, and he nodded. She unzipped her jacket and tossed Nico the plastic packet. He caught it with his free hand. "Finally. Just one more thing you're going to do for me before you die." He used the gun to point to Cullen. "Get Annette. Dump her in the ravine."

Cullen's stomach clenched, roiling in protest. He shook his head. "Not doing that."

Nico cocked his head, walked to Kit, and aimed the weapon at her forehead. "Yes, you are. You're the reason Simon's dead, so now you'll do his work."

Sweat burned his eyes, and his breathing grew shallow. Nico would shoot them all as soon as Cullen followed directions. He'd failed. He was going to lose Kit and Tot. The thought of watching them die, knowing he could have, should have made other, safer choices, squeezed the breath from his lungs. His gaze welded to Kit's.

Her mouth trembled, but she raised her chin. Tot wriggled in her arms, and Kit rocked her, soothing and comforting her though tears trickled down her own cheeks. She would offer what she could to the child until there was nothing left to give. Tot had survived so much, and so had Kit. Two strong women in different-sized packages. What if he could find a way out of this?

Determination slammed through him like a landslide, knocking away the defeat. He'd been forgiven for what he'd allowed to happen to Daniela, and he'd even begun to forgive himself, inch by inch. He could meet his Lord resting in that truth. But he would see to it that Kit and Tot did not have their lives cut short by this pathetic excuse for a man.

He locked on her. *Be ready.*

Her eyes narrowed. Message received. Her throat convulsed as she swallowed. So beautiful in her courage.

He faced Nico, giving voice to his disgust. "Why should I cooperate? You have no reason to keep us alive."

"Correct." Nico twitched as the ground shuddered. "But you'll do as I tell you anyway, because you don't have the stomach to watch them suffer."

But I've got plenty of stomach to watch you suffer.

Cullen walked over to the open tailgate where Annette was rolled in the mat. He could see only the toe of a pink sneaker. She'd tried so hard. Suffered so much. Too late for her, but he wouldn't let it be for nothing. He bent over, pretending to pull the bundle toward him as he grabbed the muddy pink shoe and slid it off. He clutched it in his sweat-slicked palm.

No line-of-duty heroics. Not fueled by some overblown

sense of his own capabilities. Just a desperate man with only his faith and one slender chance to preserve the life of a woman and a baby he'd grown to love.

He gripped the shoe with his right hand and pulled the wrapped body toward him to give him a few more seconds. *Lord, help me.*

Then he whirled around and threw Annette's shoe directly into Nico's face. Kit was indeed ready, and she dove aside as it left his fingers. Nico's eyes widened and he squeezed the trigger while throwing up his forearm to block the blow.

Bang.

Cullen was astounded that Nico's shot missed him. Nico recoiled as the shoe glanced off his shoulder, the gun flying loose as he stumbled. Taking the advantage, Cullen delivered a punishing kick that sent Nico's head snapping back. Kit didn't hesitate. With Tot clutched like a football, she ran forward and snatched the envelope from Nico's pocket.

Good woman. The best. Get them away now. Quick.

They'd take Nico's vehicle. Drive to safety. Odd that his legs weren't moving at the command of his brain.

He smiled at Kit, a unique woman of strength and sensitivity. Incomparable.

Who else could have survived what she had?

What other woman could look at him with such ferocity and tenderness and a mouth that made him want to kiss her? One delicate hand was thrust out as if she might embrace him.

Her outline grew fuzzy, and he blinked to keep her in focus.

"Cullen?" he heard her say.

The ground shuddered underneath him. Mount Ember would wait no longer.

Get to the SUV. But no words actually came out. His thoughts turned liquid and slow, and the ground rushed up to meet him.

He felt her pressing against him, noted the slow burn from the bullet he now realized hadn't missed after all. Tot squirmed at Kit's shoulder. *Good job, Tottie. You survived. Your mama would be proud.*

Kit put her face to his, inches away, and glared at him. "You will not die."

I will not die, he tried to repeat.

From over her shoulder, he saw a shape loom into view. The killer with nine lives.

"Nico!" he shouted, but it came out as a croak.

There was a hideous bang.

A shot?

The volcano?

Kit . . .

She screamed, curling around Tot. Cullen managed to roll onto his side in time to see Nico spin around, clutching at his ribs, falling onto the ground that was bucking visibly.

From the other direction, Archie and Gideon ran toward them, away from a familiar truck. John's. Was he dreaming? Could that actually be his brother and a very dirty Archie Esposito?

Gideon had taken the shot, the gun still held in his hand. Gideon never missed.

Archie ran, limping badly, and snagged Kit in a wiry embrace, darting a worried look at Cullen. "Truck. Now. She's gonna blow. Gotta get to the helicopter."

Archie. Thank you, God, he's alive.

Kit shoved Tot into Archie's arms. "You take her."

She returned to Cullen's side, and he felt a flash of alarm that her sleeves were dotted with blood until he realized it was his. On her knees, she joined Gideon, who was ripping his shirt loose and shoving the wad of fabric against Cullen's chest, none too gently. He wanted to protest, but his mouth didn't work.

Gideon glared at Kit. "Get in the truck."

"You first," she snapped back.

Cullen smiled. Those two were opposite sides of the same unyielding coin. There was going to be fireworks for sure.

Gideon swore softly.

Not in front of the ladies, he wanted to say.

"I didn't come all this way to haul you out of the fire and have an argument," his brother said.

"Guess your plan isn't working," Kit said. "Apply more pressure. He's bleeding too much."

The lava was now yards from them, the heat searing his face. "Go," he whispered to Kit.

She ignored him, speaking to Gideon. "We'll carry him to the truck together."

One angry shake of Gideon's head. "Too much time. Get to the truck and—"

She stood, grabbed Cullen's boots. "Are you going to help or am I dragging him by myself?"

More swearing and Gideon hooked Cullen under the arms. As they lifted, the ground fractured yards from their position, a latticework of turf above a lake of lava. Underneath it all came a soft, orange glow.

No, no, no.

Fingers of molten ground gobbled Nico's SUV, pulling it under with a hiss of steam.

Annette. I'm sorry.

Kit cried out with a desperate look behind her. "Nico's got to go to jail."

"Too late," Gideon said, voice hard and flat.

When Gideon hoisted Cullen's shoulders, he saw what his brother meant. Nico's body was being swallowed by the sizzling lava, literally devoured. In five seconds he was gone, rifle and all.

Gideon and Kit ran with Cullen to the truck, sliding him into the bed.

"I've gotta drive," Gideon said. "Archie, can you ride in the back with him?"

Kit spoke up. "I will. Archie's got the baby."

Archie started to protest, and Cullen did too.

"Get moving!" Kit commanded Gideon.

She braced herself against the metal bed as Gideon took the wheel. The truck tore off. He felt the force of the fiery mass chasing them, rattling the earth around them. From his vantage point he watched the trees disappear one by one, as if a massive tunneling beast was sucking them down.

The truck pivoted, jerked, sending the two of them banging around as Gideon desperately tried to keep moving forward.

Kit braced herself, one fist clenched in Cullen's jacket to anchor him. He saw reflected in her terrified eyes the stream of fire that chased them, the ground opening into a chasm that sought to join the lava-filled ravine.

It was a race now.

Cullen forced his fingers to curl around hers.

"Don't you die," she whispered, tears flowing down her face. "You big galoot."

As the heat became unbearable and the metal bed of the truck began to feel like a griddle, they catapulted onto a different road, free from trees. A scattershot of gravel raked the chassis, but above that cacophony came a glorious sound. The whapping of helicopter blades.

The truck jerked to a stop, and suddenly there were people, uniformed and one in a yellow vest.

"Them," he said to the first one who climbed into the truck bed. "Get them aboard."

"No," Kit said. "Archie and Tot are being loaded in. I'm waiting with you."

"Yes," Cullen grunted as forcefully as he could, giving her the full impact of a law enforcement command. "You will get in that chopper right now or Gideon will drag you."

Gideon stood at the edge of the truck bed, hands on his hips. Kit looked from Cullen to Gideon, probably trying to work out how much of the stubborn, bossy traits was genetically shared. She huffed out a breath and climbed out of the truck. The medic applied a clotting agent to his wound, and he and Gideon rolled Cullen onto a stretcher and carried him to the helicopter where they strapped him down.

Archie was belted into a seat next to Kit, Tot clutched to his chest.

They lifted off, rotors whirling up a storm of debris. The helicopter danced and dipped, angling so far to one

side that he caught a view through the window of the catastrophe unfolding below them, the mountainside falling
away, rivers of red devouring whatever and whoever had
been left behind.

Annette.

Kit turned toward him and stretched out her hand to
take his. He knew she was thinking what he was. Annette
had risked everything to ensure her baby wasn't a prisoner
like she had been. *You done good, Annette.*

He closed his eyes, feeling the weight of every arduous
mile they'd traveled, and prayed for the woman who'd
offered up her life for her baby's.

His senses grew fuzzy, and he fought to stay conscious
while the rescue worker monitored his vitals for the flight
to an airstrip a safe distance from the spewing mountain.
In a haze, he was aware of the helicopter landing, of being
moved into a vehicle—an ambulance, he supposed—to be
transported to the hospital.

And the beautiful sound of a baby crying.

. . . .

He woke up in a hospital room. *Kit* . . . He jackknifed
to a sitting position, head swimming.

"Slow down or you'll rip out all the tubes." Gideon sat
with his heels on the edge of the hospital bed. He looked
freshly showered and shaved, his muscular frame relaxed.

"How long?"

"Have you been out? Two days."

"Kit . . . ?"

"Was treated for dehydration and a concussion and
various minor injuries. She's been here practically the whole

time, but Tot's grandmother arrived an hour ago, and she went with Tot to meet her at the airport."

"So Tot's . . ."

"In perfect condition, the best of all of you."

He let out a huge breath and silently thanked the Lord. He felt a pang at what was about to happen for Tot and her grandmother. It wouldn't be easy for Kit to navigate that emotional firestorm alone. He wished he could have been there with her.

"When am I getting out of here?"

"If you're a good boy, this afternoon. Maybe they'll give you a sticker if you don't try to hurry them along." He got up. "Going for coffee, and no I'm not getting you any because you called me names and you didn't do the smart thing and bail before the volcano blew, like a normal person with adequate brain capacity."

If he had, Kit and Tot would be dead.

And he wouldn't have a whole new way for his heart to beat.

At the door, Gideon paused. "She's perfect for you, you know. Stubborn, thinks she knows best, smart. But she's way better than you deserve. Nonetheless, somehow you got her to like you."

"You think so?"

He pointed to the table by his bed. "She brought you a present."

Cullen waited until after Gideon left before he grabbed the small bag and opened it. He laughed so hard his body ached at the jar of green olives inside.

It was a solid month before Cullen was allowed into the obliterated Pine Hollow to see the remains of his cabin. The ruin wasn't unexpected, but it added to the ache of his healing bullet wound. His property, like everyone else's, was buried under the broken skeleton of Mount Ember. The only thing still standing was the brick chimney and a section of twisted gutter sticking up from the rubble.

He was staying in a rented room in Grandlake while he firmed up his plans. The town had largely survived somehow, except for the bait and tackle shop, which had lost a corner due to a massive rock flung loose during the explosion.

The first thing he'd done upon his return was to repay the shop owners for the supplies they'd taken. They'd protested loudly. He'd cheerfully ignored them. Fortunately, the school district had excellent insurance and declined Cullen and Kit's offer to pay for the bus they'd intentionally jettisoned. Since Archie was still bunking above the library, the two of them had helped the local cleanup efforts. Some of the roads were painstakingly cleared, and communities reopened. Many would never be.

Thanks to the coordinated efforts from dozens of agencies, the eruption only claimed fifteen lives, not including Nico, Simon, Annette, and John. It had been merely by the grace of God that he, Archie, Kit, and Tot hadn't been added to the fatality list. Gideon too.

That morning Archie had looked up from sorting the library's Zane Grey collection and winked at him as he left for Kit's, a journey he took almost every day.

"Got your hair cut finally?"

"Yes, sir."

"Shipshape."

"Yes, sir."

"Well, move out, then. You're late."

With a grin, he'd saluted before jogging to the vehicle on loan from Gideon. The arrangements for his surprise required a few hours of coordination, so he didn't arrive at Kit's trailer until after lunch.

"We're invited to Lucy's birthday party," she said when he let her out of his hug, showing him an invitation covered with tiny pink balloons.

He felt a stab of both pain and pleasure. The police had discovered the baby's correct name on a birth certificate, Lucy Elizabeth, but he could not seem to convince himself of it. In his heart she'd always be the chubby, energetic Tot.

Annette's memorial service had been a beautiful affair with flowers and music, and he and Kit had done their best to comfort the mother who'd lost her daughter twice. Mrs. Bowman had a granddaughter who would be solace and comfort to her as she mourned.

And Tot had a father, since Kyle was picked up by a rescue unit after he'd escaped Nico and Simon at Cullen's cabin. He'd submitted to a DNA test, which proved that Tot was indeed his child.

At present, Tot would remain with her grandmother while the legal issues were resolved about who would have custody and how visitation would be arranged. In any case, Cullen felt sure they would find a way where they could all love Annette's little girl. After all, they'd all loved Annette, and that was enough to bind them together.

Cullen and Kit had visited Tot regularly too, the foster aunt and uncle. Weird, since none of them quite knew how to behave around each other. Tot's grandma settled on plying him and Kit with coffee and every conceivable type of pastry and showing them photos of Annette when she was an infant. He had no idea how the whole matter of the harrowing escape would be explained to Tot one day, but he intended to be there to share how amazingly brave her mother had been, how she'd given her life to protect her baby daughter. Maybe he'd even write it down to preserve the details.

Kit did not say much during their visits, but she dutifully examined each and every photo Mrs. Bowman presented of her daughter. In the rare moments when Mrs. Bowman relinquished the baby, Kit walked Tot around and around the living room when she fussed, as she'd done in the wrecked trailer and throughout their sprint for survival. When Kit cuddled the baby, he could see how the action soothed her heart.

And it had become his single focused mission in life to do the same.

Kit was the woman he called every day and fixed sandwiches for as she waited on hold for hours with the insurance companies. He helped sweep the ash from the sidewalk outside her trucking office and wiped the filth from her windows. She was his first thought in the morning and the last prayer of the night.

Together, they'd worked to process their immense disappointments. They hadn't saved Annette. And Nico hadn't been called to account for what he'd done to her or any of the other women he'd enslaved. But the cops had assured them they would work diligently to bring closure to the families of those he'd murdered, track down the women who were still shackled by his trafficking, and provide help and rescue. They'd already made strides thanks to the photos Kit had plucked from Nico's pocket before he'd been swallowed by Mount Ember.

It wasn't enough. Not nearly, but Nico and Simon wouldn't damage any other women, and Tot would be raised in safety by people who loved her. That would have to do. Countless conversations and many more cups of coffee and tears and talking and venting, and they'd come to a peace about it, a tentative one, anyway.

Kit had been nervous at first, when he started coming over, unaccustomed as she was to having someone jabbering away in her space, but she'd gradually allowed him to chat, bring pizza, and even deliver a skinny, freezing cat he found on the side of the road. The animal was now queen of the castle with an intense attachment to Kit and a duty to keep Cullen a safe distance away.

The cat had eerily green eyes that seemed to peer into his soul. Kit had named her Olive.

As he climbed Kit's front step, Olive gave him a haughty look as if she knew what he was planning and didn't approve.

Ingrate.

The box felt heavy in the pocket of his barn jacket. His fingers were cold as he reassured himself it was there for the dozenth time. *Nerves, Cullen? Aren't we past that stage?* He wasn't some knock-kneed high schooler, and he knew Kit about as well as one person could know another.

In spite of the bond they'd created during their harrowing journey, he wasn't totally sure how she'd react to his offering. There was still that wild and untethered part of her nature that relished the solo path, the solitary journey. He cleared his throat and stifled the nerves. *Here we go.*

He joined her in the kitchen, where she'd stacked a pile of paperwork.

"I . . . got you something."

She cocked her head at him. "Why? It's not my birthday."

He smiled. "Kit Garrido, you don't have to have a birthday for a gentleman to present you with a token of his esteem." *Annnnddd . . . I've suddenly become my grandfather.* He straightened and took a breath, gave her the box. "I wanted you to have this."

She opened it, her brow crimping as she pulled out a key. Then she turned those glimmering eyes on him, and the moment had come.

He felt cold. Then hot. He took her hand and guided her outside, around the back, and up the road to the Freightliner tractor parked under the trees. Not yellow—he hadn't been able to find one—but a luminous white that dazzled the vision.

"It's an older model than you had. No way yours could be salvaged, but I thought this one would get you back in business until the insurance settles. At that point you'll have a spare rig, or you can hire another driver, grow your fleet if you want to."

She blinked—gaped, in fact—staring at the freshly stenciled logo on the side.

Garrido Trucking.

She stood as if she were made of wood, key still dangling from her fingers.

"See if the key works," he urged, guiding her gently by the shoulder.

She walked, somewhat dazed, to the truck, opened it, climbed up, lithe as Olive the cat. Her shoulders hitched when she laid eyes on her teddy bear strapped carefully in the passenger seat. The toy had been bundled in Tot's clothing when they'd barely escaped the trailer, saved by the narrowest of margins like all of them had been. Archie had carefully stitched the ear back on for him, since he wisely said Cullen would make a mess of it with his clumsy, fat fingers.

Without a word, she climbed down again, and for a moment she just breathed, staring at her shoes. His stomach tightened. Should he say something? What was she thinking? Feeling?

Her foggy gaze slid to him. "You bought this? For me?"

"Yes, ma'am."

"How?"

He shrugged. "Had a little account I cashed in." At a steep penalty, but somehow that part didn't seem to hurt at all. Unless she rejected the whole thing, of course. Then he'd be crushed and financially unwise. *Go big or go home, Landry.*

"Why?" she demanded. "Why did you get this for me?"

"I know how important your truck was to you, and I . . ." His throat was sand dry, and he forced a swallow. Three little words. Why did they weigh so much? "I love you."

There it was, dropped between them like a boulder launched from a volcano. The closer they'd grown since their rescue, neither had dared to use the L-word aloud. Until now.

He was buried in the most profound silence of his life.

He could actually hear a pine needle flutter to the ground. Each second stretched his nerves tighter.

She stared at the truck, then back at him, shaking her head. Shaking, not nodding. A bad sign.

"But it's not a package deal," he mumbled, realizing he should have handled the conversation completely differently. "The truck, I mean. If you don't feel the same way about me in the love department, I can deal with it." *Somehow.* "The truck's yours one way or the other. What would I do with a big rig? Horses are plenty, and where would I park it anyway?"

"You bought me a truck. You love me." It was as if she were reciting something she'd learned at school as a kid.

"Yep. That about covers it."

He couldn't handle another extended silence. His nerves were banging like an old screen door. "And there is no way you can tell me we don't know each other well enough for me to love you because when you spend three days together crammed in an ATV with a stranger's baby, running from a killer and a volcano, dodging bullets and lava, you learn all you need to know about a person's character. The month after was icing on the cake."

She jutted her chin at him, black eyes gleaming. "And what exactly do you know about me, Cullen?" It was a challenge that ignited sparks in his soul because he heard the throb of hope in it.

He stepped closer. "I know you got moxie. You got faith. And you're not afraid to face down whatever this world throws at you."

She spoke, chin up, defiant. "I've had a man tell me I was his world before, and look where that landed me."

"Yeah, but he was a galoot and I'm not, no matter what you say. And you're magnificent, and if he couldn't see that, he's a clueless galoot."

"Magnificent?"

"Oh yeah."

Her mouth quirked down at one end. "If I'm brave it's because I had to be, that's all. That's not why you should love a person."

"No, it's not. I love you because you're Kit Garrido. You're strong enough to use a hanger against a bad guy and you're tender enough to sing 'Take Me Out to the Ball Game' to a baby even though you can't remember the words. You don't play games and you don't lie. And you got so many thoughts and plans in here"—he tapped her temple—"that you're bursting with them. I love you, Kit." He leaned close. "And you know what?"

He saw himself mirrored in her irises, and he knew. The tickle of joy kicked up as a slow smile spread over his face.

"What?" she breathed.

"I think you love me back," he whispered.

"I . . ."

But loving someone was one thing. Living it out was altogether different, a road she had not traveled for a long while. The moment of truth. The answer that would change his life. He could not draw a full breath.

Gradually, she looked down and said nothing at all. Not one word.

His heart plummeted. That was that. Miscalculation. He tried to swallow the pain. "Okay. Well, anyway, the truck's yours."

She didn't say anything, do anything to stop him when

he turned away, his heart falling into jagged pieces in his chest. Maybe she needed more time? Or was this the way things would remain?

If so, he'd learn to live without her, of course, but he'd always ache for what they might have had, should have had. She cleared her throat.

"I don't like it when you're right," she said in a very small voice.

He snapped around. "What?"

"You're kind of insufferable when that happens."

He stood there gaping, mouth open. "When I'm . . . right?"

Her grin flashed and she laughed, a long, buttery, rich laugh that pushed all the sadness clean out of him. "I do love you, Cullen Landry. Can you believe it?"

He leapt toward her, grabbed her in an embrace, and whirled her so vigorously the key flew from her hand and landed in the grass. Their kiss was completion, a mending of broken places, a tender seal of trust, a promise. When he finally put her down, they were both breathless.

"It's not just because of the truck?" he teased. "You sure about that?"

"Yes, but if you give me a semi for a one-month dating anniversary, you'll be bankrupt by our second."

Now he laughed too. "I'm willing to risk it."

"Because all I can afford to give you while I'm building my trucking business is that measly jar of olives. You'll have to learn to love them, Landry."

"For you, Kit Garrido, I will do my very best."

And he would. Every day, every mile, every moment God let them share.

ACKNOWLEDGMENTS

I love an everyman hero, don't you? A regular guy or gal who counters extreme challenges not with an arsenal of skills or fancy tools but simply with sheer grit, buoyed by the need to save himself and his loved ones. I think God has put plenty of people like that in his world, even though they don't often make the headlines. People like my husband, who quietly toiled in the fire service for more than thirty years, long-distance truck drivers who sacrifice to keep the supply chain flowing, nurses who suffer the impacts of their jobs physically and emotionally, animal rescue workers who see the best and worst in society. Heroes are all around us, every day.

Thank you, Agent Jessica Alvarez and Editor Kelsey Bowen, for helping me bring my everyman (and every-woman) heroes to life. I have enjoyed every moment of the adventure.

Dana Mentink is a *USA Today* and *Publishers Weekly* bestselling author. She's written more than fifty mystery and suspense novels for Love Inspired Suspense, Harvest House, and Poisoned Pen Press. Winner of two ACFW Carol Awards, a Holt Medallion Award, and a Romantic Times Reviewer's Choice Award, Dana lives in Northern California with her husband. Learn more at DanaMentink.com.

Be the first to hear about new books from Revell!

Stay up to date with our authors and books by signing up for our newsletters at

RevellBooks.com/SignUp

FOLLOW US ON SOCIAL MEDIA

   @RevellFiction

Sign Up for Dana's Newsletter

Keep up to date with Dana's latest news on book releases and events by signing up for her email list at the website below.

DanaMentink.com

FOLLOW DANA ON SOCIAL MEDIA

Dana Mentink   @Dana_Mentink   @DanaMentink

A Note from the Publisher

Dear Reader,

Thank you for selecting a Revell novel! We're so happy to be part of your reading life through this work. Our mission here at Revell is to publish stories that reach the heart. Through friendship, romance, suspense, or a travel back in time, we bring stories that will entertain, inspire, and encourage you. We believe in the power of stories to change our lives and are grateful for the privilege of sharing these stories with you.

We believe in building lasting relationships with readers, and we'd love to get to know you better. If you have any feedback, questions, or just want to chat about your experience reading this book, please email us directly at publisher@revellbooks.com. Your insights are incredibly important to us, and it would be our pleasure to hear how we can better serve you.

We look forward to hearing from you and having the chance to enhance your experience with Revell Books.

The Publishing Team at Revell Books
A Division of Baker Publishing Group
publisher@revellbooks.com